THE TREE THAT SAT DOWN

THE
TREE THAT SAT
DOWN

by

BEVERLEY NICHOLS

Illustrated by
ISOBEL AND JOHN
MORTON SALE

JONATHAN CAPE
THIRTY BEDFORD SQUARE
LONDON

FIRST PUBLISHED 1945

JONATHAN CAPE LTD.   30 BEDFORD SQUARE, LONDON
AND 91 WELLINGTON STREET WEST, TORONTO

BOOK
PRODUCTION
WAR ECONOMY
STANDARD

PRINTED IN GREAT BRITAIN IN THE CITY OF OXFORD
AT THE ALDEN PRESS
BOUND BY A. W. BAIN & CO. LTD., LONDON

CONTENTS

For the PRRP

CHAPTER I

JUDY MEETS A STRANGER

JUDY was out in the wood, collecting Sleepo.

She was carrying a big glass jar, and already it was nearly full. *You* would have said the jar was empty, but it wasn't. It had heaps of Sleepo in it — even though you couldn't see it. There was quite five shillings worth, which is enough to send about sixty-seven children fast asleep for eight hours.

In case you do not know about Sleepo, I will explain. It was one of the things which Judy's grandmother sold in The Shop Under the Willow Tree. It was really her own. invention, though other people in the wood had tried to copy it. But nobody's Sleepo was as good as Mrs. Judy's; it did not send you to sleep nearly so quickly, and sometimes it gave you bad dreams. Mrs. Judy's Sleepo never gave you bad dreams . . . in fact, she had an extra special variety, which cost a penny an ounce more, which gave you the most beautiful dreams. She put a dream in each of these special boxes, which were tied up with green ribbon. Sometimes, if she thought you looked sad, she would pop in an extra dream for luck. The ordinary boxes, which had not got a dream in them, were only tied up with string. But even so, they were very good value for money.

There were two reasons why Mrs. Judy's Sleepo was so much better than anybody else's. One was because she always sold it quite fresh, and the other was because it was all collected by her grand-daughter Judy, who took the greatest pains in getting only the best.

Now I will explain how to get Sleepo, because you might like to try to collect some yourself.

Whenever a cat or a dog or a dormouse or any other animal is sleeping, the air it breathes out through its mouth or its nose has got a little Sleepo in it. You cannot see it, any more than you can see the air itself, but it is there.

Now if the animal just goes on sleeping, the Sleepo drifts away, like smoke, and goes up to the ceiling or flies out of the window. But if you take a glass jar, and hold it near its nose, a lot of Sleepo goes into the jar and settles down. And if you bottle it up and recite the right spells over the bottle, it will keep for a whole month; and when you pour it out of the bottle again, it will send you to sleep.

Now that sounds very simple, but it isn't really quite as simple as all that. First of all, the jar has to be specially treated before it will hold the Sleepo properly. It has to be put under the branches of a willow tree at midnight — (an elm or an oak will do, but they are not quite so good . . . a poplar is *no good at all*, and will lead to dreadful complications). And then you have to wait until three willow leaves have fallen into the jar. It must be three; two is no use at all, and four is very bad. And they must fall in *of their own accord*; it is not the least use putting them in yourself, or shaking the branches of the tree.

When the three leaves have fallen into the jar, you must carry it up to your bedroom, and put it as near as you can to your pillow. And every night, before you go to sleep, you must take the jar in your hands and look at the leaves and say . . .

> Sleepo, sleepo, three times three,
> Out of the branch of a willow tree;
> Sleepo come and make me wise,
> Give me rest and close my eyes.

You do this for three nights running; and when you wake up on the third morning you find that something very exciting has happened. The leaves of the willow tree have flown away, and in their place are three pennies. You must take these pennies and buy something with them to give away . . . you must not spend any of it on yourself. When you have done this — (which will be a very nice and kind thing to do) — you will be able to collect as much Sleepo as you want. And perhaps you may be able to sell some of it for more than the three pennies that you gave away.

III

Now let us get back to Judy in the wood, and see how she is getting on.

She had just been holding the jar in front of the nose of a baby leopard. It was lying fast asleep in the sun and a lot of Sleepo was coming from its nose. And then a fly settled on its tail, and the baby leopard began to twist and turn, and not so much Sleepo came. So she closed the jar and walked on.

She came to a cornfield in a clearing and wondered if she should go in to look for dormice. They were always sleepy, and it was a very good quality of Sleepo which one collected from them, because they were such amiable animals, and always had the nicest thoughts. However they were also very small, and it took a dreadfully long time to collect any quantity; you had to hold the jar in front of at least twenty dormice before you got more than half an ounce. What she really wanted was somebody like old Mr. Sloth, who hung from a tree, with Sleepo pouring from him in bucketfuls.

9

Then, through a gap in the trees, she saw something lying on the ground. It was covered with stripes, and at first she thought it must be a rug which somebody had left behind after a picnic. But when she looked more closely, her heart beat fast with excitement, because she saw it was a little zebra, sound asleep. And when zebras slept, they slept very heavily indeed. If she could only tiptoe across without waking him up, she would be able to fill her jar in no time, and go home to tea.

Very cautiously she began to creep through the bushes. Now and then the branch of a wild rose caught in her skirt, and once she nearly stumbled over a stone. But step by step she drew nearer to the zebra. What a pretty little thing he was! He looked so tired — his front legs were crossed over each other, and his head was thrown back into a cluster of ferns; she could see the Sleepo rising regularly, in tiny puffs, through the ferns, like pale blue smoke.

She was nearly on him now, and was just about to undo the lid of her jar, when suddenly the air was rent with a shrill cry. Out of the shadows leapt a boy, with a ragged shirt and red hair. Over his head he waved a glass jar. With a single jump he landed on the zebra's back and clamped the jar over its nose. For a second the poor little beast seemed stunned, then it jumped to its feet with a loud neigh. The boy was still holding the jar to its nose, but when the zebra leapt up, he was thrown from its back into a bramble bush. As he fell, he clutched his jar very closely to him.

The zebra darted away into the woods and the boy scrambled to his feet. Judy wondered where she had seen him before; then she remembered ... of course, it was Sam, whose grandfather had just bought the only other shop in the wood, which was called The Shop in the Ford. (We will tell you more about this shop later.)

Judy did not like the look of Sam very much, but she was a polite little girl, so she said: "Good afternoon."

"What's good about the afternoon?" snapped Sam. "And who are you, anyway?"

"I live in The Shop Under the Willow Tree."

"That old dump!" Sam made a rude face. "I wouldn't live in a place like that if you paid me a thousand pounds."

Judy was about to say that it was not very likely that anybody would want to pay him a thousand pounds, when she noticed that his knee was scratched.

"Oh, you've hurt yourself!" she cried.

"It's nothing," he retorted. "And anyway it's none of your business."

"Really," thought Judy, "he is the rudest boy I ever met." However, she made another effort to be pleasant.

"Were you collecting Sleepo?" she asked.

"Sleepo! That stuff! Of course not. I was collecting Wakeo."

"Wakeo? Whatever's that?"

"It wakes you up. Every time you startle an animal out of its sleep its breath has got a lot of Wakeo in it. Only don't *you* go collecting it, because my father's going to patent it."

"I certainly shouldn't dream of collecting such a thing," replied Judy indignantly.

"You couldn't even if you tried," sneered Sam, "because you have to have a magic jar, or it escapes. And anyway, you'd be too frightened."

"No I wouldn't."

"Yes you would."

"No I *wouldn't*." Judy stamped her foot. "It isn't because I'd be frightened but because I think it's very unkind to go jumping about on animals' backs when they're tired out and want to sleep."

"Pooh! Who cares about being kind to a lot of silly animals?"

"I do. Besides, I'm quite sure it can't be good for people to take Wakeo."

"Oh, yes it is! It makes them jump and sing and go on like mad. Old Mrs. Parrot bought some the other day; she's a hundred and eight; and after the first dose she climbed to the top of a tree and began to sing hymns."

"I don't think people ought to sing hymns on the tops

of trees, not if they're a hundred and eight," replied Judy severely. "She might have fallen down and broken her neck."

"All the better," chuckled Sam. "Then we could have sold her some Necko to mend it again."

"Don't you ever think of anything but selling things and making money?" asked Judy.

"Not very often. I'm going to be a millionaire. That's more than you'll ever be. In fact, if you don't look out, you won't have anything left at all. You'll be turned out of that old shop of yours."

Judy felt a little cold shudder run down her spine, for her grannie was very poor, and was always afraid of being turned out of the shop.

"How do you mean?" she whispered.

"I mean that all the animals are going to come to *our* shop. We're going to sell all sorts of new things, and they'll be much cheaper, and we're going to advertise."

"Advertise? Whatever's that?"

"Of course *you* wouldn't know. It means painting things on tree trunks and writing things on leaves."

"What sort of things?"

"Things letting the animals know that we've got everything they want — telling them that we can cure them of all their illnesses."

"But can you?"

"Of course not, but we shall *say* we can. What does it matter as long as we get their money?"

"It sounds downright wicked!" cried Judy.

"You only say that because you didn't think of it yourself."

"I should be ashamed if I *did* think of such things. It's wicked . . . telling lies to poor animals."

"Oh, you *are* goody-goody!" jeered Sam.

13

"I don't care if I am. I'd rather be goody-goody than a thief."

Sam shrugged his shoulders and grinned. "Have it your own way, goody-goody," he said.

Judy could bear it no longer. She turned on her heel and ran rapidly through the wood. And after her came the harsh echo of Sam's voice, growing fainter and fainter as she plunged deeper into the shadows.

> Goody-goody Judy
> Judy, Judy
> Goody-goody Judy
> Judy . . . Judy . . .

CHAPTER II

THE STRANGEST SHOP IN THE WORLD

JUDY'S grandmother was very old. Indeed, she was so old that Miss Squirrel, who was extremely inquisitive, had once asked her if she were ever in the Ark.

"Well, I might have been," said Mrs. Judy, "but again, I might not."

Miss Squirrel took this to mean that she *had* been in the Ark, which was just what Mrs. Judy had intended; she liked people to think that she was older than she really was. Of course she had not been in the Ark at all, but there was no harm in letting the animals think she had; it was good for business.

Indeed, at the very moment when Judy was having her argument with Sam, several animals were sitting in the

Shop Under the Willow Tree, trying to persuade Mrs. Judy to tell them stories about the Ark.

"It must have been a wonderful sight," said Miss Squirrel, ". . . all those tails waving, as they walked up the gangway."

"Wonderful," replied Mrs. Judy. Which did not tell them very much.

"A little confusing, I should have thought," observed Mrs. Manx, who had no tail, and was rather jealous of Miss Squirrel.

"Very difficult to arrange, I should have thought," chimed in Mr. Snail. "Some people are always in such a hurry."

"That's better than holding up the traffic," sniffed Mrs. Hare. "Particularly in the rain."

They all looked at Mrs. Judy in the hope that she would tell them some interesting details; but she said nothing.

"There is one thing that has always puzzled me," said Mr. Peacock, whose wide-spread tail shimmered and sparkled as though it were set with precious stones. "How did they arrange who was to have the best cabins?"

This question brought a snort from old Miss Crow. "Really, as if they would bother about a thing like that."

"Some of us," observed Mr. Peacock, "have more to bother about than others." And he glanced first at his own beautiful tail and then at old Miss Crow's shabby black feathers.

"And some of us," retorted Miss Crow, glaring at his tail, "must have looked very foolish, dressed up as if they were going to a party, soaked to the skin."

Mr. Peacock pretended not to hear her; all the same, he slowly shut up his tail. He did it with great dignity, and even when he had finished it still looked beautiful, like a

SHOP
UNDER THE
WILLOW TREE

B

fan that has been folded, with all its jewels sleeping and smouldering inside.

Mrs. Judy tried to give a new turn to the conversation. She said: "It is a pity that Mrs. Dove is not here to talk to us. After all, one of her ancestors played a very important part in the Ark."

"As if we were ever likely to forget it," snapped Miss Crow, who was still sore because Mr. Peacock had been rude. "That old olive branch!"

"She never stops talking about it," added Mrs. Manx. "Anybody would think she'd carried it herself."

"She's got an old leaf which she says is part of the original olive branch," sniffed Mrs. Hare. "It looks more like a piece of brussels sprout to *me*."

Mrs. Judy sighed; she did not like to hear the animals quarrelling. She decided that it was time to close the shop.

"I'm sorry," she said. "But I must put up the shutters now. If anybody wants to buy anything . . ."

She paused hopefully, but none of the animals seemed anxious to make any purchases. They would have liked to do so, but most of them were very poor, and it was a job to make ends meet.

So one by one they went away, gliding or fluttering or hopping, as the case may be, and soon Mrs. Judy was left alone.

11

When Mrs. Judy had said she must "put up the shutters" she did not mean real shutters, of course, because there were no shutters to put up.

(Which reminds me of a little rhyme my own mother used to say to me when I was very young . . .

18

Once I heard a mother mutter
"Go, my son, and shut the shutter."
"The shutter's shut," the son did utter,
"I cannot shut it any shutter.")

But though Mrs. Judy did not have any shutters to shut, there were all sorts of other things to be done.

The Shop Under the Willow Tree might just as well have been called The Shop In the Willow Tree, because it would have been impossible to say where the shop began and where the tree ended. It was a very old tree indeed, so old that the trunk had split open, forming a sort of cave, in which there was always a candle burning at night. When it was cold, Mrs. Judy slept in the cave; otherwise she slept in a hammock high up in the branches. She used to swing backwards and forwards in the wind, and if you had looked up through the branches, on a wild night when the clouds were scurrying across the moon, you would have thought that she was some strange bird that was resting there.

The main business of the shop was conducted in what Mrs. Judy called the "Extension". This was really an immense branch which had sagged away from the trunk, through sheer age, and had come to rest on the ground, forming a sort of arch. The branch was not dead; it was just old, and it felt that it had earned the right to sit down. And so the arch was a living arch, pale green in spring, gold in autumn, bare in winter — but always strong and warm. Underneath the arch Mrs. Judy had dragged an old log, and it was this log which served as a counter.

Apart from the Tree itself and the "Extension" there was another department which Mrs. Judy called the "Bargain Basement". This had originally been only a dip in the ground, but Mrs. Judy had hollowed it out till it was about four feet deep, and cut some steps down to it, and scooped away the earth from the rocks, which were large and flat, and made excellent shelves. On these shelves were displayed an extraordinary variety of objects, ranging from coconuts for the tits to toy mice for the Manx children. Mrs. Mouse had been very angry when she had first noticed these toy mice, which were made of grey flannel, stuffed with sawdust, with little red beads for

eyes; she said it would give the Manx kittens wrong ideas. Mrs. Judy had replied that it was better that they should play with toy mice than with real mice; Mrs. Mouse retorted that the toy mice would only encourage the kittens to try for higher things; Mrs. Judy said "Nonsense"; Mrs. Mouse added that in any case the toy mice looked so natural that the Manx kittens might make a dreadful mistake — indeed, one of them had already pounced on her youngest daughter, called Aminda, when she was asleep, and when Aminda had screamed, the Manx kitten had said "Sorry, I thought you were sawdust", which was very bad for Aminda's nerves; Mrs. Judy snapped "Nonsense" once again, and there the matter rested.

All the same, Mrs. Judy had felt rather worried about the whole thing, and had pushed the toy mice to the back of the shelf, so that all you could see of them was their little red eyes.

It was really a wonderful shop, and there were hundreds of things that would have interested you, stored away in the hollows of the trunk or hanging from the branches. But we have not time to look at any more of them just now, because Judy is coming home and we must get on with our story.

III

When Judy had told her grandmother about Sam, Mrs. Judy looked very grave.

"I was afraid this would happen one day," she said. "We are faced with Competition."

"What *is* 'competition', Grannie?"

"Some people call it 'progress', others call it 'the survival of the fittest'; but whatever name they use, it is always cruel."

"Never mind. We shall pull through somehow."

"It will not be easy. I am very old."

"But the animals all love us."

"Yes — but animals are simple creatures. They are not as simple as humans, of course, who spend their whole lives being cheated and deceived. If a *man* wants to make up his mind about something, he has to read a book about it, and even then the book will often tell him lies. But an *animal* can sum up a man's character in a single sniff; an animal can tell whether a man is a friend or an enemy simply by listening to his footfall on the grass. And that is really the most important thing in life, to know who are our friends and who are our enemies."

"In that case, surely the animals will know that Sam and his grandfather are their enemies?"

Mrs. Judy sighed. "I wonder. Those two sound as if they were very cunning. And remember — they are going to give the animals something *new*, something from the outside world, of which they have no experience. For instance, you told me that they are going to use advertisements. Now human beings know that advertisements are often just another name for lies. Some advertisements are true, of course, some are half-true, but many are plain unvarnished lies. The animals will not know this, because the advertisements will be written up in print, and the only print the animals have ever seen has been in our own shop, and we have never printed anything that has not been true. So the animals will think that print and truth are the same, and if we tell them that print can tell a lie, they will only think that we are jealous."

"Oh, why did they ever come to the wood?" cried Judy. "We were so happy here."

Mrs. Judy stroked her hair. "We shall be happy again," said Mrs. Judy. "But we shall have to think. We shall have to get some new ideas ourselves — better ideas than any that Sam can think of."

"But where shall we get them?"

"From the Tree of course." Mrs. Judy spoke quite sharply. She had lived so long under the old willow, climbing its great branches by day, sleeping snugly among its giant roots at night, that she had come to regard the Tree as almost human. More than human, in fact, for she felt that the Tree had some magical power to protect them both, that no harm could come to them as long as they dwelt in its shadow.

And, in her heart of hearts, she was convinced that the Tree could *speak*; that it could foretell the future, and give warning and advice. She did not often confess this belief to her grand-daughter — to Judy the Tree was just a tree ... a very nice old tree, of course, but only a tree after all.

"I don't see how the Tree can give us any ideas," sighed Judy.

"Ssh! Don't say such things!" Mrs. Judy looked anxiously upwards; she was afraid that the Tree might hear, and be offended. And sure enough, at that moment there came a cold gust of wind that set the branches swaying and set up a thousand little whispers among the leaves, as though the Tree were murmuring to itself.

But what was it saying? What was the message it was trying to give them?

"Time will tell," she thought. And with that, she had to be content.

CHAPTER III

PLOTS AND PLANS

IT was the day of the opening of The Shop in the Ford, and we had better pay it a visit before the animals get there, or it will be too crowded to see anything.

When Sam and his grandfather had first come to the wood, the Ford had been a very battered old car, abandoned years ago by some adventurous tourist, who had wandered off the beaten track and lost his way. Brambles thrust through the windows; there was no engine, no tyres, and nettles were growing out of the radiator. However, after Sam had cleared the ground, and mended the roof, and given it a coat of bright blue paint, it looked quite smart. And the animals, who had never seen a car before, thought it was very grand indeed.

"Will it really go?" demanded P.C. Monkey. (He was the policeman of the wood, and Sam had got on the right side of him by giving him a bag of nuts.)

"Of course it will go," replied Sam.

"Where is the engine?"

"Underneath the bonnet."

P.C. Monkey, to Sam's great annoyance, had then proceeded to lift up the bonnet and peer inside.

"But there isn't anything here," he exclaimed.

Sam cursed; he would have liked to call P.C. Monkey a meddling young fool, but he did not dare to offend the law. So he thought for a moment and said, "It's an invisible engine. They go much better than the ordinary ones."

This had impressed P.C. Monkey so much that he had gone all through the wood, telling the animals about Sam's wonderful invisible engine. They had all believed him except Mr. Justice Owl, the Chief Magistrate of the wood. Mr. Justice Owl had merely sniffed, and observed:

"In the eyes of the law there is no such thing as an invisible engine."

"But the eyes of the law couldn't see it," replied P.C. Monkey, "because it is invisible." He thought this was a very clever reply.

Mr. Justice Owl glared at him fiercely. "The eyes of the law can see everything," he snapped. "Among other things they can see that you are scratching yourself at this moment."

P.C. Monkey looked crestfallen and put his hands behind his back.

"An invisible engine," summed up Mr. Justice Owl, "is not evidence." And when he said something was "not evidence" it was no use arguing with him any more. There was nothing worse than being "not evidence" in the eyes of Mr. Justice Owl; if you were "not evidence" you just weren't worth thinking about. P.C. Monkey was never quite sure what was evidence and what was not evidence, but if ever Mr. Justice Owl told him that he was *not* he felt that it would be more than he could bear; he would go and hang himself by his tail on the highest tree in the wood.

I I

On the morning of the opening, Sam was up early.

Instead of "up" I should perhaps have written "down" for Sam and his grandfather lived in a cave, and Sam slept in the top bunk. It was made of rough planks, and it was filled with hay; sometimes when Sam was getting out of it he stepped on his grandfather's long beard, because it was warmer than the stone floor. Which shows the sort of person he was, because no polite little boy would deliberately step on his grandfather's beard, however warm it might be.

Sam finished the work he was doing, and then he went

back to the cave, pushed his head inside, and shouted "Get Up!"

"Why should I get up?" growled his grandfather, who didn't like being woken so early.

"Come out and see!"

With a great many mutterings and groanings, Old Sam

shuffled out of bed . . . though "bed" is not quite the word which you would have used if you had seen what he was lying on. It was an extraordinary collection of old bits of newspapers and feathers and rags and moss and old socks. Whenever Old Sam saw anything soft he grabbed it and said "This'll do for my bed." Once he got into very great trouble for saying this at the moment when he was snatching at an old woman's wig; she thought it was a very rude suggestion.

Old Sam pulled on his shirt and stuck on his hat and wandered outside, blinking in the September sunlight. When he could see clearly he gazed with astonishment at the object which young Sam was holding up before him.

It was a huge notice-board, and it read like this . . .

THE SHOP IN THE FORD

Principal   Emporium

of

The   Animal   Kingdom

UNDER ROYAL PATRONAGE

All   the   Latest   Goods

Underneath, in smaller letters was written:

Goods Delivered to your Door
Try our Speciality — Wakeo!
Visit Our Information Bureau
Special Terms for Large Families

"What d'you think of it?" demanded Sam proudly.

Old Sam scratched his head. "Looks pretty good to me. Only . . ."

"Only what?"

"What's an emporium?"

"It's another name for a store."

"Well why not say so?"

"Oh, don't be dumb!" snapped Sam. "We want to make a splash. We want to impress these darned animals, and that's the way to do it. They'll spend much more money if they think they're spending it in an Emporium instead of just an ordinary store."

Old Sam scratched his head again. "Maybe you're right. But what's that about royal patronage? I don't remember seeing no Kings nor Queens round these parts lately."

"Gosh!" cried Sam, "Why do they call *animals* 'dumb' when things like you are walking about?"

"That's no way to speak to your grandfather," quavered the old man.

"It's the way I *am* speaking, so you can do what you like about it." Sam spat contemptuously on the grass. "Who's going to prove we're not under royal patronage? We've got a mail order business, haven't we?"

"Have we?"

"No, you old son of a lobster, we haven't. But we can *say* we have. And we can say that only this morning the Emperor of Russia wrote in for another bottle of Wakeo."

"There ain't no Emperor of Russia no longer," said Old Sam. "It's all Bolsheviks."

"How's the animals to know that?"

"They know a good deal more than you give 'em credit for."

"Well, make it the Queen of England then. There's still a Queen of England."

"Yes, but does she use Wakeo?"

"Oh, you make me tired."

Young Sam flung himself down on the grass and began to tear up large clumps of it in his irritation.

"You got the wrong idea," he said. "You're old-fashioned. Now listen. The only way we'll get the animals to come to us instead of going to that darned old Shop Under the Willow is by giving 'em something new. Or at any rate by making 'em *think* we're giving them something new. That's the reason for the telephone."

"We ain't got a telephone," muttered Old Sam.

"No. Nor has anyone else in the wood. So they can't prove it, see? All we have to do is to say to an animal, 'Call us up', and we know quite well he can't call us up 'cos he's not got anything to call with."

"That seems fair enough," admitted Old Sam.

"It's the same with 'Goods delivered to your Door.' "

"If you think I'm going round with a basket at my age, climbing trees and ferreting into burrows, you're very much mistaken," proclaimed Old Sam.

"You don't have to. Read the notice. It says ... 'To your *Door.*' Well, none of the animals have *got* a door. They've got nests and holes and hideouts, but there's not a darned door in the wood. So if we say we deliver to the door, we don't because there ain't no doors to deliver to. Got that?"

"'Pon my word," admitted Old Sam, "that's a bright idea."

"Well, I'm glad you're giving me a bit of credit at last. I sat up half the night painting that board."

He rose from the grass and went over to examine it.

"Seems to be dry now. We'll shove it up. Give me a hand."

Together they carried the board over to the stump of a blasted oak. A few bangs with a hammer and it was firmly in position.

"And now," said Sam, "we'd better have breakfast, so's to be ready for the customers."

III

News travelled fast in the wood. Humans think they are very clever, with their telephones and their radios, but long before the humans ever thought of these things, the animals had invented many wonderful ways of speaking to each other over long distances; the thump of a rabbit's paw on

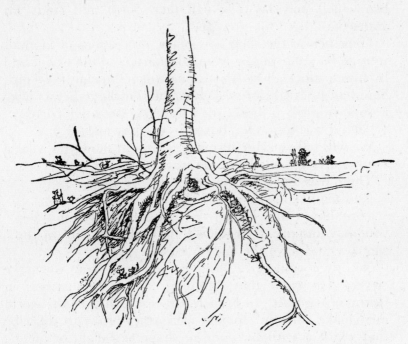

the ground, which you would not even be able to hear, flashed through the wood in a few seconds, and to the rabbits it was as loud as thunder. It was the same with the cry of birds, which you might think was just an idle cry, but to the birds themselves was a warning of peril or a sign of delight. Perhaps the most wonderful example of all was to be found in some of the Moth family, for when young Miss Moth was in love, all she had to do in order to summon her young man was to sit on a leaf and quiver her wings and think of him . . . and her thoughts sped through the night and brought him to her even if he were miles away. If you think that I am making this up, you will find it all written down, in learned language, in books which are kept on shelves too high for you to reach to-day, but which one day you will take down and study for yourselves.

Long before the shop was open, processions of animals were to be seen coming from all quarters of the wood, and by nine o'clock there was a long queue outside the Ford. Sam had put up a lot of shelves, and on these shelves were a great number of boxes, tied up with attractive ribbons.

"What was inside the boxes?" you may ask.

We will tell you, because it will help to show you what a really horrible little boy Sam was.

There was *nothing* in the boxes.

Nothing at all.

"But how could he get the animals to buy nothing?" you may inquire. "Wouldn't the animals call in P.C. Monkey and have the law on him?"

No, they couldn't. Because, you see, Sam was very clever. He knew that "nothing" has many names; in German it is *nichts*, in French it is *rien*. All over the world men make different sounds when they want to describe that which is without sound or shape or weight or life.

So Sam was going to sell the animals "Nichts" and "Rien" and if any of them made a fuss about it, he'd say that it wasn't his fault that they were so ignorant. Anyway, he had a shrewd idea that they wouldn't complain; he knew that an animal hates to be made to look a fool. If you had ever seen the look of pain in the eyes of a circus

32

dog you would know what I mean. He was meant to run on all fours, free as the wind, through the long grass, through sunlight and shadow, but men force him to spend half his life staggering over the sawdust on two legs, blinking in the glare of arc-lights.

IV

At nine o'clock precisely Sam's grandfather came out of his cave, beating a big drum. That was the signal that the shop was open, and immediately all the animals began to swarm around, twittering, and purring, and squeaking and sniffing.

Of course, there were lots of things besides the boxes full of Nothing ... real things, I mean. Most of them — though the animals did not know it — were quite useless. There were heaps of brightly coloured glass, which Sam described as rubies and diamonds and emeralds, though they only came from Woolworth's; there were all sorts of things like that. But it was the boxes full of Nothing which interested the animals most; they longed to know what was inside them; and soon there was quite a queue in front of the counter.

"What is in these boxes?" inquired Mrs. Rabbit.

"Nichts," replied Sam, with a grin.

"Nichts?" Mrs. Rabbit looked puzzled. She had no idea what "nichts" were, but she did not like to show her ignorance, because Mrs. Hare was standing beside her. And Mrs. Hare always put on superior airs, simply because she could run so fast.

"Ah, *nichts*!" repeated Mrs. Rabbit, nodding and trying to look wise. "Nichts," she said again, wondering if they were anything like nuts. Probably that was what they were — a new sort of nut. But then again they might be nothing

of the sort. They might be nightdresses or they might be
nail-scissors. She tried to find out a little more.

"What *quality* nichts?" she asked.

"Medium," observed Sam.

"Medium," repeated Mrs. Rabbit. That told her
nothing at all, though it seemed to suggest that they were
not nuts. You would not describe nuts as "medium".
Perhaps it was nightdresses after all, in which case she did
not want to buy them; she had no use for medium nightdresses, being a very fat rabbit.

She turned to Mrs. Hare. Maybe she would be able to
learn something from her, without revealing that she did
not know what "nichts" were.

"Ah, good afternoon, Mrs. Hare!"

Mrs. Hare gave one of her superior bows.

"I was just thinking of buying some nichts," said Mrs.
Rabbit, fumbling with her shopping-basket.

"Then why don't you buy some and have done with it?"
snapped Mrs. Hare. "You're holding up the queue."

Mrs. Rabbit gave a nervous giggle. "It's just a question
of whether you think the medium variety is the best?"

She looked Mrs. Hare straight in the eyes as she said this.

Now between you and me, Mrs. Hare was just as ignorant
as Mrs. Rabbit about nichts, but being so superior she did
not betray her ignorance. Without batting an eyelid, she
returned Mrs. Rabbit's stare, and drawled . . .

"Well, it depends on what you are going to use the nichts
for."

"Yes, of course. It *would* depend on that."

"What *were* you going to use the nichts for?" demanded
Mrs. Hare.

This was too much for Mrs. Rabbit. She could not say,
"I am going to eat them", because they might be nightdresses, and no lady would eat a nightdress — only shady

girls like Miss Moth ever indulged in such a peculiar diet. On the other hand, she could not say "I am going to wear them," because they might be nuts, and you could not possibly wear a nut unless you balanced it on the top of your head, which would look ridiculous. (And anyway you would be sure to knock it off if you had to dodge into your hole in a hurry). Nor could she run the risk of saying, "I am going to cut my nails with them." They *might* be nail-scissors, it is true, but again they might not. And you could not possibly cut your nails with a nut or with a night-dress. Out of the question.

So she gave no direct reply; she merely lowered her eyes, fumbled in her bag, and asked:

"How much?"

"Five shillings," snapped Sam.

"Five shillings!" gasped Mrs. Rabbit. It was far more than she could afford. It would mean that the whole Rabbit family would have to stay indoors, in the burrow, next week-end instead of going for a ramble in the wood. But she had gone too far to draw back . . . she could not admit to poverty in the presence of that dreadfully superior Mrs. Hare.

"I will have one box."

Sam wrapped up a box for her in a cabbage leaf, tied it with a few strands of hay and sealed it with a drop of gum which he had stolen from the fir tree. It looked such a grand parcel that Mrs. Rabbit felt it *must* be worth five shillings.

As Sam handed it to her, he said, "I suppose you understand how to undo this parcel?"

"How to undo it?" Mrs. Rabbit blinked at him in bewilderment. She did not know what he meant.

"You must not undo it in daylight," Sam said. "Otherwise, all the goodness goes out of the nichts. They must never be exposed to the sun."

"No," muttered Mrs. Rabbit. "I quite understand."

Poor thing. She did not understand at all. As she gathered up the parcel her brain was in a whirl. Nuts? Obviously not nuts . . . it didn't make any difference if you exposed nuts to the sun. Nor, for that matter, nail-scissors or nightdresses. What *could* these nichts be? Perhaps they were some sort of photographic film? In which case, what would Mr. Rabbit say when he learned that she had spent five whole shillings on a photographic film, considering that they were far too poor to afford a camera to fit it into?

She felt on the verge of tears. She wanted to go off, all by herself, and hide in the bracken till the darkness came and she could undo her box and see what it was that she had really bought. She was just about to hurry away when she caught Mrs. Hare's eye. For the first time in her life she thought that Mrs. Hare looked embarrassed; she kept on biting her lower lip, and there was a nervous twitch to her tail. Was it possible, after all, that Mrs. Hare had been bluffing, that she too did not know what nichts were? The thought made Mrs. Rabbit feel much better. So instead of running off with her parcel, she hovered in the background, pretending to examine some of the other goods on the shelves.

v

It was now Mrs. Hare's turn in the queue.

She strolled up to the counter, put down her bag, and sniffed haughtily.

"Good afternoon, Mrs. Hare," said Sam.

("He is much more polite to her than he was to me," muttered Mrs. Rabbit, in the background.)

Mrs. Hare inclined her head,

("I wish I could bow like that," thought Mrs. Rabbit, "but I should only get a crick in the neck.")

"May I have the pleasure of selling you some nichts?" asked Sam.

"Thank you, no." Mrs. Hare spoke in clear ringing tones, as befits a lady of quality. She had not the least idea what nichts were but she was not going to show it. Nor was she going to be such a fool as Mrs. Rabbit, and buy something she might not want.

"I have already a large supply of nichts" she said. "At 'The Burrows'."

That was the name of Mrs. Hare's house. When Mrs. Rabbit heard these words, she felt a little better. If Mrs. Hare kept plenty of nichts at "The Burrows" it *must* be all right. "The Burrows" was a very superior residence.

Mrs. Hare leaned forward over the counter. She pointed to some boxes done up in pale pink paper.

"What is in those?" she drawled.

"Rien," replied Sam.

("Heavens!" thought Mrs. Rabbit. "Something else I don't know about! What on earth is rien? It sounds like something to eat, but it might be boot-polish. I wonder if Mrs. Hare knows what it is?" She pricked up her ears to listen for Mrs. Hare's reply.)

If she had only watched Mrs. Hare's tail she would have guessed that Mrs. Hare did not know what rien was any more than she did. That tail was twitching violently — a sure sign that Mrs. Hare was ill at ease. But it was the only part of her body which she was unable to control — nobody could have guessed from her reply, that anything was troubling her.

"Rien?" she repeated. And then . . . in the same drawling tones . . . "Is it *pure* rien?"

Sam nodded. "You will not find purer rien anywhere."

Mrs. Hare sniffed. This sniff was another sign of nerves. And really, poor dear, she deserves a little of our sympathy. Although she was so superior, she was quite a nice person at heart, and a lot of her manner was due to her upbringing. She had a very snobbish mother who kept on telling her that the Hare family was much better than the Rabbit family, because when any member of the Hare family was killed in the War against Man, he (or she) was "jugged", whereas if any member of the Rabbit family fell in the same War, he (or she) was merely popped into a pie. "To be Jugged" said old Mrs. Hare, over and over again "is Something. To be Popped"—and here she would sniff contemptuously—"is Nothing."

Personally, I should have thought that it would not make much difference whether you were jugged or popped. But some people are awful snobs.

"You say that this is *pure* rien?" repeated Mrs. Hare.

She asked the question because she wanted to gain time.

"Yes madam. Nothing but rien. Absolute . . . complete . . . rien."

Sam spread out the palms of his hands to prove what he was saying. And suddenly some instinct warned Mrs. Hare to beware of him and his boxes. She could not explain what she felt; it was like one of those tremors of warning which came to her on some still summer afternoon when a tiny sound or a faint scent told her that Man was in the wood.

So she plucked up her courage, and drew herself up to her full height, and looked Sam straight in the eye.

"Thank you," she said, "I do not think I need any rien. It is one of those things which I can do without."

And though she did not know it, she was certainly speaking the truth. For we could all do without nothing; we just shouldn't miss it, in the least.

VI

So great was the success of The Shop in the Ford that dusk was falling before the animals reluctantly tore themselves away, and wandered back to their homes, bearing their parcels with them. After his experience with Mrs. Hare, Sam had decided not to sell any more boxes of Nothing; it was too risky; some of the animals might talk, and then they would not come to the shop any more.

Meanwhile Mrs. Rabbit, instead of going home, had scampered off to a quiet place to wait till darkness came, so that she might undo her parcel and see what was inside it. She did not dare to undo it in the presence of the family in case the "nichts" was something which none of them wanted.

Never had night seemed so long in coming. There had been a beautiful sunset, but though it had faded, a few gleams of gold still lingered in the sky. Surely it was dark enough now? The outlines of the trees had merged into the night; even the white wings of Mr. Justice Owl were invisible, as he soared overhead with a melancholy "too-wit too-woe".

Now!

Mrs. Rabbit stretched out her paw and with trembling

fingers she untied the ribbon. She rolled it up carefully and placed it on the grass beside her. Next she removed the brightly-coloured paper, folded it up, and sat on it to make sure that it did not blow away. And at last, holding her breath, very slowly, very gently, she lifted the lid and peered inside.

She could see nothing, even though her eyes were made to see in what we would call "darkness".

Perhaps it was very small — perhaps it was a jewel, a diamond or ruby? She put her paw inside the box and felt round the edges. She could feel nothing. Round and round moved her paw; it could find nothing. She lifted the box and sniffed it; there was no smell but the smell of paper; she turned it upside down and listened; there was no sound of anything dropping out, not even the faintest whisper. The box was empty.

Heavy at heart, and trembling with worry and disappointment, Mrs. Rabbit put down the box and stared into the darkness. Big tears came to her eyes, but she did not notice them; they fell unheeded over the coloured paper on which she was sitting. Far, far away in the distance the faintest gleam of light still lingered; it was like a single golden thread in a coverlet of deep black velvet; and as Mrs. Rabbit watched it she told herself that this was the cause of all her trouble, this little thread of light. Sam had said "wait till *complete* darkness"; she had not waited, she had been too eager.

How could she face the family? As she thought of the family the tears flowed faster. They would all be waiting for her; Mr. Rabbit would be running backwards and forwards to the front door, pushing out his nose and sniffing anxiously; and the children would be twitching their tails and asking when she was coming back with their presents. Presents! A piece of coloured paper and an empty box! It was too much to bear. Mrs. Rabbit buried her face in her paws and sobbed out loud. Perhaps you have never heard of a rabbit crying? Most human ears are deaf to the call of animals in pain. But if you listen very carefully, in some wood or secret meadow as night is falling, and if your heart is kind and you are eager to help — even if it is only a very little thing you can do, like stroking a wounded wing — then you will hear the animals. You will love them all the more for sharing in their grief.

VII

Now it so happened that Judy was walking home through the very field where Mrs. Rabbit was sitting, and Judy had been trained to hear all the cries of animals in sorrow. She knew, for instance, that there are times when even dragon-flies are depressed, when they feel that there is no point in flitting from flower to flower, and that the only thing to do is to sink on to a cool cabbage-leaf and cry. (When a dragon-fly cries it is so faint that it is like very tiny drops of rain on the roof of the smallest doll's-house in the world).

So when Judy drew near to Mrs. Rabbit, she naturally heard her crying, though most humans would have heard nothing at all.

And since we are speaking of these things, if *you* want to train yourself to hear the animals, you must begin in summer, when the fox-gloves are out. Go to the nearest wood and find a cluster of fox-gloves. Pick the *third* bell from the bottom of the tallest fox-glove. Then turn to the sun and take thirty three steps forwards. Kneel down, so that your head nearly touches the ground, and put the bell of one fox-glove to your ear. It will act as a little telephone. Wait a few moments and then whisper, very softly, the following rhyme:

> Fox-glove, fox-glove, tell me true
> Tales of grief and tales of rue.
> Fox-glove, fox-glove, tell me plain
> How to hear the wild one's pain.
> Fox-glove, fox-glove, let me borrow
> Magic powers to soothe their sorrow.

As soon as you have said this, you will hear all sorts of strange noises in the bell of the fox-glove, tiny sighs and faint groans and now and then a sharp buzz. At first you will not be able to distinguish these sounds, but gradually you will learn to understand them, and in time you will also learn how to use the fox-glove bell to guide you to the place where the animal is crying. However, that is a very advanced stage, which comes in a much later lesson.

If you ever try this experiment, you must always be very careful to pick only the third bell of the tallest fox-glove. If you use any of the other ones it is very dangerous, because you will hear the most terrible things which will frighten you out of your wits.

Well, Judy of course had no need of a fox-glove to tell her that Mrs. Rabbit was crying nearby, and as soon as she heard her she tiptoed across and whispered to her, very softly.

"Mrs. Rabbit, what is the matter?"

Instantly, Mrs. Rabbit stopped crying. Her body stiffened, her ears snapped back flat on her head, her paws were rigid. This was a Human. And Humans had only one idea, to hunt and to kill.

"Don't be silly, Mrs. Rabbit." Judy's voice was very gentle. "It's me. Judy."

Mrs. Rabbit breathed a long sigh of relief. She looked up and blinked through her tears.

"I am so unhappy, Miss Judy."

"Tell me."

42

So Mrs. Rabbit told her all about going to the shop and buying the box from Sam.

"But what did he *say* was in it?" asked Judy.

"Nichts."

"Nichts?" Judy's brow puckered. "But that is nothing."

"How can nichts be nothing?"

"I mean, it is nothing in Germany."

Mrs. Rabbit sniffed. "It may be nothing in Germany, but I do not see why it should not be something *here*." She was feeling better now, and was inclined to be argumentative.

"What I mean is . . ." began Judy.

Mrs. Rabbit interrupted her. "I might be nothing in Germany myself. In fact, I probably *should* be nothing . . . nobody at all. Most of my relations are in Australia." And as she mentioned Australia she drew herself up to her full height of nearly eleven inches, because she was very proud of her Australian relations. As well she might be. The only really sensible people in Australia are the rabbits. The rabbits saw that Australia was a great big empty place that needed a lot of people in it to make it happy and prosperous. And what could be nicer than a whole continent of rabbits . . . soft and furry, with millions of tails bobbing about the prairies like a field of daisies in the wind? Obviously, that was what Australia was meant to be. However, the Australians had other ideas.

"Besides," she went on, "there were other boxes that I might have bought. Boxes full of rien. I suppose you will say *that* is nothing too."

"Of course it is," said Judy. "It is nothing in France."

Mrs. Rabbit patted her paw nervously on the ground. She was beginning to feel impatient. "We do not seem to be getting very much further," she observed.

"Wait a minute!" There was a note of excitement in Judy's voice. "I believe I'm beginning to understand. You see . . ."

However, Mrs. Rabbit was still so nervous and upset that she did not listen. "All this talk about France and Germany . . . where does it get us?" She took up the scrap of coloured paper, sniffed it, and threw it away again. "You say that nichts is nothing in Germany. But from what I have heard about that country, things that are nothing in Germany are often something in other countries. Even . . . even Scraps of Paper." She sniffed, very rapidly. "I read that in a history book."

"You are quite right. And you are a very clever rabbit." Judy put her hand gently on Mrs. Rabbit's paw. She felt the sympathy returning between them; the paw was soft and yielding, and answered to the pressure of her fingers. "But dear Mrs. Rabbit, you must listen a minute. I have something very serious to tell you. And something very . . . very *bad*."

Whereupon she proceeded to explain.

When Mrs. Rabbit at last understood, and had learned the full extent of Sam's wickedness, her first impulse was to rush violently through the wood, stamping her feet in the secret S.O.S. which summons all the rabbits from their burrows in time of danger and crisis. But she soon realized that this would be a mistake. She would never have the courage to tell them what a fool she had been. Besides, what could they *do*? If Sam was so wicked that he would cheat animals, he might be so wicked that he would kill them too; he might even have a gun.

"What can any of us do?" she moaned.

Judy knew what she herself could do. Underneath her blouse she wore a silver locket. She was very fond of it, and it was the only piece of jewellery she had ever possessed. But Mrs. Rabbit's need was greater than her own, so with a little sigh, for she really was very fond of it, she unfastened it, and hung it round Mrs. Rabbit's neck.

"Oh, I couldn't take it," breathed Mrs. Rabbit, staring in wonder at the locket.

"Yes, you could," said Judy. "And you can say that it was what you found in the box. Look, we will actually

45

put it in the box for a minute, and then you will not be telling a lie."

"But . . . but it's so *beautiful*."

And indeed in the light of the rising moon, it sparkled like frost.

"It is rather pretty," agreed Judy. "So you'd better hurry home with it at once before I change my mind."

Mrs. Rabbit jumped up and down, giving little furry kisses to Judy's hand. Then with a final "thank you — oh, thank you!" she gathered up the box and the paper and ran into the night.

Judy watched her tail bobbing through the long grass till it was finally out of sight. Then she too turned for home.

But as she walked her heart was heavy, and she shook her head. "Something must be done," she said to herself. "Something must certainly be done."

CHAPTER IV

THE STRUGGLE BEGINS

"YES," agreed Mrs. Judy, on the following morning, when she had heard the whole story, "something must certainly be done."

It was nearly twelve o'clock, and not a single animal had come near The Shop in the Willow Tree. Not that they were not still very fond of Mrs. Judy, but Sam had been so clever with his advertisements and his smart talk, that they all thought that they could buy much better things at The Shop in the Ford.

Besides, Mrs. Rabbit had been so proud of her beautiful locket that she had been scampering through the wood ever since breakfast, showing it to all the other animals, who thought it was a wonderful bargain. And so Judy's kind action had only served to injure Judy herself. Which is often the way of kind actions, though that should not prevent us from performing as many of them as we can.

"We shall be ruined," sighed Mrs. Judy.

Judy smiled bravely. "No, we shall think of something. Perhaps Sam is right when he says we are not modern."

Mrs. Judy snorted. "Modern! Of course we're not modern. What's the point of being modern? What's better in the world to-day than it was yesterday?"

47

Judy could think of no answer.

"Are lambs better? No! Are kittens better? Certainly not. Am I better? Not at all! Is sixpence better?"

"I suppose sixpence is just the same."

"On the contrary, it's very much worse. Sixpence is always worse to-day than it was yesterday."

"Well," said Judy, changing the subject, "what we have to do is to persuade the animals to buy more."

"Buy more *what*?"

"More anything. And I really think we ought to go all round the shop now, at this very minute, and see if there isn't anything we can improve."

II

"Let's begin with the Nest Department," suggested Judy.

Mrs. Judy snorted again. "I should like to do away with that department altogether," she said. "I never did approve of it. Birds ought to build their own nests."

"All the same, we sold quite a lot of them when they were new. But I think they must be getting rather shabby now."

The Nest Department lay under the shelter of a very old and twisted branch of the Tree that had fallen to the ground so many years ago that most of the bark was crumbling to pieces. The nests were arranged in neat piles, and each pile was labelled. Like this:

Nests. Top bough.
Nests. Middle and lower boughs.
Nests. Hedge.
Nests. Eaves.
Nests. Cuckoo proof and Cat-burglar proof.
Nests. Ground floor.

There was also a little catalogue hanging on a twig, with a label on the cover, bearing the words, "Nests, sites for. . ."

Judy had taken a great deal of trouble over these nests, and at first they had been a great success, because she had been able to supply the demand of almost any bird in the wood. Thus, if a young thrush came along, very much in love, and therefore in a great hurry, asking for a quite cat-proof nest to be built, not too high up, in a wild cherry tree, suitable for a lady of moderate means but great sensibility, Judy had only to go to the pile, find the right nest, and then turn to the catalogue to see what branches were "to let". The index of the catalogue began with Acacias (white) and ended with Willows (weeping), and in a few moments she had found what was wanted. And the thrush had soared away with his lady-love, holding in his beak an order-to-view, wrapped up in a special sort of moss which brought good luck to anybody who sat on it.

But now, Judy was bound to admit, the nests did look rather dilapidated. She had been so busy in other departments that she had not had time to attend to them, and many of them were falling to pieces.

"No self-respecting bird would buy any of these," said Mrs. Judy. "Lots of them have holes in the floor so that the eggs would fall out."

"Oh dear! So they have!" Judy picked one of them and turned it over in her hands. Then she had an idea. "Supposing I made some beautiful new ones, with a partition down the middle? Then we could put in a lovely advertisement: 'Ultra-Modern Two-roomed Nests. Exclusive.' "

"With central heating, I suppose," sniffed Mrs. Judy sarcastically.

"I don't think we could quite run to that," replied Judy. "But I do think the two-roomed idea is a good one. Only

49

the other day I heard Mr. Starling threaten to leave Mrs. Starling because she never stopped chattering. If they had an extra room she could go and chatter in it all by herself."

Mrs. Judy shook her head. "It's downright pampering."

"But Grannie, we *must* move with the times."

"Very well. Have it your own way."

III

Their next visit was to the Novelty Department, which was really Judy's favourite. As they walked through it, she became so interested, and had so many new ideas, that for a time she forgot her troubles. She even forgot the wickedness of Sam.

There were all sorts of shelves and niches and pigeon-holes, containing the strangest and most exciting objects, all at the most reasonable prices. For instance, if you had been looking over Judy's shoulder, on that sunny morning, the first thing you would have noticed would have been a tiny hole labelled:

PORCUPINES — NEW QUILLS

And if you had pushed your finger into the hole, you would have pulled it out again very quickly, for it was stuffed full of the sharpest quills you can imagine. Mrs. Porcupine used to say that she only wished she could meet a human when she was wearing them; she'd teach him a lesson!

Judy paused in front of a row of pale blue bottles labelled:

GARGLE FOR NIGHTINGALES

"We haven't sold much of this lately," she said, "although the nightingales have been giving concerts every evening. Do you think it's too expensive?"

"Can't make it a penny cheaper," retorted Mrs. Judy. "It takes ages to make. First I have to get a water lily and pour in an acornful of apple juice. Then I have to add thirty drops of liquid honey and the juice of nine nasturtium seeds. Then I have to collect three dew drops off the petals of a yellow rose and drop them in,

one by one, stirring it all the time with a corn stalk. That takes time, I can tell you, apart from all the poetry I have to say."

"I didn't know you had to say poetry, too."

"Of course I do. Otherwise it wouldn't work. Listen!"

In a sing-song voice Mrs. Judy repeated the following poem:

Here's honey for the honey in your throat
To make it sweeter still.
Here's dew as pure as every golden note,
Here's magic — drink your fill.
Then to the starlight let your music float
But first — please pay the bill!

"It's very pretty indeed," said Judy. "And I don't think the gargle is at all too expensive, not with the poem. But perhaps there are some things we might make cheaper. What about this Blackbeetle Polish?"

"Yes," agreed Mrs. Judy. "We can charge less for that. It's only coal dust and olive oil."

"And then there's the Ladybird Lacquer."

"We can't charge less for that because it takes a thousand poppy petals to make a single drop."

"Couldn't we make it not quite so strong?"

"If we did, it would come out pink, and there'd be a scandal. Imagine a pink ladybird!"

"It might be rather pretty," suggested Judy.

"It might, but the ladybirds wouldn't think so. They're such snobs; they'd say it was 'unladybirdlike.' And when they say anything's 'unladybirdlike,' that's an end of it."

"What about the Food Department?" asked Judy.

"We can't cut prices much more than we have done already."

"Still, we might think of some new ideas. For instance, Mrs. Moth came in yesterday, but she flew away without buying anything."

"She was always a fussy one," sniffed her grannie.

Judy reached for a box on which were painted the words:

MENUS FOR MOTHS

She opened the lid and drew out a number of pieces of

cloth, cut into neat strips, and bearing attractive labels. For instance, there was a square of old grey silk labelled "Delicious!" And there was a piece of blue serge labelled "Very Nutritious." And there were several pieces of hearth-rug labelled "Try them . . . they're Tasty!"

"Mrs. Moth said they none of them had any vitamins in them," sighed Judy.

"Stuff and nonsense! What does she want with vitamins? Her mother brought up a whole family on half an old sock, and she never complained about vitamins."

"All the same, we have got to give the animals what they want. I think I'll cut up my red silk handkerchief."

"It would be a shame. Besides they might not like it."

"Oh yes they would. Mrs. Moth saw it yesterday and said it made her feel quite hungry."

"Very well. Only mind you charge a proper price for it. And think of some extra special label."

"I shall put 'Melts in the Mouth,'" said Judy.

They went all round the department, making notes. Judy decided to do some more crystallized acorns, which were always so popular with the squirrels, and to get some more coconuts for the tits, and paint the outsides of the shells pink and blue.

"And we're running short of ants' eggs," she said. "I must go out and buy a fresh stock."

Her grannie stamped her stick on the ground. "Ants' eggs!" she exclaimed. "I knew there was something I had forgotten to tell you! You remember the ants under the damson tree?"

"Of course. I've bought eggs from them for years."

"A nicer lot of ants I never knew. Hard-working, sober, and most patriotic — quite *devoted* to their Queen. It is too terrible."

"But what has happened?"

"Wait till I tell you. Some of them came round this morning — oh, in a dreadful state. Battered and bruised and carrying on as though there'd been an earthquake. And as far as they were concerned there *had* been an earthquake; that wicked Sam went round with a spade last night and dug them all up and carried away all their eggs."

Judy could hardly believe her ears. "You mean — he stole them?"

"Certainly he stole them. Not only that, he chopped half the nests to pieces. And when the ants said they'd have the law on him he only laughed and said that if they breathed a word to anybody he'd come and pour boiling water on them."

"Oh dear!" cried Judy, almost in tears. "This *can't* go on. We *must* do something. After all, there *is* a law in the wood."

"Yes, but it's a law for animals, not for humans."

"It isn't only the animals who will be ruined, it's us. Look at the ants' eggs, for instance. They used to be one of the most profitable things we sold. The goldfish were the richest fish in the stream and they never minded what they paid. And now Sam will be able to sell them for practically nothing. Is there *nobody* who can help us?"

"If the worst comes to the worst," said Mrs. Judy, "there is always the Tree."

"But what can the Tree do for us? It can't give us anything."

"Hush, Judy! It can give us shelter."

"But that isn't something that we can *eat*."

Mrs. Judy paid no need; for a moment she seemed to have forgotten her grand-daughter. She was gazing up into the branches of the Tree, lost in a dream. "And it can give us Beauty," she said.

Judy felt like retorting that you couldn't eat Beauty either, but there was something in the tone of her grannie's voice that made her pause — something strange and solemn, as though she were in church. She said nothing, but followed her grannie's eyes up into the topmost branches of the Tree. And as she gazed, there came a

fresh, sweet breeze, that sighed through the boughs and set all the leaves to dance, twisting and turning, green and silver, and where the sunlight caught them, pure gold. They all seemed to be laughing and happy, as well they might; for what could be lovelier than the life of a leaf, high against the sky, with the wind as your brother and the sun as your friend, and the whisper of your companions all about you? And when the end comes, and you are tired, all that you need do is to let go, and flutter down to earth. But of course it is not the real leaf that we see, drifting down from the branches in the autumn; it is not the real leaf that we trample underfoot, and sweep up with broom-sticks and burn in bonfires. The real leaf with its little green soul, has drifted upwards, and is fluttering again, brighter and greener, in the infinite and eternal forests that lie just out of sight, behind the curtain of the clouds, where there are no frosts and no angry winds, but only a sweet green peace.

"Beauty," whispered grannie once again.

And the wind seemed to catch the word, and breathe it to the tree, and the tree sang it back in a thousand gentle voices ... Beauty, Beauty, Beauty.

And suddenly Judy sat up and opened her eyes very wide and cried "Grannie, I've got it."

I V

Mrs. Judy blinked.

"Got what, my child?"

"I've got an idea. We'll open a Beauty Parlour!"

"Whatever put such an idea into your head?"

"The Tree."

"I can't believe the Tree said anything so foolish. The animals are quite beautiful enough already."

"Then why do we sell lacquer for ladybirds?" asked Judy. "And if it comes to that, why do we sell Black-beetle Polish?"

Mrs. Judy frowned, for she was a very old lady, and she did not like to be contradicted. "Well," she said, "that's a matter of *health*."

"But Grannie, darling, that makes it better still. Beauty *and* Health. What could be better?"

"We might open a Surgery," agreed Mrs. Judy, grudgingly.

"Why not both?"

"It'll mean a lot of work."

"But I could do all the Beauty Parlour. And I could help you in the Surgery too."

"You couldn't help with the Magic," said Mrs. Judy. "That would all fall on *me*." She shook her head, backwards and forwards. But Judy could see that she did not really mean it, for there was quite a bright sparkle in her eyes.

"I shall have to read up a lot of old books," went on Mrs. Judy. "And I shall have to polish my magic crystal and mend my magic wand."

"But Grannie, I didn't even know you *had* a magic wand."

"Well, it's rather old and cracked so I expect most of the magic has run out of it now," said Mrs. Judy. "Still, there's no harm in trying. Deary me. We shall be busy for the next few days!"

Judy clapped her hands. "I'm so excited. Let's begin now, this very minute. What is the first thing you would like me to do?"

Mrs. Judy thought hard for a moment. "Well, my dear, I think that the first thing you should do is to say 'Thank you' to the Tree for giving you such a good idea."

"Thank you," said Judy, rather shortly.

"You must say it much more nicely than that," corrected Mrs. Judy. "Say ... 'Thank you, Tree, for all that you have done for us, for your shelter and for your shade and for your wisdom.' "

So Judy said these words. And once again a little breeze sighed through the topmost branches, so that you would have sworn that the Tree had heard, and had bowed its head.

"And now," cried Mrs. Judy ... "and now ... to work!"

57

CHAPTER V

BRUNO ESCAPES

MEANWHILE Sam was not being idle; his wicked little head was full of all sorts of crafty schemes for enticing the animals to the Shop in the Ford; and though we very much hope that he will meet with his deserts in the end, at the moment it must be admitted that he was having a great deal of success. The Shop in the Ford was crowded from dawn to dusk, and you could hardly hear yourself speak for the purring and the twittering and the squeaking and the grunting.

And it so happened that on the very morning that Judy and her grannie were planning their Beauty Parlour and Surgery, Sam had a tremendous stroke of luck. The luck came in the shape of a bear, by the name of Mr. Bruno. He is going to play a big part in our story, so please listen very carefully.

If you had seen Mr. Bruno, lumbering happily along on that sunny morning, you would certainly never have guessed that he was a bear with a Secret; you would have said he was just a nice comfortable middle-aged bear, with a shaggy coat of which he was very proud, and a Mrs. Bruno of whom he was very fond, and three small Master Brunos, whom he was bringing up to be good citizens of the wood.

"What a happy person!" you would have said. "With a freehold cave and a quantity of honey stored away for the winter and a loving family to look after him — what more could he want?"

But he was not a happy person at all — not really,

because of his Secret. Sometimes he forgot his Secret for a while, and would dance and play and make the most amiable growls; and then suddenly he would remember it again, and stop dancing and playing, and wander off alone, to sit down under a tree and weep. Mrs. Bruno could never understand these moods, and often asked him if she had done anything to offend him. "No," he replied, with a sad shake of the head, "it is no fault of yours."

"Then is it the family? Or the honey?"

"Neither."

"Then what is it?"

Whereupon Bruno would look at her and sigh and say: "It's just Nerves."

Mrs. Bruno had to be content with this explanation, and as time went on she began to feel quite pleased with it. There was something rather distinguished about having "Nerves"; no other animal in the wood had them, not even the Rabbit family, nor Mr. and Mrs. Mouse. They only had the jumps and the twitters, which were not nearly as grand as "Nerves". So if Bruno got up from the table, when they were entertaining friends, and wandered off to sit under his tree and weep, Mrs. Bruno always turned to her guests with a proud little smile and said: "My poor husband — it's his Nerves, you know. He has *such* Nerves." And all the other animals would look very impressed, for *they* had not got Nerves, and they felt that anybody who had must be a very superior person.

But it was not "Nerves" that was the matter with Mr. Bruno; it was his Secret. It was such an awful secret that, if we tell it to you, we hope you will keep it to yourselves.

We will tell you at once, in order to get it over.

This was Bruno's secret:

HE HAD ESCAPED FROM A CIRCUS.

It was years and years ago, and you may be surprised that he had not forgotten it. But when you have heard his story, *you* will understand.

THE STORY OF BRUNO

Bruno was four years old when he escaped. Even in those days he was a big bear but he was very thin; they always kept him half-starved so that he should not grow strong enough to bite; and it was only because he had such a thick coat that you did not see his bones sticking out.

He could not remember anything about his parents, because he had been stolen from them when he was a baby. All he knew about life was his cage and the circus. His cage was so small that he had to twist his neck to get into it, and he always had cramp when he woke up in the morning. But the cage was better than the circus — oh, very much better! For in the circus he had to dance, even though his limbs were cramped, and jump through terrible flaming hoops which scorched his fur, and if he flinched or faltered, they prodded him with sharp sticks which made him bleed. The men with the sticks always had smiles on their faces, because they did not want the crowd to know how cruel they were. But though there were smiles on their faces there was sharp steel on the sticks, and if you are being beaten, it does not hurt any the less even if the man who beats you does it with a smile.

You see, it was a very wicked circus. Not all circuses are like that; there are many in which the animals are quite kindly treated. All the same, I think that they would much rather not be in circuses at all; they would rather be dancing by themselves under the green trees, and flying away where they wanted, into the blue sky.

It would be too long and sad a story to tell you all of

Bruno's life in the circus; all that you need know is how he escaped.

Although his keeper was always a little drunk at the end of the show, he usually managed to walk without stumbling. He used to prod Bruno into the cage and give him a final cut of the lash when he was inside, crying out "pleasant dreams, you ugly beast, pleasant dreams!" But this night, there was no need for Bruno to crouch in the corner, covering his face with his paws, for the keeper was too drunk to lift the whip. He just slammed the door and staggered off. And before he was out of sight Bruno realized that he had forgotten to turn the key.

Bruno gasped, and stared at the door which was swinging on its hinges. One jump through that door, and he would be free. He blinked; he felt he must be dreaming . . . but no, he was wide awake. He took a step forward and then he paused, his heart thumping against his ribs. "Careful!" he thought, "I must wait." The circus was still full of light and life and laughter; there were many people about; they would catch him before he had gone more than a few yards. Besides, he had a heavy iron chain round his wrist, which would clank and rattle and give him away.

So he lay down and pretended to be asleep. His throat was dry with excitement and his heart beat so fast that it hurt him; but he managed to stay very still.

But it seemed an eternity that he lay there, and every moment was filled with the fear that the keeper might remember, and come back to lock the door. Nobody came. One by one the lights of the circus were quenched, like coloured candles dying into the night. First the torches near the merry-go-rounds, which always made the gilded wood and the polished brass sparkle so brightly that the big stands looked like gigantic jewel-boxes . . . the torches flickered and dimmed, so that all the strange animals of the merry-go-round no longer seemed to be alive; they were like moonlit ghosts, standing stock-still in a trance from which, you would have thought, they would never awaken. Then the light in the Fat Lady's tent went out — she had a red shade over the lamp inside, which glowed through the canvas, so that the whole tent looked like a great red eye, glaring through the darkness. But now that eye was shut. And soon all the other eyes were shut; the circus magician appeared in the doorway of his booth and turned down the wick of the star-spangled lantern that swung over the entrance, casting fantastic shadows on the grass, that danced round and round like spirits conjured up by his magic wand. The Siamese twins drew back their curtain, and blew out the two Chinese lanterns that hung on poles outside . . . a puff to the left, a puff to the right . . . and then they waddled back into the same big bed. The last light to go out was the midget's; it was a very tiny candle, that glittered like a far-off star, and he put it out by waving a blade of grass over it.

And now there was no light but the moon.

I I

All this time, Bruno had been trying to get his chain off. He gnawed at it with his teeth, he tugged at it with the claws of his left paw; all to no avail. He would willingly have cut off his arm to gain his freedom, but that was impossible.

Then he had an idea. It was a very brave idea, and it made him tremble to think of it, but it was the only thing to do; he would have to tie the chain to the cage and jump, knowing that the weight of his body would drag his paw through the iron ring. It would be agonizingly painful, it would scrape all the fur off, and it might break the bone, but it was worth going through any pain to escape.

Once he had thought of this plan he wasted no more time. He tied the chain fast to one of the strong iron bars; then he shuffled to the door and flung it open. For a moment he stood there trying to pluck up his courage for the jump. Everything was very quiet; now and then there was a growl from the lions' cages and a neigh from the paddock where they kept the performing ponies, but there were no sounds of humans. There was only one danger now — that the pain of his paw, as it was dragged through the ring, would be so acute that he would cry out and would wake somebody up.

He took a deep breath. It was now or never. "Courage, Bruno," he muttered to himself. He closed his eyes.

He jumped.

There was one sharp cry; he could not possibly prevent it; he felt as though his paw, from the wrist down, had been plunged into boiling water, as though it were being crushed beneath heavy weights. But when he looked down he saw that the chain had gone; it had torn the fur away; his paw was bare and bleeding. And he did not cry out any more, he just lay there and sobbed beneath his breath, licking his paw very gently, till the pain grew a little less fierce and he felt he could begin to crawl away.

He crawled on his three legs, holding his bleeding paw close to his side, and always keeping to the shadow of the tents. Luck favoured him for a cloud had drifted over the moon; before he reached the outskirts of the circus he was able to stand upright and run, over a field, through a little coppice, over another field, and finally on to a broad road.

He was free!

Now it so happened that the road on which he found himself was one of the main highways, to the North; there

was always a good deal of traffic on it; and you can imagine that the sight of a tall shaggy bear, with a bleeding paw, hurrying down the road in the middle of the night, was not one to which the lorry drivers were accustomed. And very soon the news began to spread abroad that there was a bear on the road; the police were called out; and before he knew where he was, he was flying for his life with a whole procession after him, made up of policemen with whistles and villagers with flashing torches and dogs with sharp teeth that glistened in the moonlight.

We need not take too long in describing that chase, though it seemed to him to go on for ever and ever. He was torn by brambles, drenched with the water of bogs into which he stumbled, famished and exhausted, but after a couple of hours he had run many miles, and he began to notice something strange about the country. It was growing wilder and wilder and yet — in some way that he could not explain — it was also growing more *friendly*. You see, he was on the slopes of the Magic Mountain, and nearing the outskirts of our wood. The trees grew taller and taller, and the shadows they cast were like the shadows of gigantic soldiers; and yet they were kindly shadows, and their branches seemed like great fingers beckoning him home; the wind that sighed through the branches seemed to whisper: "Just a little further, Mr. Bruno, just a little longer, my friend, and you will be home." Thicker and thicker grew the wood, and with every step he felt a little more safe; he knew that the humans were still pursuing him but he also knew that the wood was on his side; once, turning round, he could have sworn that he saw the branches of a great pine swing behind him, like the shutting of a door, and he seemed to hear the wind cry: "Stay back, humans, stay back." Maybe that was only a trick of the wind and the shadows, but that was how he felt. You see, he was getting faint and dizzy. And at last he could go no further, and he fell down, waiting for the worst.

He lay there panting and bleeding, staring with frightened eyes into the undergrowth, waiting for his pursuers to catch up with him. Once they came very close, a whole crowd of them, led by the keeper holding a torch high above his head; he could see the cruel lines on his face, lit by the torch, and could hear the hiss of the whip which he sent curling savagely into the shadows. But he lay so still that they did not notice him, and soon they turned aside, cursing. He saw the torch drifting further and further away, and heard the curses growing fainter and fainter, till at last there was darkness again and the wood was still. About an hour later he noticed a chain of lights far below in the valley, moving towards the south. They were the lights of the circus, making for the next town. At last he knew that he was safe. With a sob of thankfulness he dropped his head on his bleeding paw and fell asleep.

It was thus that they found him in the morning — stiff, cold and almost dead.

CHAPTER VI

MORE ABOUT BRUNO

MISS FOX, who was the first to find Bruno, had thought that he was really dead, and had scampered off to Mr. Justice Owl, who always had to be told of these things before anybody else, because he was so very old and so very wise.

Miss Fox was a frivolous sort of person; she was very proud of her coat and her long brown brush; she thought she was so attractive that everybody wanted to run after her. Sometimes, when she strayed too far, beyond the outskirts of the wood, she found that they *did* run after her . . . whole packs of hounds, and humans with red coats who bounced about on horses and shouted "Tallyho!" This always thrilled her, and she flirted with them in the most shameless manner, running up hill and down dale, through coppices and over ploughed fields — "till really, my dear," she would say, "I was quite out of breath." But the hounds and the huntsmen were even more out of breath, for she could run as fast as the wind; besides, she was really quite a nice girl at heart, and never allowed the flirtation to go too far, so that she always turned back to the wood when she felt that her pursuers were getting too excited. And in the wood, of course, the hounds could not pick up her scent, because the ground was far too full of magic.

Her mother always scolded her when she returned home from these adventures. "One day," she said, "you'll go too far, and be caught."

"But, Mother darling, they wouldn't hurt me. They *adore* me."

"You are an ignorant, conceited girl."

Miss Fox tossed her head. "Then why do they run after me, and make so much fuss of me? They don't want to *eat* me, do they?"

"Certainly not. They just do it for fun."

"There you are! That's what I say. For fun. You don't run after people for fun unless you like them."

"*We* don't. Humans do."

Miss Fox sniffed. "I can't believe it," she said. "I know that humans are silly, but they can't be as silly as that."

Mr. Justice Owl was well aware of Miss Fox's little escapades, and he thoroughly disapproved of them. He knew that Mrs. Fox was right, that the humans were not chasing Miss Fox because they thought she was so attractive, but because they thought she was so *unattractive*; and though he did not pretend to understand the extraordinary stupidity of human behaviour, he realized how dangerous it was for the animals, and he was constantly warning Miss Fox about it. But she never took any notice.

So when she arrived panting at the entrance to the ruined barn where he lived, he was not too pleased to see her.

"Mr. Justice Owl," she gasped, "I have found a body in the wood."

Mr. Justice Owl blinked. He was feeling extremely sleepy, for it was seven o'clock in the morning, and long past his bed-time.

"A body?" he repeated. "Whose body?"

The last body with which he had been concerned was the body of Cock Robin, and a nice business *that* had been, trying to find out who had killed him. He sincerely hoped that this was not going to be a case of that sort.

"The body of a bear," she panted. "A great big bear."

Mr. Justice Owl woke up with a start. He opened his eyes very wide and glared at Miss Fox,

68

"Is this anything to do with one of your harum-scarum chases?" he demanded.

"Indeed no, sir." Miss Fox's voice trembled — she felt that she was being threatened by the majesty of the law. "I just found him."

"There are no humans concerned? No hounds? No huntsmen?"

"None that I know of, sir."

Mr. Justice Owl blinked at her. He was a very good judge of animal nature, and he felt that she was telling the truth. This was a case which demanded immediate attention.

He turned his head, and gave a piercing whistle. There was a scuffling sound in the back of the barn and in a moment P.C. Monkey appeared, rubbing his eyes with one hand and doing up his belt with the other.

"Miss Fox," observed Mr. Justice Owl, "has a statement to make."

"Oh no, sir," she cried. "Not a *statement*. I just found the body. That was all."

Mr. Justice Owl ignored her. "You will take her statement," he continued, "and you will warn her that anything she says may be used in evidence against her." Upon which he fluttered off his perch to snatch a bite of breakfast before setting off to see the body.

By now Miss Fox was in a fine flurry; she felt as if she had committed a murder. P.C. Monkey asked her question after question — her name, her address, even her age — the impertinence! What was she doing out at such an early hour, what she had done when she first saw the body.

"I didn't do anything," she cried. "I just ran here."

"That's *your* story," said P.C. Monkey, darkly.

"But it's true!"

"We shall see!" And P.C. Monkey closed his notebook,

put his hands behind his back, and bent his knees out. "Just as if he were a human," thought Miss Fox. "The silly fool!"

Mr. Justice Owl was not long over his breakfast; to tell the truth he was anxious. He did not like this business; in spite of what Miss Fox had said, he suspected that there might be humans at the back of it. And the one thing upon which he was determined was to keep the wood, as far as possible, free from humans.

"When a human walks into a wood," he often said, "law and order fly out through the branches."

"You will proceed with Miss Fox," he commanded P.C. Monkey. "I shall follow in due course."

P.C. Monkey clicked his paws together and saluted.

"Lead the way," he said.

Miss Fox led the way.

II

It was only a short distance from Mr. Justice Owl's barn to the spot where Bruno was lying, but by the time they had traversed it, the whole wood seemed to have learned what was happening. Through the sunlit branches there was a great fluttering of birds, all eager to learn about this new excitement; and over the grass, and under the bracken, and across the glades all sorts of animals hastened to the spot. They knew that Mr. Justice Owl was on his way, so they did not go too near the body (they all thought that Bruno was dead, he lay so still); they formed a wide semi-circle, and waited. There was a great deal of twittering and whispering, but they were very grave and reverent, for animals understand death much better than humans. No animal would think of making a vulgar procession out of death, or of doing anything so ridiculous as dyeing its fur black, or hiring other animals to make foolish bleating noises. Animals know that death is quite a natural thing, which comes to all of us, but they also think that it is a thing which is best faced alone. That is why they just wander off by themselves when they are going to die, and find a place where the shadows fall deepest and the branches are most thickly twined, and lie down and close their eyes. And that is why they were so sorry for Mr. Bruno . . . because here he was, lying dead in the open, with no shade to cover him.

There was a buzz of conversation when Miss Fox arrived with P.C. Monkey.

"Did *she* do it?" demanded Master Parrot in a loud voice.

"Ssh!" rebuked his mother.

"But *did* she?"

Mrs. Parrot was so embarrassed by his naughtiness that she immediately burst into a loud cackle: "Scratch my head, shiver my splinters! Scratch my head, shiver my splinters!" She had learnt this, years and years ago, in a human house from which she had escaped. Everybody felt that it was in very bad taste for her to come out with such remarks at a time like this. Nobody wanted to scratch her head, and as for shivering her splinters, nobody wanted to do that either. What *were* a parrot's splinters, anyway? And how could you shiver them? A lot of human nonsense!

All eyes were upon Miss Fox, when she entered, and she felt very hot and nervous, particularly as P.C. Monkey insisted on staying by her side as though she were going to try to escape.

However, they soon forgot about Miss Fox, for all of a sudden there was a shadow over the ground, and they looked up and saw that it was Mr. Justice Owl.

I wish that you could have seen all their faces, brown and grey and black, long-haired and short-haired and smooth, staring up through the shadows to the figure of Mr. Justice Owl, gliding towards them. His entrances were very dramatic; he always made sure of that: he knew that he was the representative of the law of the wood, and he felt that he would be better able to enforce respect for that law if the animals thought of him as a thing apart. So he never just fluttered upon them unexpectedly, he

never just "hopped in"—he glided backwards and forwards, sending his shadow over them as though it were a herald to announce his arrival, and only when they all knew he was coming did he finally swoop down.

P.C. Monkey ran to his side.

Mr. Justice Owl fluttered his feathers, blinked, and closed his eyes. For a moment there was silence. Then, in his best legal voice, he demanded:

"Where is the Body?"

He knew quite well where the body was because he was almost standing on it. But he felt that it would be more dignified to be led up to it.

"Here, your Honour."

Mr. Justice Owl opened his eyes, blinked again, and regarded Bruno.

Then he took three steps forward, and paused. Surely his sharp eyes had detected a faint rise and fall beneath Bruno's fur? He put his head down on Bruno's chest. There was no doubt about it. The heart was beating.

Mr. Justice Owl drew a deep breath. He looked first at P.C. Monkey, then all round the circle of the animals. And in ringing tones he proclaimed:

"This is not a Body. This bear is alive!"

III

There was an immediate sensation and a great buzz of twittering and chattering.

"Silence!" cried Mr. Justice Owl.

They obeyed him at once.

He proceeded to issue orders. There was no time to waste. The animals hurried to and fro, bringing cool water from the brook to revive him, the leaves of the giant burdock to bind his bleeding paw, honey to give him strength, a cushion of moss to rest his head. While they were getting all these things Mr. Justice Owl ordered Mr. Peacock to spread his tail and wave it gently backwards and forwards over Bruno's face . . . a task which Mr. Peacock undertook with great pleasure, for he was very proud of his tail and liked to show it off.

So when Bruno at last came to, and opened his eyes, that was the first thing he saw — the stars on Mr. Peacock's tail waving above him, green, and gold and blue, and he thought that he had died and that they were the stars of heaven.

"Thank you, Mr. Peacock," said Mr. Justice Owl. "You may desist."

Mr. Peacock slowly folded his tail. It was like somebody shutting a paint-box or rolling up a precious canvas. And when the stars faded from Bruno's eyes, and he saw all the animals sitting round, watching, he no longer thought he was in heaven; he knew that he was back on earth, and the animals seemed to him like the crowds who used to watch him in the circus. You see, he was delirious. He thought he was back in the Ring.

A great fear seized him. He knew that he ought not to be lying down; they always beat him when he lay down — not in front of the crowds, but after the performance, when he had been led away. He must get up quickly, or he would be beaten — he must get up and dance.

He tried to stagger to his feet. But he sank back again exhausted, on to the moss.

"I can't," he panted, "honestly I can't . . . give me a minute . . . just another minute." And he covered his head with his paws to ward off the lash of the whip which he felt would come hissing through the air.

But no whip came. Instead he heard the kindly voice of Mr. Justice Owl:

"Calm yourself!" he murmured. "Calm yourself! You are among friends."

"Friends?" Mr. Bruno was not quite sure what "friends" were; he had never had any friends; but the word had a pleasant sound. Friends . . . they did not sound as though they were the sort of people who would whip you or starve you or lock you up.

"Friends?" he muttered, in a sort of daze.

"Indeed," said Mr. Justice Owl. "We are all friends; we wish to help you."

His voice was so kind that Mr. Bruno slowly took his paws away from his face. And at last his head cleared; he remembered his escape, he remembered coming to the wood, he remembered, above all, the strange feeling of kindness and comfort that he had known as he had plunged deeper and deeper into it, as though the very branches were there to protect him. And as soon as he remembered all those things he began to revive very quickly — he was able to sit up and drink some water and take a nibble of the honeycomb.

All the animals were delighted to see him so much better; tears came to Miss Fox's eyes, and even Mrs. Hare, who was supposed to be very cynical, blinked in a suspicious manner.

But Bruno's troubles were by no means over. Mr. Justice Owl, seeing that he was now well on the way to recovery, decided that he was well enough to answer a few questions. He liked the look of Bruno; he was prepared to welcome him to the wood, but first he would have to explain where he came from. They could not have mysteries in the wood ... and after all, the sudden appearance of a large bear in the early morning, seriously wounded, and lying in a bramble bush, was something of a mystery. For a moment Mr. Justice Owl wondered if Bruno were in any way connected with the Human War which was raging in the world outside, if he were some sort of spy who had come down in a parachute. Mr. Justice Owl knew all about parachutes and heartily despised them — he regarded them as a typical example of Man's constant efforts to turn himself into something which Nature had not intended; animals would never be so foolish. Could one imagine a tortoise in a parachute, for example? Or a rabbit or a snail? If animals like that had gone tying parachutes to their backs and floating all over the place, it would have been quite impossible to keep any law and order, nobody would have known who was doing what, the whole wood would have become a sort of Bedlam. No . . . parachutes were a very undesirable form of amusement, in Mr. Justice Owl's opinion.

However, he did not think that Bruno had come down in a parachute. He looked far too sensible — besides, a parachute was a great clumsy affair which would certainly have been discovered if it had been left lying about.

How then, had he come to the wood? What was his secret? It was Mr. Justice Owl's duty to find out. So as soon as Bruno had finished his honeycomb, and was sitting up, and letting P.C. Monkey bind the burdock round his paw, Mr. Justice Owl stepped forward.

In grave tones he demanded:

"Do you feel well enough to answer a few questions?"

Bruno closed his eyes for a moment. He had been afraid that this would happen. However, he would have to go through with it; he might as well get it over.

"Yes," he whispered.

"Good!" Mr. Justice Owl preened himself. "Now, first of all — where have you come from?"

IV

It was the question Bruno had been dreading.

He looked round him desperately, trying to think of a reply. They said they were "friends" — these animals, but he did not trust them — not yet. How could he trust the animals, seeing that he knew nothing of their nature? He only knew *human* nature, and he had every reason for distrusting that.

"Where do I come from?" he repeated. They were waiting for his answer. At all costs he must avoid telling them the truth; they might give him away. He thought of the hundreds of cities to which he had been dragged, North, South, East and West, but he could not remember any of their names; they were all the same to him, just a glitter of bright lights, a blare of music, a roaring of thousands of people, and then — the solitude of his tiny cage. Besides, even if he told them the name of some city, they might suspect. "What was a bear doing in a city?" they might ask themselves.

Then he had an inspiration. He remembered the big paper placard that they used to hang over his cage when the circus went on the road. It had been a long time before he had been able to read it, because he had always been inside the cage, looking through the placard, so that he had been obliged to read it backwards, and even then only when the sun was shining on it. This was what he had read:

BRUNO
THE CELEBRATED DANCING BEAR
ALL THE WAY FROM
THE STEPPES
OF
RUSSIA

If you take this book to the looking-glass you will be able to read the words on the placard. You will not be surprised to know that it took Bruno a long time to understand them, considering that he had to read them backwards in a tiny cage, with no mirror to help him.

"The steppes of Russia." The words floated through Bruno's head — it was as though they were coming to his rescue. He had never been to Russia, but he knew that it was hundreds of miles away, and that none of the other animals would have been there either. Besides, he had learned a little about it because there had been a Russian dancer in the circus who had sometimes slept in a tent near his cage, and late at night he had heard her talking about her country, which seemed to be very vast and always covered with snow. He never quite understood what the steppes were; he thought they were a sort of staircase, and it seemed very odd to spend your life on a staircase. However, none of the other animals knew either, so it did not matter.

He took the plunge.

"Where do I come from?" he said. "I come from Russia."

"From Russia!" There was a great rustling and panting and squeaking and twittering among the animals; this was indeed exciting.

"From Russia?" repeated Mr. Justice Owl. He blinked, very wisely, at Bruno. To tell the truth, Mr. Justice Owl knew even less about Russia than Bruno, but he had no intention of betraying his ignorance. From the way he blinked, you would have said that he knew it inside out.

"What part of Russia?" he inquired.

"The steppes," gasped Bruno.

"The steps?" echoed Mr. Justice Owl. There was a rather sharp note in his voice. He wondered if Bruno was trying to make a fool of him. What did he mean — the steps? The doorsteps? The steps leading up to the attic? He was about to rebuke Bruno, when he stopped short, and a melancholy "Too-wit, too-woe" echoed from his beak.

For Bruno, exhausted by all he had gone through, had fallen into a dead faint.

CHAPTER VII

BRUNO RECAPTURED

AND now we can go on with our story, which we left
on a bright sunny morning when Bruno was lumbering through the wood on his way to The Shop in the
Ford.

Many years had passed since all the sad things which
we have been recalling in the last two chapters, and to-day
if you had seen Mr. Bruno, you would have said that never
in your life before had you met a bear so happy, so plump,
and so prosperous; he had developed into one of the most
respected citizens in the wood.

"Top of the morning, Mr. Bruno! . . . All the best, Mr.
Bruno! . . . My! Mr. Bruno, you're looking fine!" Such
were the cordial greetings that welcomed him, all along
the way. Miss Fox gave an extra twitch to her brush when
she saw him, and Mrs. Hare gave a very gracious bow.
And even Mr. Peacock, who only spread his tail on very
special occasions — (except, of course, when he was by
himself, standing by the edge of the lake watching his own
reflection, which was so beautiful that sometimes he felt
quite giddy and fell into the water) — even Mr. Peacock
greeted Bruno by spreading his tail to its fullest extent.

"My word, Mr. Peacock," said Bruno. "I almost need
my sun glasses to look at you, you're so bright!"

And indeed, standing there all spread out in the sunlight,
Mr. Peacock was like a regular display of fireworks.

"You are going to The Shop in The Ford?" inquired Mr.
Peacock.

Mr. Bruno nodded.

"They will be honoured by your patronage."

"Kind of you to say so. Coming along too?"

Mr. Peacock shook his head. If he went along with Bruno he would have to shut up his tail again, for he could only walk very slowly when it was open. And now that it was open, he simply could not bring himself to shut it. It felt so beautiful; it seemed to tingle all over; he could feel all the emeralds and the opals and the turquoises sparkling and shimmering in the air around him, and sending delicious tremors down his spine. No, it would really be a sin to shut it all up; and in a moment he would go down to the lake and look at himself, and go on looking and looking and looking; and he only hoped that this time he would not fall in.

So Mr. Peacock shook his head to Bruno's invitation. "I regret," he said, "that I have a previous appointment." Which in a way was true, because after all there is no reason why one should not make an appointment with oneself. "But," he added, "do not let me delay you. It is an Interesting Establishment." His tail quivered all over when he pronounced these long words. "They sell Something of Everything. In fact ..." and here he lowered his voice, as if he was very important indeed. "I should not be surprised if they sold Something Russian."

"Something Russian?" There was a sudden note of anxiety in Mr. Bruno's voice, and his tail gave a nervous twitch. Then he smiled again. After all, what had he got to fear? It was all so long ago. "Something Russian!" he repeated. "That *would* be a pleasant surprise!"

And with a wave of his paw, he went on his way.

Poor Bruno! If he had only known!

II

And now — we can conceal it no longer — we must confess that Bruno, in the last few years, had been telling the animals a very big untruth. He had been telling them that he could speak Russian, whereas of course he did not know a single word, not even the word DA, which is the Russian for "Yes", and a very nice word too.

Mind you, we are not blaming Bruno, at least not very much. It was not as though he were doing anybody harm. If ever a bear had an excuse for telling an Untruth, *he* had, after all that he had been through.

Besides, as the years had gone by, he had almost come to believe that he *could* speak Russian. For instance, when he was dozing in the sun, with a half-eaten honeycomb by his side, he would say to himself, "I have just five minutes more Sleepsky before I go home to Mrs. Brunovitch." And he would feel that he was speaking Russian. Which was not really quite the case. And then, when he fell asleep, he would dream of quantities of beautiful white staircases, with banisters made out of ice, which were lovely to slide down, and he was almost certain that he was dreaming of the Russian steppes. And that was not quite the case either, as we have all learnt in our geography classes.

So obviously it would have been better if Bruno had not told his Untruth. However, it is too late to think of that now. The Untruth had been told and he was about to pay for it, to the bitter end.

III

Sam was sulky this morning ... the morning that Bruno was approaching.

In spite of all the money that he was making, he still

wanted to make more. And though it was very gratifying
to see how all the animals were thronging to the shop, he
did not care for animals, indeed, he actually hated them...
particularly the small, timid animals like Miss Fieldmouse
and old Mr. Caterpillar. He was not at all like Judy, who
would pay just as much attention to the humblest of the
Beetle family as she would, let us say, to Mr. Peacock
himself.

For the moment the Shop was empty, and Sam was
adding up the morning's takings. They were quite a lot,
but in his opinion they were not nearly enough.

"At this rate," he said to Old Sam, "we shan't be able
to retire till Doomsday."

"But ain't we doing well?" queried Old Sam.

Sam did not answer, but only spat on the ground contemptuously.

"At any rate we made a nice profit out of them ants'
eggs," Old Sam reminded him.

"Pshaw!" muttered Sam. "What's a few ants' eggs?
Chicken food!"

"But I thought ants' eggs was for goldfish?"

Sam made a rude face. "You make me tired," he said,
"Don't you know what chicken food means?"

"Scraps and potater peelings?" suggested Old Sam.

Sam made an even ruder face. "That's what you are!"
he said. "Scraps and potater peelings. Scraps for legs and
potater peelings for brains." Which is not at all the way in
which little boys should speak to their grandfathers, particularly when their grandfathers are over three hundred
years old, and look their age.

"You get worse and worse," growled Old Sam.

"You couldn't!" retorted Young Sam. "You was born
worse. You couldn't get any worser."

"That's not grammar."

"Maybe. But it's sense."

And Sam, just to show his spite, gave an angry pinch to the rubber bulb of the motor horn, which was only a few inches from Old Sam's ear, making the old man jump in the air as though a bee had stung him.

"What this shop wants," said Sam, when his grandfather had ceased rubbing his ear, "is Class."

"What's Class?" demanded Old Sam, keeping a watchful eye on the motor horn.

"Class is everything that you aren't, you old buzzard. Class is dough. Class is front row in the stalls. Class is throwing a clean shirt into the laundry basket just because you can't wear it twice."

"Sounds like a lot of hooey to me."

"It is hooey. But it's what we've got to have."

Old Sam scowled and scratched his ear.

"What we want's new blood," continued Sam. "A partner. Somebody all these darned animals respect. Somebody can sell 'em a lot of junk and make 'em believe it's the real article. Somebody who . . ."

Suddenly he stopped, right in the middle of his sentence. His eyes lit up and a wicked grin twisted his mouth.

"Gee whiz!" he muttered. "Here he comes!"

For down the glade, happily ignorant of his fate, wandered Mr. Bruno.

I V

He was not alone. On one side of him was Miss Fox and on the other side was Mrs. Hare. They had all met on the way, and had come along together.

No meeting could have been more unfortunate. For hardly had they walked a few paces before Mrs. Hare, like Mr. Peacock, had said to Mr. Bruno how nice it would be

if he could find somebody in the shop who spoke Russian,
and poor silly Mr. Bruno, instead of changing the subject,
had pretended that this was just what he wanted, and that

he was only too eager to have the chance of speaking
Russian again.

They walked up to the counter. If Bruno could have
seen the expression on Sam's face at that moment, he
would have turned and fled.

For Sam had recognized him!

Often, in the old days, he had sat in the circus and
watched Bruno as he danced and plunged through hoops.
When Bruno had escaped, Sam had been one of the hottest
on his heels. "Oh, this is rich!" thought Sam to himself.

"This is the biggest stroke of luck I've ever had. I've got this Bruno, and I'm going to hang on to him."

However, for the moment he kept these thoughts to himself. Bruno was much too valuable a prize to be treated lightly; he would be much more use to Sam as a partner than as a slave, because he was one of the most important citizens in the wood.

Sam came forward with a pleasant smile, and his manner was very respectful when he said: "Good morning, ladies, good morning, sir, and what can I do for you, this morning?"

Mr. Bruno really wanted to buy a sponge cake. But since Mrs. Hare and Miss Fox were both expecting him to speak Russian, he thought he had better get it over, once and for all. It never entered his head for a moment that he was walking into a trap.

And so it was with a jaunty smile that he stepped forward and demanded, "Do you speak Russian?"

As he asked the question he looked proudly round at his two friends, as if to say, "See how clever I am!"

"Of course I speak Russian," lied Sam, who could not speak a word.

Mr. Bruno blinked. He could hardly believe his ears. "You . . . you *do*?"

"Like a native," said Sam, who was thoroughly enjoying himself.

If Mr. Bruno had been able to turn pale he would have gone as white as his Uncle in the North Pole. What on earth was he to do? They were all looking at him. He must say *something*. So he muttered. . . .

"So do I."

"What did you say?" demanded Sam.

"I said *so do I*," repeated Bruno. He could not stop his voice from trembling. Mrs. Hare was looking at him

86

eagerly, waiting for him to begin. So was Miss Fox. What *could* he say? Then he had a sudden inspiration.

"But not on Thursdays," he went on, "I never speak Russian on Thursdays. It . . . it gives me a pain."

There! that was a splendid idea. Nobody could expect him to speak Russian if it gave him a pain.

"But to-day's Wednesday," said Mrs. Hare.

"Yes," chimed in Miss Fox. "It's completely Wednesday."

"It's as Wednesday as it can be," agreed Mrs. Hare. "So now you can speak Russian after all."

Bruno cursed the two ladies under his breath. Why did they want to come butting in?

What *could* he say? He wanted a sponge cake; supposing he asked for a sponge cakeski? That sounded like Russian, but it mightn't be Russian at all. Sponge cakeski might mean poison. Or it might mean blackbeetles. Or it might mean a cold in the head. And whatever would they think of him if he said he wanted to buy blackbeetles or a cold in the head? They would think him quite mad.

They were still waiting. He began to feel desperate. He lifted his eyes, and looked at Sam, hoping that perhaps Sam might see his plight and take pity on him.

And as his eyes met Sam's his heart nearly stopped beating. For there was something in those eyes that reminded him of another pair of eyes that he had known long ago — the eyes of his keeper in the circus — staring at him with a cold hatred.

"Well, Mr. Bruno," said Sam, "I'm waiting."

Bruno shivered. How often had he heard those words before . . . "I'm waiting" . . . snarled at him through the clenched teeth of his keeper, as he stood over him with a whip!

"Oh *please* . . . just a few words . . ." murmured Mrs. Hare.

"Such an education, it would be . . ." pleaded Miss Fox.

He must, he *must*. If he did not, he would never be able to face the animals again; he would be exposed as a sham and a fraud; he would have to leave the wood for ever.

He took a deep breath and said:

"Stavolinski."

It was the name of his old keeper. He dared not look at Sam as he said it, for he knew, in his heart of hearts, that Sam had already guessed his secret.

"Stavolinski!" echoed Mrs. Hare. "Fancy that!"

"Stavolinski!" giggled Miss Fox. "What a funny word! Whatever does it mean?"

Sam's voice cut in. "*We* know what it means, don't we, Mr. Bruno?" For he had recognized the keeper's name.

Bruno could only gulp and nod.

"It means bright lights, doesn't it, Mr. Bruno? And big crowds, and brass bands."

"Gracious me!" cried Mrs. Hare. "To think that one word can mean so much!"

"Oh, but it means a lot more than that, too," declared Sam. "It means lions and tigers and giants and dwarfs. And it means . . ." His voice sank almost to a whisper, so that only Bruno could hear him . . . "It means a CAGE." As he said the word he burst out laughing, and he laughed so loud that Mrs. Hare and Miss Fox both joined in.

"I must be going," muttered Bruno, desperately. But somehow his feet would not move.

"Oh no, Mr. Bruno. I couldn't hear of it." Sam leapt over the counter and seized his arm with an iron grip. "You and I's going to be friends, Mr. Bruno. More than friends. We're going to be Partners."

"Well, well!" cried Mrs. Hare. "Whoever would have thought it?"

"It's a great honour for Mr. Bruno," tittered Miss Fox.

"That's just what it is, an honour. Ain't it, Mr. Bruno?" And he gave Bruno's arm a cruel pinch.

Bruno was speechless. He could only hang his head.

"And now ladies," said Sam, "if you'll excuse us, me and Mr. Bruno's got business to discuss. This way, Mr. Bruno!"

Very timidly, as though the whip was already poised above him, Bruno looked up. His eyes met Sam's. As he saw their cruel glare, he knew that he was doomed; he had to obey.

Slowly he shuffled off into the cave. And Sam followed him, with a final bow to the ladies who went on their way through the wood to spread the news.

And there, for the time being, we must leave poor Bruno, crouching miserably in the cave, with Young Sam chuckling over him on one side and Old Sam wheezing over him on the other, and both of them prodding him in the ribs with their sharp fingers, while they told him all the wicked things that he would have to do for them unless he wanted to be sent back to the circus.

CHAPTER VIII

A PEACOCK SPREADS HIS TAIL

MR. PEACOCK was feeling very proud.

As well he might, for it was the morning of the opening of the Beauty Parlour; and all over the wood there were notices pinned to the tree-trunks, announcing. . . .

Miss Judy's Beauty Parlour
All the Latest Methods
Tails a Speciality
Open To-day
The Opening Ceremony will be performed
by
MR. PEACOCK

In smaller letters underneath it was printed:

Mrs. Judy's Surgery will Also be Opened to-day
All the Oldest Remedies.   Strictly Confidential

"Well, really," said Mrs. Peacock, who looked rather a dim little figure as she stood by the side of her magnificent husband reading the notice, "I'm sure it's a great honour."

Mr. Peacock turned his head to look at her.

"An honour for whom?"

Mrs. Peacock had meant an honour for Mr. Peacock, but she realized that as usual she had said the wrong thing. So she quickly added: "An honour for Miss Judy, of course."

"Thank you." He bowed. "It certainly is an honour for her. But it is an honour that I feel justified in granting, in such a Cause." He drew himself up proudly, and swelled out his chest. "The Cause of Beauty." And as he said these words, his tail, which was carefully folded and shut up, began to quiver violently.

"Oh, dear," thought Mrs. Peacock to herself, "he is going to Open. Far too soon. And his tail will get all creased and dusty . . . after all the trouble I have taken." For Mrs. Peacock had been up half the night, ironing and brushing and polishing Mr. Peacock's tail, and when it was finished she had folded it with the greatest care and wrapped it up in tissue paper, begging him not to open it again till he mounted the platform to make his speech.

"The Cause of Beauty!" repeated Mr. Peacock, his tail quivering more violently than ever, and little bits of gold and purple beginning to peep out from under the folds.

Mrs. Peacock could not bear it. "Were you . . ." she ventured very timidly, "were you thinking of Opening already?"

"Certainly not," snapped Mr. Peacock. "Why?"

"I only thought . . ." she began, casting an anxious eye on his tail.

"Then you should not think," he interrupted. All the same, he was glad that she *had* thought, for if she had not checked him, he would certainly have Opened.

"I'm sorry," breathed Mrs. Peacock, noticing with relief that the tail was closing up again.

Mr. Peacock felt that he was not being quite fair. He gave her a playful peck. "That's all right, my dear. It was my fault. To tell the truth I'm a little nervous about my speech."

"Oh, Mr. Peacock! The idea of *you* being nervous! Why—the minute you Open, you'll speak like an angel."

Mr. Peacock bowed. No doubt she was right; she usually was. He gave her another peck for luck. And then, very slowly, with long dignified struts, they walked together towards the shop, through glades that were still ghostly with the early morning mist.

II

At The Shop Under the Willow, Judy and her grannie were giving the final touches.

"Have we enough Fur Lotion, do you think?" asked Judy, arranging the bottles on the shelf. There were three kinds: "Long Fur" in a purple bottle with a fir-cone for a cork; "Short Fur" in a yellow bottle with a little chain of red daisies round the neck; and "Medium Fur" in a green bottle with a bluebird's feather gummed below the label.

"Well, we certainly can't make any more at this hour," grumbled Mrs. Judy. She had been working very hard and she was inclined to be cross. "Besides, nobody may buy any at all."

"Oh, Grannie, don't say that, after all our trouble!"

"We shall see." She bent over and sniffed one of the jars. "I must say I'm pinning my faith to this Honeysuckle Cream."

"Why don't you use some yourself, Grannie dear?"

"Don't be foolish, child. At my age!" All the same, when Judy's back was turned, she popped her finger in the jar and dabbed some on the end of her nose, where it remained like a pat of butter, slowly melting. It looked very strange, and not at all beautiful, but it smelt delicious, so what did she care?

"They're *bound* to like the Magic Eyedrops," said Judy, giving a row of bottles a final flick with her duster.

"If they don't," sniffed Mrs. Judy, "they don't deserve to have a Beauty Parlour at all."

And now that we have mentioned the Magic Eyedrops,

we will tell you how to make them yourself. We have several minutes to spare before the animals arrive, and we could not spend them better than in learning about the Eyedrops, because they are really wonderful things and will help you a great deal. This is what you have to do:

Recipe for Magic Eyedrops

To be used whenever you feel like crying, or, in acute cases, when you actually ARE crying, and do not see any reason to stop.

First, collect a glass of rainwater. If you live in the country, this is easy, for you can just run along to the waterbutt, or catch it in a bucket as it runs off the roof. But if you live in a flat in the city it may not be quite so easy, and you will probably have to put an enamel basin on the window ledge.

Next, take a small pebble — any little stone from the road or the beach or the flower-bed will do—wash it very clean under the tap and press it gently on your eyelids, first on the left eyelid and then on the right.

Then, take a very tiny piece of blotting paper, only a quarter the size of a cent or a sixpence. And put the rainwater in a jug.

Then take a quarter of a teaspoonful of salt.

Pour the rainwater very slowly into a clean cup, and as you are pouring — (remember to do it *very* slowly) — repeat the following rhyme:

> As the rain falls in the cup
> *(Start pouring)*
> Take my tears and dry them up
> *(Finish pouring)*
> Blotting paper . . . pebble . . . salt
> *(Drop them in, one by one)*
> P'raps it really is my fault
> *(Stir with clean spoon)*

Maybe if I only try
(*Go on stirring*)
I shall never want to cry!
(*Finish stirring*)

Pour the contents of the cup into a saucepan, bring to the
boil, and keep boiling for exactly sixty-nine seconds. Pour
the water — (*without* the pebble or the blotting paper) —
into a small bottle, and put it on the top of your head and
keep it there for nine seconds. Then put it away in a dark
cupboard and leave it to cool, and to get full of magic, for
three days and three nights.

Now comes the great test. Sooner or later — it may be
in a few days or it may be in a few weeks, according to all
sorts of circumstances over which you have no control —
you will probably want to cry. Perhaps you will fall down
and cut your knee, or perhaps you will have a pain, or
perhaps you will just be very sad because all grown ups
are so silly, and always stop you from doing what you want.
Never mind what the reason may be, the Magic Eyedrops
will stop you crying if you only use them rightly.

You must run at once to your mother or father, or whoever it may be who keeps the bottle — (for I am afraid that
it *must* be kept by a grown up, otherwise the magic goes out
through the cork) — and you must ask them to put three
drops *at once* on to each eyelid. They MUST OBEY you —
(which is nice, for a change; if they do *not* obey you, they
will have a very bad pain). As soon as they have obeyed
you, and put on the drops, you will cease crying; you will
not be able to cry even if you try, and very likely you will
begin to laugh.

But this is not the end of the story. For if you put out
an ordinary glass of water on the window ledge, next time
it is raining, and pour into it two of the magic drops, and

go away into the next room for five minutes, you will find that each of the drops has crystallized into a penny. These, of course, you may spend as you like.

But mind that you never cry just to get pennies. I once knew a little girl who cried to get pennies, and she was stung all over by bees. This would also happen to you, if you followed her bad example.

III

The animals were beginning to arrive, and although it needed nearly half an hour to the opening ceremony, there was already quite a fluttering and cooing and purring and sniffing, among the ancient roots and branches.

However, Judy was rather worried, because they all seemed very shy, and not at all sure whether they ought to buy anything or not.

Mrs. Dove, for instance, was longing to order some of Judy's Pearl Powder to sprinkle on her chest, but she simply did not dare to do so because Mrs. Pouter Pigeon was watching her, and she was sure that if she ordered any, Mrs. Pouter Pigeon would say something unpleasant.

"You really *should* try some," urged Judy.

"What is it made of?" queried Mrs. Dove.

"It is made of powdered mother of pearl and the seeds of white moon-flowers; then it is mixed together with the juice of white cherries and spread out to dry on white toadstools in the moonlight."

"It sounds beautiful," sighed Mrs. Dove. But out of the corner of her eye she could see that Mrs. Pouter Pigeon was watching her like a hawk. So she shook her head, murmuring "Some other time, perhaps," and passed on.

Which was really very foolish, for Mrs. Pouter Pigeon was longing to buy some of the powder too.

"It will be better as soon as Mr. Peacock has made his speech," thought Judy. And she hurried off to see how he was getting on.

Mr. Peacock, who had arrived with Mrs. Peacock before any of the others, was resting in the "Annexe", which was really a withered branch round which an old honeysuckle had twined itself into a sort of arbour. In spite of his grand manners he was very nervous indeed, for he had never made a speech before. (Except, of course, to Mrs. Peacock.) And he showed his nervousness by all sorts of angry little pecks and pouts.

"I hope," he said to Judy, "I *sincerely* hope that when I speak there will be silence?"

"But of course, Mr. Peacock. Nobody would be so rude as to. . . ."

"No sniffs? No crunchings?"

"Certainly no sniffs. As for crunchings. . . ."

"Who would dare to crunch at a moment like this?" interposed Mrs. Peacock.

"Mrs. Rabbit," snapped Mr. Peacock. "*She* would crunch. She crunches out of sheer nerves."

"Well, I am sure she will do no such thing to-day."

"Let us hope not." Mr. Peacock closed his beautiful eyes. "What is the time?" he breathed in a faint voice.

"There is still about twenty minutes to go," said Judy.

"Are you sure?"

"Well — fairly sure."

"Have you blown the dandelion clock?"

"Not for the last hour or so."

Mr. Peacock tapped his foot impatiently. "Then kindly bring one here and blow the time immediately. I cannot keep My Public waiting."

He did not really care two hoots about the time, but he was so nervous that he had to go on talking, and complain-

ing and fidgeting. Judy understood just how he felt, and did
not blame him in the least, for she would have been quite
as nervous herself. So she ran off to get a dandelion clock.

Dandelion clocks are far more sensible than human
clocks, for you can make them tell just the time you want.
If you want to be early you blow out your cheeks like bal-
loons and puff very hard, and lo and behold, it is Early.
If you want to be late, you breathe softly, and puff very
carefully, so that the soft seeds of the dandelion drift away
one by one, and lo and behold it is Late. And you stand
there watching them, floating off into the distance so lazily
that you can see them for quite a long time . . . over the
hedge, through the boughs of the apple tree, then a little
higher, up, up, till they vanish in the blue, each one of

them on their way to heaven, where they will be kept until our coming, little symbols of time to be lived again, far more happily than we ever lived it here.

Time is an airy, feathery thing, like the seed of the dandelion; it flies away all too swiftly on the summer air; we should treat it gently; above all, we should treat it with love.

And so, when Judy brought back the dandelion clock to Mr. Peacock, and began to show him the time, she breathed very softly, so that he should not feel too agitated. Nevertheless, the seeds flew away merrily up into the tree tops, for it was growing late, and though a dandelion clock can be very obliging, and can grant us a few moments' indulgence, it can never really tell a lie. Time can do almost anything but that.

The last delicate feather of a seed flew off the stalk, hovered above them, twisted, turned, and then danced up to the sky.

Mr. Peacock watched it go.

Then he rose to his feet. He was trembling all over, and his tail, which was still firmly folded, was on the point of opening. It was only with the greatest effort that he could keep it shut—it felt like a whole bundle of rockets that only needed a match to set it alight in a thousand flaming stars.

"Come!" he said, in a hoarse voice. "We must proceed."

Slowly he emerged from his retreat, and made his way to the platform.

IV

At the very moment when Mr. Peacock was mounting the platform, accompanied by the wild applause of all present, a plot was being hatched by Sam, at the other end of the wood. It was such a wicked plot, and it seemed so likely to succeed, that if Mr. Peacock had known of it he would probably never have dared to get up and make a speech at all.

Let us pay a quick visit to The Shop in the Ford to see what it is all about.

When Sam had gone out in the morning and had seen the advertisements of Judy's Beauty Parlour and Mrs. Judy's Surgery, he had been so angry that he could hardly contain himself. He rushed back to the cave where Bruno and Old Sam were sleeping, gave Bruno a vicious kick and tugged hard at Old Sam's whiskers.

"Get up . . . get up!" he shouted. "We've been double-crossed!"

"Double-crossed?" growled Old Sam, staggering to his feet. "Who by?"

"Those two witches under the Willow."

When Bruno heard this, his heart gave a leap of joy. If only it were true! However, of course he concealed his feelings.

"What've they been up to now?" demanded Old Sam.

Sam explained. As Bruno listened, he felt that it was a splendid idea! He was sure it would be a success. Perhaps it might even be so successful that Sam would be ruined and would have to leave the wood. He was so cheered by the thought that for the first time in many days he began to smile.

But not for long. Another kick, harder than ever, brought him back to reality.

"You there!" shouted Sam. "Take that darned grin off your face! And go and get our breakfast and look snappy about it. Scram!"

When Bruno had scrammed, Sam began to pace backwards and forwards, scowling and snarling.

"We got to do something," he muttered. "We got to do something, and do it quick."

"What sort of thing?" queried Old Sam.

"We got to wreck that meeting. We got to make it the biggest flop this wood's ever seen. We got to see to it that she don't sell one cent's worth of her phoney stuff."

"How're we going to do it?"

"That's what I'm asking you, you old son of a buzzard, you old petrified beetle, you . . . you old blue-nosed toad-in-the-hole."

"That's not a respectful way for a boy to talk to his grandpa," complained Old Sam, with some truth.

"It's too darned respectful for *you*!" retorted Sam. And he continued to pace up and down, and snarl and splutter, trying to think of some idea which would show him how to wreck the Opening of the Beauty Parlour.

But no idea suggested itself. Breakfast came and went. Still no idea. Sam began to feel desperate.

"Couldn't we just go round and smash things up?" ventured Old Sam.

"You make me tired," snapped Sam. "What d'you think we are? Gangsters?"

"Well . . ." began Old Sam, and then thought better of it. He had been going to say that Sam was not a bad imitation of a gangster, but perhaps the suggestion would not be very well received.

"We're not going to get in wrong with the law," continued Sam. "What's more, none of the animals have got to suspect that we've had anything to do with it." He beat his hand on his forehead, scowling more blackly than ever.

Suddenly the scowl gave way to a wicked grin. He clapped his hands and sprang to his feet. "I got it!" he cried. "Gee — it's a swell idea, too!" He put his fingers in his mouth and blew a shrill whistle.

From out of the cave shuffled Bruno.

"Hi you!" yelled Sam. "Bring me a pen and paper!"

Bruno brought it.

"Stand there while I write," ordered Sam. "You got to take a note in a minute."

Bruno began to tremble. "Oh dear!" he thought. "Whatever is he up to now?" Out of the corner of his eye he watched what Sam was writing. And when he saw what it was, he felt worse than ever.

This is what Sam wrote:

To Mrs. Badger,
     Badger Bungalow,
     The Wood.

Dear Mrs. Badger,
     This morning we are opening our new Beauty Parlour and Surgery. Mr. Peacock is making a speech at the beginning. This is a Special Invitation, because we all so much hope that you will be able to come.

                                   Yours truly,
                                        Miss Judy.

Sam folded up the letter, wrapped it in a dock leaf, and handed it to Bruno.

"Take that," he snapped, "and mind you run all the way."

Bruno shuffled miserably from one foot to another. How could he do such a thing? The letter was a forgery . . . the wickedest forgery that was ever written. For if Mrs. Badger attended the meeting, all would be lost.

"What you waiting for?" cried Sam.

Bruno gulped and made as though to speak. But Sam did not give him a chance. He rose to his feet, and stepped forward and glared straight into Bruno's eyes.

"Don't you think you'd better do as you're told, Mr. Bruno?" he hissed. "Or do you want to be sent back, Mr. Bruno? Back to the Circus?"

At the mention of that dreadful word, poor Bruno gave a low moan, snatched the letter from Sam, and ran off on his hated mission, with tears in his eyes.

V

And now, why all this fuss about Mrs. Badger?

Well, we must be quite frank. The trouble about Mrs. Badger was that she . . .

Really, it is very difficult to say. It makes us feel quite hot and bothered to say it, because it sounds so rude.

But it must be said. Once again, the trouble about Mrs. Badger was that she. . . .

Oh dear! This is very awkward. If only there were somebody else to say it for us! However, there is nobody else. So we must take a deep breath and make a real effort. For the last time. The trouble about Mrs. Badger was that she *smelt* quite terrible.

There — the truth is out. It was most unpleasant to have to tell it, but there was no avoiding it, because otherwise you would not have realized the wickedness of Sam's plot against Judy. Mrs. Badger smelt so terrible that she had only to appear on the horizon for all the other animals to run away. If she were to go to the meeting it was almost certain that the whole thing would break up in disorder.

She smelt like burnt feathers and very bad eggs and very old dustbins. Even if she crossed the path quite a long way ahead you said, "Oh dear, whatever is it? It must be the drains. Or perhaps it's the gasworks. Or maybe . . ."

The Family Failing — for that is the nicest way in which we can describe it — was shared by Mr. Badger and the three Master Badgers. They all smelt like nothing on earth. If you were to put even the youngest Master Badger in the middle of Trafalgar Square, and leave him there, playing with his toys, you would find that in a very short time the square would be empty, the traffic would have been diverted, the pigeons would have flown to the South of France, and the lions would have been straining at their leashes. It really was as bad as that. And it was only the fact that the wood was a magic wood, where all things were made a little better than in the outside world, and where even the ugliest sights and sounds and smells were softened and sweetened . . . it was only this fact that made the Badgers even tolerable.

The tragedy of it was that in every other respect they were such nice people, kind and generous and gentle, anxious to be on good terms with their neighbours. As far as they knew, they *were* on good terms, for the animals were very polite, and never dreamed of telling them. All the same, the Badgers were nearly always left out of things. And whenever any of the animals called, out of a sense of duty, they only stayed for a very short time, and even then they kept fanning themselves and sniffing their handker-chiefs and pretending that they had a cold in the head — or, if they could think of no other excuse, complaining of the drains.

All this seemed very strange to the Badger Family, who thought that the animals were most eccentric. They hap-pened to be discussing it on the very morning that Bruno was on the way to the Badger Bungalow with Sam's note.

"The animals seem to have only one subject of conversation," sighed Mrs. Badger. "The drains!"

"Quite," agreed Mr. Badger. "They seem obsessed with the idea of drains. I had not been in the club for five minutes yesterday before they were all talking about the drains."

Mrs. Badger nodded. "They have drains on the head," she observed.

"How can you have drains on the head, Mummy?" asked the youngest Master Badger.

Mrs. Badger smiled and patted him. "At any rate, my dear," she said, "*you* will never have drains on your head."

"And then they are so fidgety," resumed Mr. Badger. "Always fiddling with fans, and sniffing things."

"I can't understand it," murmured his wife. "Do you remember the time that Mrs. Hare came to call?"

"Indeed yes!"

"Never have I seen such a restless creature," she said. "She couldn't sit still for a moment and kept complaining of the draught. She said she had to get out of the wind, but when I went and sat in the door, to protect her from it, she only seemed to get worse. She came over quite faint."

"She did indeed," agreed Mr. Badger. "A very nervous type, obviously. Do you remember how she asked for smelling salts?"

"And lavender. . . ."

"And onions. . . ." chimed in the youngest Master Badger.

His mother stared at him in astonishment. "You mean to say she asked for onions?"

"Yes, Mummy, when your back was turned. Just to smell. She said that anything would be better than *this*."

"What did she mean by 'this'?" demanded Mr. Badger somewhat sharply.

"She didn't say. She just said '*this*'. Perhaps she meant. . . ."

But before he could finish the sentence there was a knock on the door. It was Bruno, with the note.

Five minutes later, Mrs. Badger, beaming all over, wearing a new hat and smelling, if possible, more terrible than she had ever smelt before, out of sheer happiness, was hurrying on her way to The Shop Under the Willow Tree.

VI

Mr. Peacock was in the middle of his speech, and it was being an enormous success. The animals were in raptures, and Judy whispered to her grannie, "After this, we shall sell out the whole stock."

It is true that right at the beginning there had been an awkward moment. Just as he had mounted the platform, and was slowly spreading his tail, to loud applause, one of his feathers had caught in a bramble bush and Mrs. Peacock had been obliged to rush out and disentangle it. However, the embarrassment of this accident was quickly forgotten in the sensation caused by his opening sentence.

Spreading his tail to the fullest extent, and taking a step forward so that he was in full brilliance of the early sunlight, Mr. Peacock cleared his throat and proclaimed:

"Some are born with tails . . ." (Here he turned slightly to the left).

"Some achieve tails . . ." (Here he turned slightly to the right).

"And some . . ." (Here he paused, and by chance his eye met the eye of Mrs. Manx, who, poor dear, had no tail at all) . . . "Some have tails pinned upon them!"

The excitement caused by this statement was intense. Everybody turned to look at Mrs. Manx, to see if she had bought a tail and pinned it on. When they saw that she had done no such thing, they turned and looked at each other, this way and that, twisting and turning, and shifting in their seats.

Mr. Peacock called them to order. "Ladies and gentlemen, if you *please*! No personal reference was intended. I was speaking . . ." and here he paused to let the full effect of his statement sink in . . . "I was speaking Poetry."

All the eyes of the animals were again riveted upon him. Poetry! Fancy that! It was really wonderful. "And to think," whispered Mrs. Rabbit, "that we are getting all this for nothing!" Which drew an outraged "ssh" from Mrs. Hare, who was sitting just in front of her.

Once he had begun, Mr. Peacock lost all his nerves; he was like a ship flying with a fair wind over coloured water—a ship whose sails glittered with stars of green and purple. From the subject of tails he passed to beauty in general, and told the animals that it was for them to set an example to their less fortunate brothers, the Humans.

"With all apologies to our charming hostesses . . ." he said, bowing gracefully to Judy and her grannie, "even the Humans must admit that the animals start with a tremendous advantage, from the moment they are born to the moment they pass away. Compare, for example, a baby with an egg . . . the egg, let us say, of one of our own citizens, such as Mrs. Thrush." (Here he bowed to Mrs. Thrush, who preened herself and fluttered her feathers.)

"Who could possibly fail to vote in favour of the egg, either for colour or for shape and for general convenience? The egg is pale blue; whoever heard of a pale blue baby? The egg is delicately moulded, like a turquoise; the baby on the other hand . . ." And here Mr. Peacock shook his head sadly as though a baby were really too ugly to think about.

"It is the same throughout life," he continued. "What Human has ever been able to grow a single feather? None! Can the Queen of England grow feathers? Not one. Not even if she sat up all night, and tried and tried . . . not even then could the Queen of England grow a single feather." ("Poor thing," whispered Mrs. Thrush, feeling very sorry for the Queen, "she must feel it dreadfully.")

"It is the same with fur," went on Mr. Peacock. "What Human can grow a coat of fur? Can the Emperor of Japan?" Mr. Peacock shook his head again. "The Emperor of Japan is supposed to be a very Important Human. He has millions of slaves. He lives in a great palace. But even if he were to sit on his throne for a hundred years, thinking of nothing but how to grow fur, trying to grow fur at breakfast, at dinner and at tea, he could NOT GROW FUR. Not even as much as — let us say — the youngest of Mrs. Rabbit's charming children, who grow fur as naturally as they scamper through the buttercups, without the smallest effort."

"And so . . ." proclaimed Mr. Peacock . . . when suddenly he paused. From far away, carried by the breeze, there drifted a faint but sickening odour. Mr. Peacock sniffed. Surely there was something familiar about it? He sniffed again. It was unmistakable. It was Mrs. Badger.

Surely she could not be so mad as to have decided to come to this meeting? Surely she must *know*? But then, Mr. Peacock remembered, Mrs. Badger, poor creature, did *not* know. What on earth was to be done? Here he was in

the middle of a sentence, before a great audience, with this
terrible odour coming nearer and nearer. And he noticed
that many of the animals were also sniffing suspiciously,
and that Mrs. Hare had begun to fan herself.

He must make a great effort; he must set an example.

"And so," he began again, "it is for us, the representa-
tives of the animal kingdom . . ."

Once more he paused, and this time he almost choked,
for a little breeze had sprung up and had carried the overpowering essence of Mrs. Badger right among them. It was
quite impossible to pretend that nothing was happening;
already several of the animals were hastily making for the
exit, and the others were all fanning themselves violently;
in a moment there would be a panic.

It was then that Mr. Peacock made his great decision,
and rose to the occasion as only he could have risen.

Stepping forward, and using all his power of command, he cried:

"Ladies and gentlemen, this is no time for flight!"

They all paused and stared at him.

"I share your . . . your feelings," he continued, with a gulp. "But I entreat you to control them. If the source of the approaching . . ." he paused to find the right word, " . . . the approaching Disturbance . . . is, as I suspect, Mrs. Badger, I must remind you that in spite of her . . ." he paused again . . . "in spite of her affliction, she is a fellow citizen. And in times like these, we must stand together. We owe it to ourselves; we owe it to our hostesses; we owe it to . . ."

He had no time to finish the sentence. For round the corner, all smiles, in her new hat, came the Disturbance herself.

And now Mr. Peacock was really magnificent. Feeling as though he were walking to the executioner's block, and holding his breath as long as possible, he stepped down from the platform and offered Mrs. Badger his wing.

The animals were so thrilled that for the moment they forgot their own discomfort. To think of it . . . Mr. Peacock showing Mrs. Badger such an honour! Mr. Peacock who was so grand and so standoffish!

As for Mrs. Badger herself, she was in such a flutter that she hardly knew whether she was standing on her head or her heels. She had been prepared for the usual behaviour, the usual sniffs and polite withdrawals, the usual hasty conversations about the drains. And now, nobody was withdrawing, nobody had — as yet — mentioned the subject of drains, and Mr. Peacock, of all people, who had never even condescended to look at her before, was actually offering to escort her round the shop, in front of all the other animals! She was so excited that she began to breathe very quickly. Which was really most unfortunate, because when Mrs. Badger breathed quickly, the result on the surrounding atmosphere was indescribable.

Mr. Peacock knew that he had to act at once, if he was to avoid disaster. So he stepped nimbly to the windward side of Mrs. Badger, and said, in a loud voice:

"I have heard, madam, that the Perfume Department is quite excellent." He spoke loud so that Judy could hear him, and cast an agonized glance in her direction as though to say, "Quick, quick, sell her something very strong and pour it all over her at once!"

Judy caught his eye, and he was thankful to see her reach for a big yellow bottle.

The other animals heard him too, and they all stopped fanning themselves in their anxiety to hear Mrs. Badger's answer.

"Well," she said slowly, "I had been thinking of a permanent wave."

The fanning began again, and they all prepared to escape.

Mr. Peacock groaned inwardly; he felt that at any moment he might grow faint; and in desperation he plucked at a stray laurel leaf and held it to his nose. It was not a very pleasant smell, but it was better ... oh, infinitely better ... than Mrs. Badger!

"Perfume, madam," he said, as firmly as his condition would allow him ... "perfume is what you need."

Mrs. Badger was not quite sure if she liked that remark, even from Mr. Peacock. After all, it was a lady's privilege, to pick and choose.

"Well ..." she began.

But Mr. Peacock could not bear any more.

"And perfume, madam, is what you are going to get!" He took one final, agonizing breath, and added ... "In fact, I am going to get it for you. I am going to Give You a Present.''

So saying, he staggered to the counter and seized the yellow bottle, which Judy was holding out in readiness.

Mrs. Badger was overwhelmed. Never in her life had anybody given her a Present before — (except, of course, Mr. Badger, who had very odd ideas about Presents. *He* thought that if he gave her a nice long lick on the ear he was giving her a Present. Which is not at all what a modern girl is entitled to expect).

And now, to be given a Present by Mr. Peacock, of all people. In full view of all the public! It was too wonderful. What *would* Mr. Badger say? She hoped he would not think that she had gone too far. She hoped there would not be a scandal. But really, she was so happy that she hardly cared. And when Mr. Peacock came over to her and undid the bottle, and poured it all over her from head to foot, she felt that she had really gone to heaven.

"Oh, thank you," she murmured. "Thank you, Mr. Peacock. You are *too* kind!"

As the beautiful perfume spread among them, a sigh of relief swept over the whole assembly. And the sigh of relief changed quickly to a series of delighted sniffs and snorts and grunts as all the animals flocked closer to Mrs. Badger. What was it? What could it be? It was like nectar; it was like wine; it was like sunshine.

"I must certainly have some of *this*," announced Mrs. Hare, hurrying to the counter, and her movement was the signal for a general rush. Judy could hardly wrap up the bottles quickly enough. And as she handed them over she told them some of the things that had gone to make up the beautiful perfume — lilies of the valley, cut with silver scissors in the moonlight, and yellow roses, cut with golden scissors in the rain. But there were many other fragrances, of course, that could only be captured in a magic bottle — the sweet drift of wood-smoke, the faint tang of moss, the odour of new-mown hay.

"And one very special scent," she said, with a twinkle in her eye. "But that is a secret."

Which only made them all the more anxious to buy it.

And so the meeting, which might have been such a disaster, ended as a triumphant success. Judy and her grannie were nearly run off their feet, selling things; all the animals were delighted; and Mr. Peacock stalked about in a cloud of glory, the hero of the hour.

But the happiest person of all was Mrs. Badger. Till late that night she kept the whole family enthralled with the stories of her great adventure.

"And nobody," she kept on saying, again and again, "*nobody* mentioned the subject of the drains!"

CHAPTER IX

QUEER CUSTOMERS

BUT would they be able to keep it up?

As the days drew by, Judy began to wonder.

The opening morning, of course, had shown a wonderful profit, but after that, things were strangely quiet. They sold one or two bottles of Fur Lotion, and a little more of the scent, that was all.

"They'll come back for more as soon as they find out how good it all is," said her grannie.

"I hope so." But in her heart of hearts Judy was not at all certain. Perhaps it had been a mistake to try to sell beauty to the animals, perhaps they were beautiful enough already!

"And anyway," added Mrs. Judy, "there's always the Surgery."

Judy had almost forgotten the Surgery; in the excitement of Mr. Peacock's speech, and all the to-do about Mrs. Badger, the Surgery had been overlooked, although Mrs. Judy had been constantly popping about in the background selling odd bottles of balm, and giving advice about sore tails.

"Once they know what I can do for them they're bound to come flocking along," continued Mrs. Judy. "Why, I declare that here are some patients at this very moment!"

Judy saw a strange trio approaching.

Mrs. Judy blinked, and fumbled for her spectacles.

"Who are they, my dear? My sight's not too good."

"It's Mr. and Mrs. Chameleon," said Judy. "And . . . and someone else."

"What do you mean, someone else? Isn't it their son?"

"No, it can't be. Because it's bright pink."

Mrs. Judy peered at the approaching animals. Now you all know about the chameleon family, how they always change colour according to their surroundings, how they are green when they are sitting on the grass, or brown if they are sitting on the earth. And there was no doubt that this *was* the chameleon family, for both Mr. and Mrs. Chameleon were bright green when they walked across the clearing, but as they crossed the little bridge over the stream they turned blue, and when they came into the shadow of the willow tree they were grey and green with little specks of yellow.

But all the time, Master Chameleon remained a brilliant pink.

"It is most extraordinary," said Judy. "Whatever can have happened to him?"

"Whatever has happened," replied her grandmother, "we must cure him, because he is our first patient."

And she pulled her wig straight, and polished her spectacles and looked very wise.

Mrs. Chameleon came straight up to Mrs. Judy.

"We need hardly explain why we have come," she panted, for she was slightly out of breath. "He speaks for himself." And she glanced at her son, who stood there with down-cast eye, as pink as a raspberry ice-cream.

"But that is exactly what he will not do," observed Mr. Chameleon. "He will not speak at all. He refuses to explain how he got like this."

"Never, *never* in our family has such a thing happened before." Mrs. Chameleon's voice was trembling, and she wiped a tear away from her eye. "We have always been quiet, simple people who liked to keep ourselves in the background . . ."

"And to fit in with our surroundings," chimed in Mr. Chameleon. "To adapt ourselves, in fact."

"If we have a fault as a family," Mrs. Chameleon continued, "it is that we are too modest, too afraid of striking out on our own. I have often thought that if my husband would only assert himself a little more . . . ."

"One moment!" Mrs. Judy held up her finger. "Before we go any further I must examine the patient."

Mr. and Mrs. Chameleon bowed their heads and waited.

"And in order to do that I must take him into the Consulting Room."

"The Consulting Room!" exclaimed Mrs. Chameleon. "Is there *really* a Consulting Room?"

"Of course there is."

"Oh, *please* show me where it is. I've never seen a Consulting Room before!"

Mrs. Judy pointed to a thick bush of may, which grew only a few yards away. Mrs. Chameleon stared at it, and blinked.

"It looks to me just like a bush of may," she said.

"It *is* a bush of may," retorted Mrs. Judy. "But that's no reason why it shouldn't be a Consulting Room too, is it?"

Mrs. Chameleon blinked again. "No," she murmured, "I suppose it isn't." But she felt very puzzled. She glanced at her husband, hoping that he would explain. However, he knew no more than she did, and so he played with his tail and echoed, "No reason at all." And to add point to his remark, he took a few steps towards the bush, sniffed, and murmured, "Obviously a Consulting Room". Whereupon he stepped back again and went on playing with his tail.

Master Chameleon's shrill voice suddenly demanded, "What is a Consulting Room, Daddy?"

Mr. Chameleon stared at him with great disapproval, "Little boys," he said, "should be seen and not heard."

"It's only too easy to *see* him," wailed Mrs. Chameleon. "You could see him from miles away."

"But what *is* a Consulting Room, Daddy?"

"You will soon see," said Mrs. Judy, stepping forward. "Come with me!"

Master Chameleon looked at his father, then he looked at his mother, then he looked at Mrs. Judy. And though she was smiling at him kindly, he was obviously very frightened, for he squeaked, "No!" and drew back as though he wanted to run away.

His father took him by the tail and gave it a sharp tweak. "It is not for you to say 'No.' Do as you are told. Go with the lady."

Mrs. Chameleon was all in a flutter. "You will not hurt him? It will not be a painful operation?"

"Certainly not," said Mrs. Judy. "In fact, he will enjoy it."

Master Chameleon still held back. It was not till his father gave his tail another tweak that at last he shuffled off with Mrs. Judy.

The minutes passed very slowly when he had gone. Judy tried to make conversation, but the Chameleons were too worried to listen to what she was saying. Mrs. Chameleon kept walking to and fro, shaking her head, and now and then she sat down on a big black rug which was lying on the grass. Each time she sat on it she went as black as soot.

"Please do not sit on that rug, my love," said Mr. Chameleon. "You look so very sad."

"I *am* sad."

"But there is no need to take such a black view of things. We are not in mourning . . . *yet*."

The word "mourning" and all that it meant was too much for Mrs. Chameleon. Tears sprang to her eyes; her mouth dropped; and heaven knows what a moaning and wailing there would have been in the wood if, at that very moment, there had not been a stirring behind the bush of may. Mrs. Chameleon blinked, gulped, and then suddenly uttered a cry of delight. For suddenly Mrs. Judy stepped from behind the bush, closely followed by Master Chameleon . . . and what a transformation it was! For there was not a single speck of pink left on him. He was green and brown and dappled, just like the shadows under the willow tree.

"Look, Mummy . . . watch, Daddy!" he cried happily. And he rushed backwards and forwards, out into the sunlight, where he turned as green as the grass, on to the little blue bridge where he changed to a perfect blue. Suddenly he saw Mrs. Judy's pink shawl which she had left out to dry. He took a flying leap at it and was again as pink as a raspberry ice.

"No! No!" cried Mrs. Chameleon, "not on *that* . . . you may not be able to change back again!"

But hardly had she spoken before he had turned and jumped back on to the grass, where he turned green, and had run to his parents under the willow, where he was as dappled as they were themselves.

It was a very happy ending.

"I shall never forget this," said Mr. Chameleon, when he had paid the bill (which was quite a large one). "There is only one thing I would ask . . . how did you do it?"

Mrs. Judy looked very wise and shook her head.

"I am afraid that must be a secret."

"Perhaps our son might explain to us?"

"He might, but I don't think he will." And here, Mrs. Judy gave a broad wink at Master Chameleon, who blushed all over. (It is very strange when a chameleon blushes, because it is like a pink bloom over all the other colours . . . as though you were looking at him through tinted glass). "In any case," she added, "I am quite sure that it will not occur again."

With that the Chameleons had to be content, and they took their departure.

"How *did* you do it?" asked Judy, when they had gone.

"Ah!"

"But, Grannie, *please* tell me!"

"Come and see."

Mrs. Judy led the way to the Bargain Basement. She pointed to a rocky shelf on which all sorts of bottles of sweets and candies were displayed. In the centre was a bottle of bright pink sherbet — almost empty.

"Last night," said Mrs. Judy, "when I was shutting up, I found that somebody had been at the sherbet. The jar was lying on its side and a lot had been spilt on the ground. Of course I was very angry, and was just going to send for P.C. Monkey when I saw a little note lying on the ground. Here it is. "

She handed Judy a piece of crumpled paper, on which a message was printed in a childish handwriting:

> YOU WAS OUT AND I COULD NOT WAIT. I AM
> VERY SORY TO HAVE SPILT THE SHEBERT.
> THIS IS ALL THE MUNEY I HAVE.
>
> SIGNED
MASTER C.

"Lying beside the note," said Mrs. Judy, "were two pennies. Of course it was not enough for all that he had taken, but it showed that he was not a thief. I tried to think who it could be, but 'Master C' might have been so many people — Master Crow, or Master Calf or Master Caterpillar or Master anybody. So I decided to say nothing and just to wait. Of course, when I saw Master Chameleon I guessed at once what had happened. It rained heavily last night, and he was covered with the bright pink sherbet and the colour came off on his skin."

"So what did you do?"

"I gave him a wash," said Mrs. Judy. And then, with a smile . . . "And I gave him some more sherbet, too!"

II

But Master Chameleon was the only patient they had; it seemed as though all the animals had suddenly decided never to be ill again. Which was all very well in its way, but not very satisfactory when you are running a Surgery.

To make matters worse, it was at about this time that they suddenly lost one of their best and oldest customers, Mrs. Manx. Since there was afterwards a great deal of discussion among the animals about this affair, we must give the true facts of the case.

It happened like this.

Ever since she had listened to Mr. Peacock's speech, Mrs. Manx had been restless and ill at ease, for Mrs. Manx, as you know, belonged to that branch of the cat family whose members have no tails, and though she would never have admitted it in public, she felt her lack most bitterly. It had gone to her heart when Mr. Peacock said, "Some are born with tails, some achieve tails, and some have tails pinned upon them". She would never forget how all the animals had stared at her. As though she would ever pin on a tail! It would be most vulgar, apart from the fact that it would also be extremely painful.

However, Mr. Peacock's words had put an idea into her head. Why should she not *achieve* a tail? Surely that would be quite a proper thing to do. To pin — certainly not: to achieve — a very different matter. The more she thought of it, the more she liked it. She would not tell Mr. Manx about it, of course — not until it was actually achieved — for Mr. Manx had absurd old-fashioned ideas about tails. But achieve it she would; and the obvious place to achieve it was at The Shop Under the Willow Tree. Was there not a notice there, in large letters, saying "Tails a Speciality?"

And so, one bright morning, Mrs. Manx set out for the shop. She went very early, because she did not want any of the other animals to see her.

"What can I do for you, Mrs. Manx?" asked Judy, when she arrived.

Mrs. Manx looked over her shoulder to see that they were not observed. Then she leant forward, and spoke in a very confidential voice:

"It was about tails."

Judy looked surprised. "Tails? I should not have thought that tails would have interested you, Mrs. Manx."

"Oh, but they interest me very much," protested Mrs. Manx. "Very much indeed."

"Really?" replied Judy, wondering what she was getting at.

"After all," continued Mrs. Manx, "tails *are* being worn."

"Not by your family," suggested Judy politely.

"Maybe not," agreed Mrs. Manx. "But I have often felt that my family was a little eccentric. A little *lacking*, if you know what I mean."

"Not lacking in manners, surely?"

"Not in manners, no. But in . . . how shall I say? . . . In *dash*; in what I might perhaps describe as 'finish'". And as she said the word "finish" she twitched the back part of her body in a movement that struck Judy as so odd that she wanted to laugh. If Mrs. Manx had possessed a tail, the movement would have been very grand and impressive. As it was, it only looked absurd.

"You see what I mean?" said Mrs. Manx, guessing her thoughts. "One has nothing in reserve."

"I do see, in a way," agreed Judy.

"I often feel that a tail is rather like a fan," went on Mrs. Manx. "When one is at a loss, it fills in the gaps. When one can't speak, one *waves*. That at least is how *I* see it. If one has no tail, one is stumped. In more senses than one."

"So it would seem."

"And so," she continued, "as I have decided to . . . to embark on this adventure, I thought I would do it properly. No half measures. It would look ridiculous, at my age, to make a sudden appearance with — let us say — the tail of a small stoat attached to my . . . well, attached behind."

"It would indeed."

"On the other hand, I do not want to look vulgar. I do not want to blossom out into ostrich feathers."

"Certainly not," said Judy; who was wondering how long she would be able to stop laughing.

"I suppose the *chief* difficulty will be to make it look natural," continued Mrs. Manx. "I do not wish for a tail that sticks up like a flag-pole all the time. I wish it to *wave.* But I do not wish it to wave so much that there is any danger of it waving *off.* That would be very humiliating." She sighed, and glanced behind her, to where her tail would have been if she had owned one. "You see," she said, "I don't want anything in the least showy . . . just a *tail.*"

There was a moment's silence. "Just . . . a *tail,*" repeated Mrs. Manx. As she spoke, Judy seemed to hear something sad in her voice, something wistful, as though she had never known what it was to be happy in life.

All the same, Judy felt that it would be all wrong to fit a tail on to Mrs. Manx. To begin with, she was sure that Mr. Manx would not like it. He was always very contemptuous of the tails of other cats, which he said were useless and old-fashioned.

Judy put her thoughts into words. "What does Mr. Manx say about the idea?"

"I should not dream of asking him," replied Mrs. Manx, "and I sincerely hope you will not mention it till the tail is fitted and I can wear it home. Which reminds me that I really should like to see a selection *now.*"

Judy still hesitated. She had a number of tails in stock, but they were all meant for fitting on to animals who had lost theirs in accidents. She felt that it would be unnatural and foolish to fit one on to Mrs. Manx — you might as well fit wings on to a tortoise. And she was sure that all the other animals would jeer at her and make her sorry that she had wasted her money.

"Well," she began, "I don't know if it will be possible *now.*"

"But I'm in a hurry. I want it to-day."

"Oh, I'm afraid that is *quite* out of the question," said Judy. "It may take weeks."

"*Weeks*? But when Mrs. Persian had the top of her tail bitten off by that dreadful Mr. Fox, you fitted a new top in half an hour."

"That was different," said Judy. "Mrs. Persian had a very easy figure to fit."

"Really!" Mrs. Manx sounded quite indignant. "I suppose that means that I've got a very difficult figure."

"Not at all, but . . ."

"Never in my life," continued Mrs. Manx, her voice growing more and more shrill, "have I been told that my figure was difficult. I simply don't know what you mean."

Judy tried to calm her down. "You misunderstand me," she said. "I didn't mean that there was anything *wrong* with your figure, I simply meant that it would be more difficult to fit a tail to it than to Mrs. Persian's, because Mrs. Persian has long hair and you have short."

"Oh! Oh!" snorted Mrs. Manx. "So now it's my *hair* that's wrong!" She rose to her feet, and her stump twitched backwards and forwards so angrily that if she had been wearing a false tail it would certainly have fallen off. "I shall not stay to be insulted any more."

"Please, Mrs. Manx, *please* don't go!" Judy felt very distressed and unhappy. The last thing she had wanted to do was to offend Mrs. Manx, not only because she was an old customer, but because she liked her so much for herself. However, it was in vain that she pleaded. Mrs. Manx was already gathering up her belongings, muttering to herself, and giving angry little noises that sounded like gas escaping — a noise that you would write like "hhichchh". When a cat says "hhichchh" it is a very bad sign.

At last she was ready to go. She looked Judy straight in the eyes and she spoke as follows:

"I am very sorry that this has happened, Miss Judy.

But you cannot expect me to continue to patronize your establishment any more."

"Oh, Mrs. Manx . . . after all these years!"

"Quite. After all these years. That, in my opinion, only makes it worse. I come to your Beauty Parlour with a perfectly simple request. A tail. Just a tail. It is not much for a hard-working cat to ask." Here her voice trembled, as though she were trying not to cry. She went on: "If I had asked you to fit me with a pair of horns, I should not have been surprised at your behaviour. Horns would be vulgar, expensive, and dangerous. I would not entertain the idea of wearing horns for a moment." She shook her head vigorously.

"Nobody suggested that you should wear horns," began Judy.

"So I hope that you will not suggest it now," retorted Mrs. Manx, not very fairly. "Again," she continued, "if I had asked you to put diamonds on the ends of my claws or to give me luminous whiskers, I should have understood if you had protested. Luminous whiskers would be in very bad taste . . . ."

"Particularly in the dark," said Judy.

Mrs. Manx ignored her. "But all I asked was a tail. A modest simple tail. And you insulted me. You *insulted* me!" Her voice rose almost to a mew. She leant forward and shook her paw in Judy's face. "Well, let me tell you," she cried, "I shall *have* my tail. I shall buy it Somewhere Else. There is Another Place. And *that* is where I am going now!"

And before Judy could say another word she leapt over the tree trunk, whisked through the bush of may, and vanished in the undergrowth.

When Mrs. Manx had gone, Judy began to shut up the shop, for it was nearly closing time, and she felt tired and depressed at the bad way in which everything was going.

She was just drawing the last branch over the counter when she heard a strange squeaky noise just behind her and a voice saying:

"Excuse me!"

Judy started, and looked around her. Wherever did that funny little squeak come from?

"Excuse me!" there it was again. Like the scratchy sound that a pencil makes on a slate.

Suddenly she saw who it was. It was a very tiny, very old, very shabby tortoise, who was standing at the foot of the counter, blinking up at her with weak, bleary eyes.

"I beg your pardon," said Judy. "Is there anything I can do for you?"

"Yes, there is."

Judy hesitated. "Well, we were just closing . . ." she began.

"Never mind. You can open again."

Judy smiled. "Very well. What is it you wanted?"

Slowly the tortoise ambled towards her; then it stayed at her feet, still looking at her through its bleary eyes.

"I wondered if you could do anything about my shell," he said.

Judy knelt down to examine the tortoise's back.

"Oh, it *is* in rather a bad way, isn't it?" she exclaimed.

And indeed it was. There were several holes in it, and it was wearing thin.

"You've said it," said the tortoise.

"Some of it seems to be . . . well . . ." Judy hesitated for

the right word; she did not want to hurt the tortoise's
feelings . . . "well, sort of missing."

"Sort of missing?" The tortoise gave a croaking laugh.
"I should say it was. It's just an old patchwork. Hardly
any of it's really *me*. And what's more, it leaks."

"Oh dear! Won't you catch cold?"

"Of course I shall catch cold. I'm always catching cold.
That's the worst of *being* your own house."

"I suppose it is," said Judy.

"Nobody ever sees a tortoise's point of view," he went on. "Supposing *you* were your own house? Supposing your back was your roof, and your chimneys grew out of your head and your spine was in the attic? Supposing that when you were ill you had to call in the plumber to mend your pipes? And supposing, when you wanted to lock up at night you had to lock *yourself* up, and draw in your head through your own front door? Like this!"

And suddenly Mr. Tortoise drew in his head, and all that Judy could see was a shell, lying at her feet, like a sort of little tank. It looked so funny that she could not help smiling.

"It's no laughing matter," squeaked the tortoise, darting his little head out again. "It's a tragedy. Sometimes I wonder what I really am — a house or a person. In fact, if I ever had to put an advertisement in the papers, asking for a wife, I don't know how I should word it. What do *you* think? Should it be 'Distinguished tortoise (male) wishes to meet distinguished tortoise (female)?' Or should it just be 'Desirable Residence to Let'? "

"I don't think I should bother about advertising," said Judy, who could not see the solution of this strange problem. "I'm sure you will meet her some day."

"Maybe I shall," sighed the tortoise. "In the meantime, I'm *not* a desirable residence."

"I'm afraid you *are* a little dilapidated," agreed Judy.

"It's the roof that's the trouble," he went on. "If I had a proper roof I could go to sleep all the winter. But you *can't* sleep if the rain's trickling through your roof. That's why I came to you. I want you to mend my roof."

Judy thought for a moment. She wanted to help the tortoise but it would not be easy. It would be a long job, and the materials would all have to be specially ordered.

"Tortoiseshell is very expensive," she began. . . .

"Oh, I'm not particular about what the roof's made of," said the tortoise. "As long as it keeps out the rain. Any old thing will do. Bits of silver paper. Sealing wax. Anything."

"But wouldn't that look rather odd?"

"I can't help it if it does. Beggars can't be choosers. I haven't a cent in the world."

"Oh dear!" Judy was taken aback. She had not expected to make much money out of the tortoise, but she was so poor that she did not see how she could undertake such a big job for nothing, however anxious she was to help.

"Does that make a difference?" asked the tortoise. "Having no money?"

"Well, it does rather," admitted Judy. "You see, this is a shop."

"And a shop has no soul." The tortoise sounded suddenly bitter.

"*Please* don't say that," protested Judy. "A shop *has* a soul. At least, I like to think that this one has."

She looked up into the great branches, twisted and tangled against the sky, with its thousands of leaves shimmering in the dying sunlight, and all the lights and shadows and patterns that they made . . . and she felt that she had spoken the truth. And the tree, as it had so often done before, seemed to give her a message. It seemed to say: "Be kind to this little creature . . . be kind, be kind!" Not that Judy really needed to be told, for it was as natural to her to be kind as to sing or to smile.

So she bent down, gave the tortoise a stroke on the back, and said, "Follow me."

The tortoise followed her, walking so slowly that Judy had to sit down after every few paces to wait for him to catch up. (She did not like to lift him for fear that he should be offended.) And then she began to work on his roof.

She found an old hair-brush with a tortoiseshell back and cut it into strips. There was not enough of this, however, so she cut off part of the lid of a biscuit tin, and painted it brown and stripped it into small squares. Then she measured the tortoise's back, and shaped the pieces of shell and tin so that they fitted beautifully; and after that she drilled a lot of little holes and fastened it all on with strong brown string.

"It's not a bad fit," said Mr. Tortoise, when it was all on. "Not at all bad. What do I look like? A tortoise or a salvage dump?"

Judy laughed out loud.

"I like to see you laughing," observed Mr. Tortoise with a twinkle in his eye, which was surprisingly bright for his age. "Why aren't you always laughing?"

"Well," said Judy . . . And her face became grave again. "I have not very much to laugh about just now."

"Come, come! That's not the way for a pretty little girl to speak." He shook his head at her. "Look here! I can't pay you for this job. Not with money."

"That doesn't matter," said Judy.

"Oh, but it *does* matter. I don't like being in debt. But though I can't pay you in money, I can pay you in something else."

He fumbled for a moment and then produced a small round object which he held out to her.

Judy took it and looked at it curiously. "It looks just like a bean," she said.

"It *is* a bean," replied the tortoise. "But not an ordinary one. It's a magic bean."

"Really?" Judy was not very impressed. "What does it do?"

"If you rub it, it makes you laugh."

Judy was so surprised by this strange news that she began to laugh again.

"There you are, you see!" exclaimed the tortoise. "What did I tell you? You're laughing."

"But I didn't rub the bean," said Judy, "I only held it."

"Yes, you did. I saw you." (And indeed she had been rubbing it, without knowing).

"Well anyway, I'm not rubbing it now. And I'm not laughing."

"No, but you look much happier."

"Do I?" Judy smiled and gave him a pat. "Thank you. That's your doing."

"Thank *you*," replied the tortoise. "Now I must be off." And with a farewell wave he turned and went away.

When he had gone Judy stared at the bean, turning it over in her hand. What a strange idea! She gave it a rub, just to see, and sure enough, she began to laugh again. But then — she told herself — that wasn't because of the bean itself — it was just because the whole idea was so funny. Judy was a modern little girl, and she was never quite sure how much she really believed in magic.

So she put the bean in her pocket and forgot all about it.

However, she laughed again several times before she went to bed that night. She felt strangely happy, as though she had found a friend. Which indeed she had . . . a very great friend indeed.

But we cannot tell you why, not just yet.

CHAPTER X

THE WICKEDNESS OF MISS SMITH

IF Judy had known of all the wicked plots that Sam was preparing at The Shop in the Ford, she would not have felt at all like laughing.

For Sam had made up his mind to ruin her. Although he was doing very big business — particularly since he had

made poor Bruno his "partner" — he was still unsatisfied. He was not content with a fair share; he wanted All.

The problem was — how to get it?

"I've been thinking things over," he said to Old Sam, "and we want some new blood in this place."

"We've got Bruno," replied Old Sam. "Ain't he new blood?"

"He ain't blood at all." Sam spat contemptuously in

Bruno's direction. "He's fur and water, that's what he is. We want somebody with pep."

"Human or animal?" inquired Old Sam.

"A bit of both, I guess." He scratched his head. "Say, that's an idea . . . a bit of both. What about a witch?"

"Witches run expensive, these days," grumbled Old Sam.

"Well, we can afford it. We made a nice turnover on that honey I borrowed." (By "borrowing" Sam meant that he had raided the hives of the bees, in just the same way that he had raided the nests of the ants).

"Besides," he went on, with growing enthusiasm, "if we get a witch she'll be able to tell us how to deal with those two she-cats in the Willow Tree. 'Set a witch to catch a witch' — that's my motto."

"She'll be terrible expensive," repeated Old Sam. "And she'll probably want to sleep in the cave and turn me out. And the nights'll be getting nippy soon."

"And I hope they freeze that old goat's beard of yours," snapped Sam. "If I say it's going to be witches, it's going to be witches, see?"

"That's easy said, but how'll you get her?"

"Advertise, of course."

"But there ain't no newspapers in these parts."

"Not in the wood, there ain't, but there's newspapers outside, ain't there? I'll take the day off."

So Sam took the day off. And when he got outside he went to the nearest Wicked Newspaper Shop. Of course, only a very bad boy would have been able to find it, for the Wicked Newspaper Shops are always hidden away in dark alleys and crooked side streets. A red candle splutters in the window, the blinds are half drawn, and a raven sits on the doorstep, uttering gloomy squawks. If you ever get lost, and pass such a shop, never, never go inside. It is full of the most dreadful books and pictures which will make you wish you had never been born.

However, all these things were nothing to Sam, and as soon as he had found the shop he went inside, aiming a careless kick at the raven, who flapped away to the nearest chimney, spitting curses at him.

"What's the best paper to advertise for a witch?" he demanded, throwing down a silver coin.

The old hag behind the counter stretched out her hand to grab the coin, but Sam was too quick for her and snatched it back.

"Business first," he chuckled, "that's my motto. Come on. Out with it."

"Well, there's *The Weekly Cauldron*," wheezed the hag.

"Too highbrow. The last time I saw a copy the leading article was all about Vested Interests in Broomsticks. And most of the letters were from refugee witches complaining about conditions in this country. They ought to be darned glad that we let 'em come in at all."

"That's true," agreed the hag, nodding her withered head. She looked through a pile of magazines. "What about the *Hag's Home Journal*? That's very well spoken of."

"Too respectable," growled Sam. "Full of articles on how to make salads out of toadstools."

"Well, then, that only leaves *The Witch's Evening Wail*."

"That's the one," exclaimed Sam. "Nice and spicy."

"Now what shall I put in?" asked the hag.

"Say, 'Witch wanted for Country Shop. Must hate animals, old women and children. Extra wages if prepared to be thoroughly disagreeable.'"

"That's a nice advertisement," agreed the old woman. "They're always more willing to take a job where they feel they'll have a chance of expressing themselves."

Sam threw her the coin, and gave her his name and address. While she was copying down the advertisement he turned over some of the magazines. What a wonderful, fascinating world they revealed! There was a murder on nearly every page. And there were stories of blackmail and theft and treachery, beautifully illustrated with pictures of the criminals and their victims. They made him long to live again in the Human world, which was so far better, so far more advanced than the silly wood, with its lonely dells, its foolish animals and its senseless birds . . . creatures who had never even heard of blackmail and would not know how to forge a cheque if you gave them one!

He felt quite homesick, and bitterly regretted having to return. Never mind; he'd take it out of those darned animals yet. And when he'd made his fortune he'd shut up the shop and leave the wood for ever. And then he'd be able to come to the Wicked Newspaper Shop every day of his life.

So thinking, Sam bade the old hag good-day, and swung out of the shop on his way home. The raven watched him vanish down the street, and squawked its curses till he was out of sight.

II

The witch arrived a few days later, but not at all in the way that Sam expected.

Evening was falling, and he was sitting at his desk playing patience. He was in a worse mood than ever; trade had been very bad all day; he had toothache; and now, as the last straw, the patience would not come out.

He was so annoyed that he began to cheat.

He was such a wicked boy that when he could not find anybody else to cheat he cheated himself. He took a black queen out of the pack and put it down where a red queen had been before. Now the patience was bound to come out.

He was just about to move a card when he paused and blinked. The black queen had turned red again! What on earth had happened? Surely he had put down the right card? He bent over to see if he was being fooled by some trick of the light. No — the queen was red as red. He supposed he must have made a mistake, though he could not understand how or why.

"It's this darned toothache," he muttered to himself. And once again he removed the red queen, searched the pack for a black one, and placed it firmly down on the table.

"Now!" he exclaimed. "Now I'll be able to get on with it."

He lifted his hand to play. But suddenly a gurgle of fear came from his lips and his hand remained poised in mid-air.

The black queen had turned bright green!

"Snakes alive!" he whispered. "Jumping Jehus! What's going on?"

Trembling, he shifted away from the table, as though the cards might spring up and bite him. But nothing happened. He rubbed his eyes and stared. There was no question about it. The queen was as green as grass, and as he stared at her she seemed to wink at him.

He stretched out his hand to touch the card and then

drew it back hastily. Better not; it might give him a nasty shock; it might be red hot; it might even be poisoned. If there was any touching to be done, Old Sam was the person to do it. He decided to go and fetch him.

He rose to his feet. And as he did so, he got a sharp crack on the head.

"In the name of all that's holy, who's that?" he cried.

"Not in the name of all that's holy, Mr. Sam . . . in the name of all that's wicked, if you please!"

It was a very sweet voice, and it came from directly behind.

He turned and he saw a very pretty young lady, dressed in a pink gown, with a pale blue feather in her hat.

It was Miss Smith, the witch.

III

Miss Smith held out a visiting card.

"Was it you playing those tricks?" demanded Sam.

"Certainly," she replied. "Allow me to present myself."

Still growling and rubbing his head, Sam took the card and examined it. This is what he read:

MISS SMITH

M.A., W.I.T.C.H., E.T.C.

Member of the Union of Hags
and Sorceresses

Haunting a Speciality

"This you?" asked Sam.

Miss Smith bowed.

"Sure?"

"Quite sure."

Sam gave her a good look-over. She really was very pretty indeed. She had blue eyes and fair hair and her nose was slightly tilted.

"You don't *look* like a witch," he grunted. "Still, if you're sure, I suppose it's O.K. In fact, it's quite a pleasant surprise."

He lurched over to her and gave her a chuck under the chin. But as soon as he did so sprang back and uttered a yell of dismay. For Miss Smith's chin was as cold as ice and as rough as a brick.

"Say," he cried, "what's that you've got there?"

"Just a chin," replied Miss Smith demurely.

"Are you like that all over?"

"Of course. Feel!" And she held out her hand for him to touch.

"No, thank you!" muttered Sam, edging away from her. "I've had enough."

"Just as you wish." Miss Smith seated herself on a log and crossed her legs. She looked as pretty as a pin-up girl. "After all," she said, "I can't expect to appeal to a young man like you, not at my age."

"Why, how old are you?"

"To be frank," replied Miss Smith, "I'm three hundred and eighty-three."

"Holy Smoke!" gasped Sam.

"That is to say, I shall be three hundred and eighty-three to-morrow. It's my birthday to-morrow," she looked at him very coyly and swung her legs.

"You don't get any present from me," snapped Sam. "Not with a chin like that."

"I didn't come here for presents," retorted Miss Smith, rather shortly. "I came here on business."

"Well, you can start right now," he replied. "I've got toothache. Get busy and do something about it."

"Really," she said, "that's hardly my line. I came here to give people toothache, not to cure them of it."

"If you can't cure this one you can hop it, right away."

Miss Smith sighed. It was really very hard, the way one's clients overworked one, these days. Still, she supposed she had better try. She did not want to hop it, not after having come all this way; besides, she was sure she would like the place very much. It looked nice and bad ... just the right atmosphere. And she had taken to Sam at once, such a nice wicked little boy. Yes, she must certainly try to cure the toothache, particularly as she was badly in need of a job. Which was not surprising, for she was really a very poor sort of witch. At school, in the reign of Charles II, she had been the dunce of the class, always forgetting her spells, and losing her dog's tongues and newt's eyes; she had never even really learnt to cackle properly. She was, in fact, a very second-rate sort of witch, but Sam could not be expected to know that.

"I'm waiting," growled Sam.

Miss Smith knitted her brows. "A cure for toothache?" What did one do? She seemed to remember, rather dimly, that

you had to have some sort of powder. Then what? You had to do something with three dead worms. But what? Mix them up in it, probably. Then what was it she had learnt about the cross-eyed toad? Did you put the powder on the cross-eyed toad or did you put the cross-eyed toad on the powder? For the life of her she could not remember. Still, it probably amounted to the same thing. She would get the powder and the worms; in her bag she already had three cross-eyed toads to whom she was very much attached; they were called Shadrach, Meshach and Abed-nego; between them they could probably do something.

She unfastened her bag and out hopped the toads. For a moment they sat there, blinking at the sunlight with their crossed eyes and then, with one accord, they opened their mouths very wide and burst into song.

> Three little toads are we, are we,
> We are as bad as bad can be,
> Three little worse toads you won't find,
> We spit in your eye and you're stone, stone blind!

"Aren't they little darlings?" cried Miss Smith, when they had finished. "As ugly as sin itself!"

"They're ugly all right," retorted Sam, scowling.

"And their behaviour is just as bad as their looks," she continued, stroking them affectionately. "Isn't it, my tweets?"

"You've said it," replied the three toads, all together.

" 'Ugly is as ugly does' . . . that's what I always think," she said.

"Well, what are they going to do?"

Miss Smith thought hard for a moment. Then she had an idea.

"I want a piece of string, the nail of a murderer's coffin

141

and the wing of a bat that was struck by lightning," she declared.

"I can manage the piece of string. But how'm I to get them other things?"

Miss Smith sniffed. "I should have thought that one would have found them in any modern home," she retorted. "However, if you haven't got them I shall have to make do with a rotten dodo's egg. I imagine there will be no difficulty about *that*?"

"Never heard of such a thing," snapped Sam.

Miss Smith raised her eyebrows. "Really," she said, "we do live in the wilds, don't we? You'll be telling me next that you haven't any hangmen's nooses!"

"Not a one. What's more, you ought to provide them things yourself."

"If I'm expected to do that," she said, "I shall have to charge extra."

"I don't care what you charge," shouted Sam, "so long as you stop this darned toothache."

"What's more I shall have to have an assistant."

"That's easy."

Sam blew a shrill whistle and out of the cave lumbered Bruno.

Miss Smith regarded Bruno with marked distaste. "Oh, dear!" she exclaimed, "I don't like the look of him at all. He looks good."

"He's not as good as all that," growled Sam.

"He looks quite good enough to do a lot of mischief," she retorted. "He looks as though he was shockingly honest and disgracefully kind; I can't abide such people."

Poor Bruno lowered his eyes. He could not understand why it should be such a crime to be good. All he knew was that he disliked Miss Smith just as much as she disliked him. She was very pretty but she was bad; she reminded him of some of the people he used to know in the circus, like the Fairy Queen who had thrown boiling water over him when she was drunk.

"He's the only assistant you'll get, so you'd better make the best of him."

"Well, I must say it's all putting a great strain on me," sulked Miss Smith. "However, we'll see what we can do." She was not really feeling nearly as sulky as she looked; in fact she was quite glad that Bruno was there, because if anything went wrong — as it probably would — she could put all the blame on him.

She took Sam's piece of string, laid it on the ground, muttered a few wicked spells over it, and then beckoned to Shadrach, Meshach and Abed-nego.

"Now, darlings," she cried, "spit on this beautiful piece of string."

They hopped forward obediently, and spat.

"Once more, lovebirds!"

They spat again.

She lifted up the string and gave one end to Bruno.

"Hold this!" she snapped, in a very different tone of voice. Then she went over to Sam.

"Open wide!"

Sam started back. "You're not going to tie that round my tooth?"

"Yes, I am, but it won't hurt at all, because my darlings have spat on it, and all the pain will go into the string."

"I don't approve of this," growled Sam. All the same, he allowed her to tie the string round the tooth.

Miss Smith turned to Bruno. "Now," she said, "it's up to you. If you pull properly it won't hurt Mr. Sam at all. But if you are a wilful, stubborn bear, and don't pull properly it will hurt a lot."

Which was very unjust of Miss Smith, for no matter how

poor Bruno pulled, it would have hurt and well she knew it.

Miss Smith raised her hand. "One . . ." she cried.

"Wait a minute!" shouted Sam. "It's slipping off!" He adjusted it again, and braced himself for the shock. "And mind you pull properly!" he growled to Bruno. "If you don't, you're for it!"

"One!" cried Miss Smith again. "Two . . . Three!"

Bruno gave a huge tug.

Sam yelled and leapt in the air.

The next few minutes were a scene of wild confusion. Miss Smith darted round, chasing Bruno, screaming that it was all his fault; Sam hopped up and down, howling and yelping, and aiming kicks at the cross-eyed toads, who got in everybody's way, because they were so cross-eyed that they could not see where they were going. To make matters worse, Old Sam, who had been sleeping in his cave, was awakened by the uproar, and rushed out, shouting "Murder! Police!"

It was late at night before they all went to bed. By that time Sam's pains were over, and Miss Smith — who had put a magic potion in his tea — had convinced him that Bruno was the culprit.

So on the whole he was satisfied.

"She's a good girl, she is," he growled to Old Sam, just before he went to sleep. "She's going to make things hum around these parts."

He spoke more truly than he guessed.

CHAPTER XI

WITCHCRAFT

MISS SMITH began her wicked work at once; on the following morning she was up early, making her preparations to call on Judy.

"Are you going visible or invisible?" demanded Sam, at breakfast.

"Invisible at first, visible afterwards," she replied.

"What's the idea of being visible at all? Why don't you just hang around and put poison in things, and give her a crack or two on the head?"

Miss Smith tapped her beautifully manicured fingers impatiently on the table.

"Sometimes you seem to forget that you're speaking to a lady," she observed.

Sam guffawed. "That's good ... that's rich! You a lady!" He lay back in his chair and bellowed with laughter.

Miss Smith shrugged her shoulders, and rose from the table. Really — the people one had to work for nowadays! Quite impossible! Very different from the sort of clients she had been used to in the past, like that charming old murderess in the reign of Queen Anne, for instance; she had given her everything she wanted, whole belfries full of bats and whole lakes teeming with cross-eyed toads — (from a pair of which, incidentally Shadrach, Meshach and Abed-nego were descended).

That reminded her, she must take the toads with her. They might come in handy; besides, they were always good company. She whistled, and they came hopping out of the cave.

"Drat them things!" growled Old Sam, when he saw them. "One of 'em spat in my eye last night."

"Then it's lucky you didn't go blind," she countered. "He must have done it for fun, otherwise you would have done."

"That's not my idea of fun, not spitting in a gentleman's eye, it ain't," he muttered.

"Then the sooner you change your ideas the better!" She patted the toads lovingly on their bald heads. "There, darlings, never mind what the nasty old gentleman says. He doesn't understand your little ways. Are you feeling nice and wicked this morning?"

"Yep!" croaked the toads.

"How wicked are you feeling?"

Instantly they burst into song:

> Three little toads are we, are we,
> Ready for any sinful spree,
> If you do not treat us well
> We'll spit in your eye and you'll go to . . .

"Ssh!" cried Miss Smith, putting her finger on their lips, and pretending to be shocked. "Aren't they *marvellous*?" she giggled, turning to Sam.

Sam grunted.

"Such high spirits!" she went on. "Such naughtiness! When they grow up I'm going to let them join our local scouts. One bad deed a day, that's our motto."

"Well, they'd better get busy and do some bad deeds right away if they're going to earn their keep," he growled.

"*They'll* be busy, all right, won't you, my poppets?"

"You've said it," croaked the toads.

"Come along then, my lambs," she cried, opening her bag. "We've got work to do!"

The toads hopped into the bag, one by one, and in the next second, Miss Smith had vanished.

Old Sam blinked. "Has she gone?" he inquired.

"Just going!" breathed a sweet voice, so close to his ear that he jumped as though he had been bitten.

A tinkle of laughter echoed in the air. It grew fainter and fainter, and finally died away at the end of the clearing. Miss Smith really *had* gone, now.

"I don't like it," grumbled Old Sam. "All these tricks. I never know whether she's coming or going. I hope she's worth it."

"Well, if she ain't, she'll get the sack," snapped Sam. With which, for the moment, they had to be content.

II

While Miss Smith was on her way to The Shop Under the Willow Tree, Judy was attending to the first of the morning's clients in the Beauty Parlour. It was still very early, and she was washing up the breakfast things when the bell rang.

Wiping her hands on her apron, and pinning a wild rose in her hair, she hurried out.

There, standing at the counter was a squirrel. She was a very pretty squirrel, with a long, bushy tail, which she kept swishing backwards and forwards, as though she were nervous about something.

"Miss Squirrel, I believe?" said Judy, advancing.

"Yes — that is my name," she replied, with a little giggle. "How ever did you know?"

"I think everybody in the wood knows the members of your distinguished family," replied Judy, with a polite bow.

Miss Squirrel simpered. "It's very nice of you to say so," she said. "But that's just the trouble — people don't know us. At least, they mix us up. Only last night I was mistaken for my cousin Etty. Do you know her?"

"I don't think I have the honour . . ." began Judy.

"It isn't much of an *honour*," retorted Miss Squirrel. "She's a very common girl. She doesn't even know how to eat an acorn like a lady. And her tail's at least an inch shorter than mine."

"Really?" said Judy, wondering where all this was leading to. "It seems very strange that anybody should have mistaken her for you."

"That's what I say," replied Miss Squirrel eagerly. "And I don't want it to happen again. In fact, it mustn't happen again."

"But how can I help you?"

Miss Squirrel looked very coy, and took a little nibble at an acorn which she was holding in her left hand. Then she leant forward and whispered . . .

"This is a beauty parlour, isn't it?"

"Yes, of course."

"A real beauty parlour . . . not a make-believe?"

"No . . . it's absolutely real."

"In that case, I thought . . ." Again she hesitated, and blushed, and swished her tail over her face as though she didn't dare to come out with what she wanted to say.

"What did you think?"

Miss Squirrel made a great effort. "I thought I'd have it dyed!" she proclaimed. And then she sat down on a log, and buried her face in her tail, and kept darting bright little glances at Judy through the fur.

"Have it dyed?" echoed Judy, bewildered. "Have *what* dyed?"

"My tail, of course!"

Judy was so astonished that she could not think of the right thing to say.

"But . . . but . . ." she stammered.

"Oh, please don't go on saying but-but," cried Miss Squirrel. "But *what*?"

"But what *colour*?" gasped Judy, just to gain time till she could think of something else.

Miss Squirrel beamed all over, and took her tail away from her face, and stroked it in a very elegant way. "I thought a nice pale pink."

"Pale pink?" echoed Judy.

"You think a brighter colour?" Miss Squirrel looked at her sideways, with the silliest expression.

"Well, not exactly *brighter*."

"Pale blue, then?" Miss Squirrel took another nibble at her acorn, and continued to gaze at Judy with the silly expression.

"Well," said Judy, "I'm not sure about pale *blue*."

"I believe it would become me," observed Miss Squirrel. "When we had a picnic in the bluebell glade last Spring, I had a great success."

"I'm sure you had," said Judy. "But you didn't have your tail dyed then."

"But if it had been dyed, I should have had an even greater success."

"Do you think so?"

"Of course I think so." There was a hint of sharpness in Miss Squirrel's voice. "Really, Miss Judy," she said, "you aren't being much help."

"I'm very sorry."

"I thought this was a *Beauty* Parlour," went on Miss Squirrel, speaking more sharply than ever.

"It is."

"Well, it doesn't sound like the Beauty Parlours I've read about. In those, the great idea was to make people look different from what they really were. If you had a grey tail you dyed it pink. If you had a straight tail you gave it a curl. If you had a curly tail you made it straight. If you had long fur you cut it off, and if you had short fur you bought extra fur to make it look long. That's my idea of a beauty parlour."

She looked quite hot after this long speech, and fanned herself violently.

Judy sighed. It was all very difficult. She hated the idea of Miss Squirrel with a pale blue tail almost as much as the idea of Mrs. Manx with an artificial one, but if she did not do as she was asked Miss Squirrel would only run off to The Shop in the Ford. And heaven knows what they would sell her *there*!

So she forced herself to smile and said: "You . . . misunderstand me, Miss Squirrel. The reason I hesitated was because I thought you looked so charming as you are."

"Well, of course, that's a matter of opinion," replied Miss Squirrel, tossing her head coyly.

"However, of course I shall be happy to oblige you."

"Pale blue?"

"Yes, I have a very pretty pale blue in stock."

And indeed she had. It was made by blue butterflies fluttering over the cups of blue Canterbury bells in the rain, and flicking the raindrops into the bells, one by one. And there were many other things in it to make it bluer still, such as the dew from fresh violets, plucked on a blue morning under a cloudless sky.

"Can I put it on straight away or shall I wait till I get home?"

"I think you had better wait till you get home," said Judy, "as it takes a little while to dry. If you will excuse me, I will go and mix it up."

She went to the back of the shop and for a moment Miss Squirrel was left to herself.

Meanwhile Miss Smith was walking through the wood. And as she walked, all the evil things of the wood raised their heads and gave her welcome.

Evil is a very powerful force; there is only one force

more powerful, which is Good. Evil is infectious; it spreads itself far and wide. If there is anything evil at large, all the other evil things know it by instinct; they rejoice and grow strong.

So as Miss Smith made her way towards the Willow

Tree, all the evil things in the dark corners knew that she was passing; it was as though a foul mist were drifting over them, and they sniffed it and savoured it, chuckling with delight. The snakes felt the poison tingling in their tails, and made vows to sting something as soon as possible. The ragged toadstools oozed with more of their deadly slime; it was as though they were licking their lips at the thought that somebody might soon come and eat them; and if you had been able to watch them, through a pair of magic spectacles, you would have seen them joining their pale clammy hands, forming an unholy ring, and dancing. In many dark caves wicked old spiders, who had long given up hope of catching a fly, began to weave again with tattered pieces of web, muttering to themselves as they mended the knots. And the mosquitoes and the blight flies rose in swarms from the stagnant ponds, with a buzz of triumph, and flew away to spread disease and havoc.

Miss Smith arrived at about the same time as Miss Squirrel, but she did not declare herself at first; she wanted to study Judy. So she sat down on a log and listened, quite invisible. It did not take her long to make up her mind. "A dreadful little girl," was her verdict. "Good through and through. Not a single decent nasty thought about her. Almost as good as that awful old Bruno." Miss Smith shivered and felt quite sick; real goodness always had that effect on her.

She listened to the argument about the blue tail, and when it was over, and Judy had gone to prepare the mixture, she decided that it was time to make herself known. So she walked a little distance away, stepped behind a tree, and made herself visible again. Then she let the toads out of her bag.

"Now darlings," she said to them, "we're calling on a

silly girl who may not like you as you are, so I'm going to change you into three little puppies."

"No!" croaked the toads, very crossly. They hated being turned into puppies; it made them hot and itchy.

"Only for ten minutes, my poppets."

The toads shook their heads.

"Three little ugly puppies," she pleaded. "As ugly as sin!"

They shook their heads more than ever.

"Mother will be angry if you don't do as she asks."

"Spit in your eye," observed the toads, coldly.

Miss Smith was beginning to get angry. And yet she could not help loving the toads; they were so wicked. In fact, they were so wicked that she did not dare to offend them; if she changed them into puppies against their will they might rush after her and give her a lot of poisonous bites.

"You're making it very difficult," she pleaded.

The toads merely shrugged their shoulders. As there was evidently no arguing with them, Miss Smith sighed, and led the way to the shop.

Miss Squirrel was the first to see her.

"Oh, what a beautiful lady!" she cried.

Judy turned round. "Whoever can it be?"

"It might be a Princess!" exclaimed Miss Squirrel. "Oh — if only I had my new tail!"

Miss Smith approached the counter.

"Good morning," she said, in a very sweet voice. "Is this a shop?"

"Yes madam," replied Judy. "May I have the honour of selling you something?"

"I expect there will be lots of things you can sell me, later on," lied Miss Smith who had no intention of buying anything. "But first may I look round?"

"Of course, madam," replied Judy. Then she noticed the toads, who were glaring at her with a very wicked expression, and she could not prevent a little gasp of dismay coming from her lips. "Are these . . . are these with you, madam?" she inquired.

"Yes, indeed they are, the little darlings," cooed Miss Smith. "Aren't they precious? Aren't they little honey-bags?"

"Yes, I'm sure," stammered Judy, though anything less like little honey-bags she had never seen.

Miss Smith smiled and nodded. "Would you believe me when I tell you that of all the toads I have ever known these are much the wickedest?"

Judy stared at her in surprise, and even Miss Squirrel was startled by such a recommendation.

"The wickedest?" echoed Judy.

For a second an ugly look came over Miss Smith's face. What a stupid mistake to make! She was always forgetting that these humans thought that it was wrong to be wicked. Then she smiled again.

"Whatever was I thinking of?" she exclaimed. "I meant the *best*. That's what I meant. Didn't I, my poppets?" She turned to the toads, and gave them a broad wink. "Aren't you the best toads in the world, my love birds? Aren't you good?"

"You said it," proclaimed the toads. And at once they burst into song.

> Three little toads are we, are we,
> We are as good as good can be,
> We wouldn't hurt the smallest fly,
> We never spit in mother's eye.

"You see?" cried Miss Smith. "What did I tell you? However, we mustn't allow the little angels to distract us."

She bowed to Miss Squirrel. "I see that this lady is waiting to be served."

"Oh, it's of no consequence," declared Miss Squirrel, though she was really longing to take her bottle and run home and dip her tail in it.

"Was it a perfume you were buying?" inquired Miss Smith.

"Well, not exactly a perfume," admitted Miss Squirrel, beginning to blush all over.

"Surely not an aid to beauty? Not with your looks?"

Miss Squirrel blushed so deeply that her fur, which was a delicate grey, seemed to grow quite red, as though she was sitting in front of a fire.

"It's . . . it's a sort of a change," she giggled.

"Well! Well!" Miss Smith eyed the bottle with a hungry look. Here, she felt, was her chance to do something really wicked. "It's certainly a beautiful bottle, and a beautiful colour, too." She gave one of her sweetest smiles to Judy. "May I be allowed to see it?"

"With pleasure." Judy handed it to her.

Miss Smith held the bottle up to the light; it sparkled in the sun like a sapphire. "I declare that it might have dropped straight from heaven!" she exclaimed. "May I have just a teeny sniff?"

She undid the stopper. "Oh, but it's wonderful! Like violets and sunshine."

Of course she really hated the scent of it, her own favourite perfume being made out of burnt feathers, garlic, and dead shrimps.

She sniffed and sniffed, and suddenly she had a brilliant idea. "I must let my darlings have a teeny sniff too!" And before Judy could prevent her, she had knelt down and was holding the bottle to the noses of the toads. As she did so she whispered "Spit in it!" The toads instantly obeyed her, and they spat so quickly and with such skill that neither Judy nor Miss Squirrel had any idea that they had spat at all.

Miss Smith rose to her feet, put back the stopper and handed it to Miss Squirrel. "I do congratulate you," she said. "You will hardly know yourself after you have used this beautiful lotion!"

Which was a far truer remark than poor Miss Squirrel guessed. If she were to put on even a few drops all the hair would fall off at once and her tail would be as bald as a rat's.

Miss Squirrel made a low curtsy, and scampered away with her bottle.

"Now, you must let me see all over your wonderful shop!" cried Miss Smith, who had not nearly finished her wicked work. So Judy, who hoped that she might prove a good customer, proceeded to show her; and wherever she went the toads went too, hopping on to shelves, peering into tins and boxes, jumping in and out of nests and even slithering under the counter. When they were sure that nobody was looking, they spat, spreading their poison over almost every article in the shop. Judy, of course, did not know what they were doing; even so, she wished Miss Smith would keep them under better control. She did not like to think that there were any animals that she could not learn to love, if she only understood them, but she had to admit to herself that it would take her a very long time to learn to love the toads. In fact, they were so slimy that they gave her the creeps.

By and by the toads had spat so much that they had no more poison left. So they hopped down from the shelves, went up to Miss Smith and tugged her skirt.

"Want to go home!" they croaked.

Miss Smith guessed that they had run out of poison.

For a moment she thought she would give them some more, but she was afraid that Judy might see her. Besides, they

had done such good work that there was no need for them to do any more.

"Tired, my sweets?" she asked.

"Exhausted," croaked the toads.

"Poor little cherubs! Poor precious ones! We won't stay a moment longer!"

"Have you a long way to go?" ventured Judy, who was longing to find out who she was.

"Some might call it long, and some might call it short," she replied. Which was not very helpful.

"Do you . . ." Judy hesitated. She wanted to know if Miss Smith lived in a palace, because it would have been wonderful to be able to put up a sign . . . "Under Royal Patronage" . . . though, to be true, Miss Smith had not actually bought anything. However, she felt that the question might sound rude. So she said, "I expect it's a very beautiful home you live in?"

Miss Smith was just about to reply, "Yes, it is," when the toads, who were getting crosser and crosser, now that all their poison was gone, croaked with one accord:

"It's a dump!"

Miss Smith gave a startled laugh, and opened her bag nervously. "Oh, the little wicked ones!" she cried. "Saying such untruthful things! Jump in, my jewels!"

The jewels jumped, very sulkily, and flopped into the bottom of the bag, glaring at her with unconcealed hatred.

"Such mischievous darlings!" she laughed, closing the bag firmly. "Always having their little jokes! When I think of our beautiful home, with its marble halls, and its fountains, and its swimming pools . . ." She felt the bag give an ominous lurch, as though the toads were trying to get out, so she decided that it would be wiser to say no more. She glanced at her watch.

"Heavens!" she cried. "I had no idea it was so late. I must be flying."

And before Judy could ask any more questions she was gone.

CHAPTER XII

A TORTOISE TO THE RESCUE

NEXT day the dreadful news about Miss Squirrel's tail was all over the wood.

Miss Squirrel's mother had been the first to tell the story. She had arrived at The Shop in the Ford in a terrible commotion — ("Never," she exclaimed, "shall I set foot in The Shop Under the Willow Tree again!") — announcing that her poor daughter's tail was as bald as a rat's, and that she was in a state of complete nervous collapse, all because of some poisonous mixture that Miss Judy had insisted on selling her.

"It is wicked!" she cried. "Downright wicked, selling people things like that! There should be a law against it!"

The other animals could hardly believe their ears. They had known Judy and her grannie for so long, they had bought so many things at their shop; never before had there been any complaints, though, of course, they were a little old-fashioned. However, surely they were as honest as the day? Was not Mrs. Squirrel making some mistake?

"Mistake?" squeaked Mrs. Squirrel. "Mistake? You should see my daughter's tail, that's a mistake all right. Eleven inches of mistake!"

"Perhaps Mr. Sam might be able to sell you something to put it right?"

"That's what I'm hoping!"

She began to examine all sorts of worthless ointments that Sam was eager to sell her. As she did so, Sam pretended to be very upset about the news, and kept on saying how careful one had to be these days, and how important it was to be quite certain about the quality of everything one sold.

"I don't think any of *our* customers will ever have to complain about such mistakes in *this* establishment", he said, loud enough for all the animals to hear him.

Meanwhile, the poison that the toads had spat into all the other things in the shop was beginning to do its work, and strange rumours ran through the wood. There really must be something wrong at The Shop Under the Willow Tree. Consider the case of Mrs. Badger. Her first bottle of scent had made her smell so beautiful that she had gone round to buy another. But as soon as she had put it on she smelt far, far worse than she had ever smelt before — so overpowering that when she passed by the lake Mr. Peacock, who was as usual admiring his reflection, fell fainting into the water and was nearly drowned. In fact, if P.C. Monkey had not possessed a gas-mask, Mr. Peacock probably would have been drowned, for all the other animals were too breathless to go near him.

Then there was Mrs. Hare . . . up all night with a violent stomach-ache after eating a few beech nuts which Judy had sold her. And Miss Fox, who had taken only one sip of Mrs. Judy's tonic and had promptly felt quite — well, really quite intoxicated — and had reeled home in the most suspicious condition, looking very wild and strange, hiccupping and laughing immoderately, and occasionally bursting into snatches of most unladylike song, such as:

Can it be wrong to kish?
Seeing I feel like thish?

Even the nests, which had always been so reliable, seemed
to have been affected. When Mrs. Pouter Pigeon's nest

was damaged in a storm, she hurried round to Judy's to
buy another one, for Mr. Pouter Pigeon was ill and she was
too busy to build one herself. No sooner had she tucked up
the family for the night than the whole bottom of the nest
fell out, and the four little Pouter Pigeons, who had been

very slow in learning to fly — (because they had been so busy pouting) — went tumbling down through the branches and were so badly bruised that they howled all night.

Yes, there really was something very wrong indeed. The animals could not understand it at all, and shook their heads and whispered among themselves. They were so fond of Judy that instead of feeling angry with her they were only sorry. All the same, they kept away from the shop. It really was not safe to go there any longer.

I I

Even so, Sam was not yet satisfied.

"You're earning your keep," he admitted grudgingly, when Miss Smith reminded him of all the wicked things she had done, "but you don't work fast enough."

"I like that!" she retorted indignantly. "You wouldn't get any girl to work faster, not for double the money."

"Why didn't them toads use deadly poison, so that it killed people instead of just making 'em sick?"

"That's the silliest question I've ever been asked," she snapped. "Isn't the whole idea to make the animals come to your shop instead of hers? How can they come if they're all dead?"

Sam saw her point. "Well, why can't we kill *her*, then? And her precious old grannie?"

"We can," replied Miss Smith calmly. "With the greatest of ease, provided that you are prepared to pay me at least three times what you're paying now. And to give the toads a bonus into the bargain. Killing good people is extremely expensive."

"Not another cent," growled Sam.

"Then all we can do is wait." And she sat down on the

grass, looking as pretty as a picture, and began to stroke the toads.

Suddenly she had an idea. "There *is* something we could do," she suggested.

"What's that?"

"We could make the animals think she was a witch. Then they'd never go near her again, and that old Mr. Justice Owl would have to send her to prison."

"They'd never believe us."

"They'd believe their eyes, wouldn't they?"

"How do you mean, their eyes?"

"I can't explain till I've done it, otherwise it would break the spell. But if I do it . . ." and here she looked him very sharply in the eye . . . "do I get a bonus?"

Sam scowled. He hated parting with money but he could see no way out of it. "O.K.," he muttered.

"And my poppets too?" she demanded.

"Your which?"

"My angels . . . my jewels . . . my love-birds . . . do they get a bonus too?"

Sam saw that she was referring to the toads. The idea of giving them a bonus was really intolerable. "I can't see why . . ." he began.

"If you don't agree," she interrupted, "you know what they'll do?" she turned to the toads. "What will you do, my chocolate drops?"

The toads took one leap into the air and landed on Sam's shoulders.

"Spit in his eye!" they hissed, looking as though they really meant it.

"O.K.! O.K.!" growled Sam hastily, brushing the toads from his shoulders.

He was beginning to think that it wasn't all honey, having a witch about the place.

"Very well, that's settled!" Miss Smith rose to her feet and beckoned to the toads. "Come along, my little wonderfuls! We must get to work!"

III

It was nearly a week later before Miss Smith again called at The Shop Under the Willow Tree. This time she did not take the toads with her, partly in case they aroused Judy's suspicions, but principally because they had been so naughty that she really felt they ought to be punished.

By "naughty", of course, Miss Smith meant "good"; for what was good to other people was naughty to her. During the last few days the toads had shown the most surprising tendencies to be good; they had not croaked any of their wicked songs; they had not even threatened to spit in anybody's eye. Miss Smith did not like it at all ... she supposed it must be the weather, which was quite perfect — sunny, calm, and sweet-scented. A nice storm and a few sharp winds, and the toads would be her darling wicked ones again.

When Miss Smith arrived, Judy was not quite sure whether she was pleased to see her; her last visit seemed to have brought such bad luck, what with the terrible business of Miss Squirrel's tail and all the other things that had gone wrong. However, she did not really blame Miss Smith for it, and she was relieved to see that this time she had not brought the toads. Instead, she was carrying a large brown paper parcel.

"Good afternoon!" crooned Miss Smith, laying the paper parcel on the counter. "It is so nice to see you again. And I have brought you a present."

"Me? A present?" exclaimed Judy. "How very kind of you! May I see what it is?"

She stretched out her fingers to undo the string, but Miss Smith quickly stopped her.

"Not yet!" she cried. "You must not touch it till I have gone, or you will put it out of order. But I can show you how it works."

She undid the parcel, and there on the counter was a beautiful new Hoover.

"What a wonderful thing!" cried Judy. "Whatever is it?"

"Wait and see!" laughed Miss Smith.

She disentangled the coil of the Hoover, went over to the tree and plugged it into the bark. (You may not have heard that all trees are full of electricity, if you know how to treat them. But only people who have lived at least a year in a tree, without ever putting their feet to the ground, are able to get the electricity out of the tree. If you live a year in a tree you will be able to do the same. And then you will be able to take a reading lamp or an iron or a radio, and plug it into any old tree, and it will work beautifully. Miss Smith had once lived for thirty-nine years in a tree without ever coming down, so of course she got a lot of electricity.)

She plugged in the Hoover and immediately it began to work, hissing away as though it were alive, and sweeping up all last year's leaves and twigs and dead moss.

"You see?" cried Miss Smith. "I noticed that it was very untidy round here. And I thought you looked too tired to do much sweeping. So I brought along this wonderful invention to do all the sweeping for you, and now you will have the tidiest place in the wood."

"That *is* thoughtful of you," declared Judy. "I do not know how I can ever thank you."

"There is no need," replied Miss Smith. "I am only too happy to oblige." She turned off the Hoover, and leant it against the tree. "Only too happy!" she repeated. Then suddenly she stopped and put her hand over her mouth. She had felt somebody coming, somebody very good, somebody so good that he might do her a lot of harm. She must go quickly, before it was too late.

"I must go," she muttered.

"Already?" asked Judy in surprise.

"At once," replied Miss Smith, who could feel the good person, whoever it might be, drawing nearer and nearer.

"I hope you will come again very soon," said Judy. "And thank you once more!"

Miss Smith muttered an inaudible reply, blew her a hasty kiss, and hurried away.

IV

When she had gone, Judy sat down and waited. She wanted to be quite certain that Miss Smith was well out of the way before touching the Hoover; it was such a lovely present that it would be a shame to spoil it.

What a perfect afternoon it was! The sky was so blue and the breeze was so cool! Though it was still summer, one or two leaves had already begun to fall, and in a few weeks they would be scattering down in their thousands. Judy watched them — first a big scarlet one, then three little yellow ones, all together, then two that were still green, though flecked with gold. She wondered why some leaves fell before others. Were they tired of staying on the trees . . . were they eager to hasten off on their great adventure? Or was it that they loved their party dresses, and could not wait to deck themselves out in their reds and their golds? How wise are the leaves, she thought to herself! When they say good-bye to the tree — which is their life on earth — they flutter off gaily, in their brightest clothes; and all the other leaves begin to dress up as though they were going to a party, which indeed they are. Whereas Humans, when they say good-bye, are all gloom and misery; and their friends dress in sombre black, as though they were never going to be asked to a party again. "When I go away from the earth," thought Judy, "I shall dress up in my best frock and I shall ask all my friends to dress up too — in blues and purples and in pinks and mauves and silvers. . . ."

She was so far away in her dreams that she did not hear a little voice at her side.

"Ahem!" said the voice.

"And greens and violets and crimsons ..." thought Judy.

"Ahem," said the voice, louder this time.

Judy woke up, and looked down by her side.

"Well I never," she exclaimed. "It's you again!"

It was the old tortoise.

V

"And how are you to-day?" she asked, with a smile.

"Never mind how *I* am," snapped the tortoise. "What about *you*?"

He spoke so sharply, and his head was darting about so angrily underneath his shell, that Judy felt sure his roof must be giving him trouble again. She bent down to look at it more closely.

"There's nothing wrong with my roof," said the tortoise, more sharply than ever. "So don't go scratching about with it. There's no time to waste."

"Why, what's the hurry?"

The tortoise flicked one of his paws towards the Hoover. "I want to know where you got *that* thing," he said.

Judy glanced at it with a smile. "Isn't it lovely? It was given me by a young lady who's only just left."

"By the name of Smith?" demanded the tortoise.

"Yes. Do you know her?"

"I know *of* her," he replied.

"You sound as if you didn't like her very much."

The tortoise nodded. "I don't."

"Why not?" asked Judy in surprise.

For a moment the tortoise did not reply. Then he said

very quietly, "I suppose that it never occured to you that Miss Smith might be a witch?"

Judy could hardly believe her ears. "Miss Smith might be a *what*?"

"Not a what, a witch," repeated the tortoise. "W . . . I . . . T . . . C . . . H ."

Judy went quite red in the face. "How dare you say such things? Miss Smith is a most charming girl. You've only got to look at her to see that."

"Oh yes, she *looks* all right," agreed the tortoise. "Particularly when she's dressed up as she was this afternoon. False teeth, wig, false nose and all that."

"I don't believe for a minute that she wears such things."

"Don't you? Then who dropped those?" and he pointed to the ground just by Judy's feet.

Judy looked down. Sure enough, there on the grass lay a full set of gleaming false teeth. She bent down and picked them up.

"Oh, what horrid things!" she cried.

"Quite. Property of your friend Miss Smith."

"How do you know?"

"Don't you remember how she was laughing just before she said good-bye? And how she suddenly clapped her hand over her mouth and mumbled that she had to be going?"

"Yes, I do remember. But what made them fall out?"

"She felt me coming. And she was frightened."

"Frightened of *you*?" Judy could not help laughing at the thought of anybody being frightened of a poor old tortoise. "Why should she be frightened of you?"

"Because she knows that I know she's a witch."

"I still can't believe it."

"You've *got* to believe it." There was a note of fear in the tortoise's voice. "Look over there!"

He pointed to the Hoover, standing against the tree-trunk, spotless and glistening in the sun.

"You see that thing?"

"The Hoover? Yes, of course I see it. She lent it to me to take up all the rubbish. It's a wonderful invention. Look . . . I'll show you."

She walked over to the machine.

"Don't touch it!"

Judy paused and drew back her hand.

"Why shouldn't I touch it?"

"Because it isn't a Hoover at all. It's a broomstick . . . a witch's broomstick!"

VI

When Judy had recovered from the shock of this discovery the tortoise asked her to come and sit down by his side while he told her a few things about modern witches which she certainly ought to know.

Speaking in quiet, kindly tones, this was what he said: "Modern women do not use broomsticks any more for sweeping carpets; they use Hoovers instead. So it is with modern witches. All the best witches — or perhaps I should say all the *worst* witches — use Hoovers for flying by night. Only a few very old-fashioned witches still use broomsticks, and they are usually so slow and feeble that they can't do much harm — the most they can do is to fly in at the window when you are asleep and put a wart on the end of your nose — and only a very small wart at that. Sometimes, too, these very old witches are so short-sighted that they can't see your nose properly, and put the wart on the pillow by mistake, or on the candlestick. Whenever you see a lump on the pillow in the morning it's a sure sign that a very old witch has flown in and been up to mischief. Of course, if you have said your prayers before going to bed, they can't get in at all . . . not even the most modern witches . . . but everybody knows *that*!"

"It's the modern witches who are the real trouble. Their Hoovers travel ten times as fast as the old broomsticks. Besides, modern witches *look* so much nicer than they used to look. In the old days, people used to run away when they saw them coming; even at a distance you could tell they were witches, with their wisps of white hair and their tooth-less mouths and their hook noses. But now they've all been to beauty parlours, and made themselves look attractive. It's the same with the things they use for weaving spells. The old-fashioned witches used to collect a few toad's eyes and raven's wings and newt's legs, and all the other horrible things they need in their trade, and then they used to stuff them in holes and in trees, or bury them in the ground, and of course they didn't keep very long, and soon rotted away. But the modern witches have all bought Frigidaires . . . and toad's eyes and things like that will keep in a Frigidaire for weeks. I once knew a witch who kept twelve dead tadpoles in a Frigidaire through the whole summer and they were quite fresh enough to use in October."

"What did she use them for?" interrupted Judy.

"It was a little matter of turning a film-star into a goat."

"Good heavens! Did she succeed?"

"Yes, but it didn't have at all the effect she expected. None of the public noticed the difference; the film star was more popular than ever."

Judy shook her head. "It's all very puzzling," she said. She glanced over towards the Hoover. "And very dis-appointing too. I had been looking forward so much to sweeping up the leaves with the Hoover."

For a moment there was silence, while Judy stared at the Hoover, and sighed. Then she turned to the tortoise. "One thing I don't understand. Why did she leave the Hoover here? Why did she want me to have it at all?"

"Ah!" The tortoise gave a very wise wink. "That's the whole point of it; that's where she was so wicked. She wanted to make all the animals in the wood think *you* were a witch."

"But why?"

"Because if they thought you were a witch they wouldn't come to the shop any more."

"Why doesn't she want them to come to the shop?"

"Because she's working for Sam and that awful grandfather of his. She's employed by The Shop in the Ford."

Judy stamped her foot with anger. "They are the wickedest people I ever met!" she cried.

"They are indeed. They know they can't beat you by fair means, so they use foul tricks like this."

Judy clenched her fists. "I wish I were a boy," she began . . .

"I'm very glad you're not," said the old tortoise, with another wink. "You're a very pretty girl."

Judy could not help smiling, although she was so angry. "Thank you, Mr. Tortoise." Then she became grave again. "I'm afraid you'll think me very stupid, but there's *still* something I don't understand. Why should the animals suspect me of being a witch merely because I had a Hoover?"

"They wouldn't. But the minute you turned it on, it would become a broomstick and take you flying over the wood for everybody to see."

"Are you certain?"

"Quite certain. We'll prove it now. Only you must be careful to do exactly what I tell you. Now! Take that branch over there . . . no, not that one . . . that's only birch and we want something tough . . . *that's* the one! That's good old oak."

"It's very heavy," panted Judy.

"I wish I could help you, but I'm afraid I can't. Is it too heavy?"

"I think I can manage it."

"Take it over to the Hoover. But be sure you don't touch it."

Judy dragged the big branch over to the machine. It made a harsh scraping noise as it caught the leaves and twigs of the undergrowth. She drew nearer and nearer to the Hoover, and out of the corner of her eye she seemed to see the machine making ugly faces at her. . . she could have sworn that it was scowling . . . the smooth, chromium-plated surface seemed all wrinkled up. Or was that a trick of the shadows?

"That's far enough," cried the tortoise. "No nearer!"

"What now?" gasped Judy.

"Now you must recite a poem. And after you have recited it you must make one last effort and lift the branch and bring it down on the Hoover with a great big bang. And then we will see what happens. Now, are you ready?"

"I'm ready."

"Then this is what you must say . . ."

Slowly, word by word, he told Judy the poem. Through the quiet, golden air of evening their two voices echoed — first the old tortoise, hoarse and croaking, and then Judy, sweet and clear. These were the words they chanted:

> Stick of broom and broom of stick,
> Lit by candle's weary wick,
> Come into the light of day,
> Come where children laugh and play,
> Come . . . and now . . . Away! Away!

"Quick" shouted the tortoise. "Lift the branch! Aim it! Bring it down with a bang!"

With a terrific effort Judy lifted the branch. She whirled it through the air. And it hit the Hoover with a sickening thud.

And then — the most extraordinary thing happened. Slowly the Hoover changed colour. From a glistening silver it turned to a dirty brown. And as its colour changed, so its handle began to split into dozens of little twigs. All the time that this was happening, it shivered and trembled violently, and a dreadful hiss came from it, like the hiss of a snake. The hiss grew louder and louder, until suddenly, it rose from the ground. It hovered for a few moments over their heads, a complete broomstick, twitching angrily backwards and forwards, as if it were seeking to attack somebody or hit something . . . and then, with a final hiss, like the noise made by a rocket when it takes the air, it soared through the trees, up into the darkening sky, and was lost to sight.

VII

"Well," said the tortoise, when the broomstick had finally vanished, "that was a narrow escape." His legs were trembling and his shell had gone several shades paler.

He turned to Mrs. Judy, who had rushed out on hearing the noise. "I wonder, madam, if you would be so very kind as to give me a sip of your raspberry wine?"

"I think we should all have a drop," cried Mrs. Judy, "I feel quite upset myself."

When she had brought the

wine and poured it out, Mr. Tortoise raised his glass and gave them a toast.

"To the damnation of the Witch," he proclaimed solemnly.

"It's a very serious toast," said Mrs. Judy, "but I really think she deserves it."

"She certainly does," agreed the tortoise. "Do you realize, madam, that she and her toads have poisoned nearly everything in your shop?"

"Poisoned?" gasped Mrs. Judy.

The tortoise nodded. "There is poison everywhere . . . upstairs, downstairs, in my lady's chamber. Miss Squirrel was poisoned. And Mrs. Hare, and Miss Fox, and all the rest of them."

"So that explains it!" cried Judy. "Whatever are we going to do?"

"Leave it to me!" answered Mr. Tortoise with a wise wink. "But first . . . if I might be so bold . . . another little sip?"

He held out his glass, which was quite a large one, and Mrs. Judy filled it again. He drained it at one gulp and Judy hoped it would not go to his head.

"We can't possibly afford to buy a whole new stock," declared Mrs. Judy.

"Do not disturb yourself, madam." Mr. Tortoise put down his glass, though not without another lingering glance at the raspberry wine, as though he would not have refused another "little sip".

"You know the Fairy Ring, beyond the old sycamore tree? Good! I want you to bring everything from the shop and place it in the ring. Everything — bottles, lotions, nests, foods — everything that has been touched by Miss Smith or her toads."

"But what an extraordinary idea!" exclaimed Mrs. Judy. "Why ever should we do that?"

If Mr. Tortoise had been able to draw himself up to his full height he would have done so, but he had not got a full height, his height was full whether he was sitting down or standing up. And if he had been able to speak in ringing tones he would have done that too, but his tones would not ring, they just squeaked. Nevertheless he managed to put a great deal of dignity into his reply to Mrs. Judy's question.

"I am not accustomed to being asked why," he observed. "I should have thought that after the episode of the broomstick my requests would not have been questioned."

"We would not dream of questioning you, dear Mr. Tortoise . . ." began Judy.

"I am not without influence in the Unseen World," continued Mr. Tortoise, waving her aside. "When I enter a fairy ring, I do not have to explain who I am. I do not have to show my card. I am Accepted."

"We only wondered . . ." attempted Mrs. Judy.

"Then you must not wonder, madam."

Mrs. Judy sighed; she had not meant to offend Mr. Tortoise. Then she had an idea. She took his empty glass.

"Just one more sip, Mr. Tortoise?"

Mr. Tortoise pretended to hesitate.

"The night is growing chilly," urged Mrs. Judy.

"Well, madam . . . if you absolutely insist!"

Once more he drained his glass.

When he had drunk, Mr. Tortoise felt quite mellow again. He repeated his instructions to Mrs. Judy, insisting that they must bring absolutely everything out of the shop and put it inside the Fairy Ring. "You see," he explained, "once the things are inside the Ring, the poison will begin to come out of them; some of it will sink into the ground and the rest of it will drift up into the air. But first I shall have to go ahead and recite the right spells and see that everything is in order; so let us get busy, because it must all be finished before midnight."

He waddled off — somewhat unsteadily, Judy thought — in the direction of the Fairy Ring, and Judy and her grannie began to clear the things off the shelves. They had to make several journeys before everything was in the Ring, and when at last they had finished, the pile in the middle was as tall as a little house.

All the while that they had been going backwards and forwards, Mr. Tortoise had been waddling round and round the Ring, whispering to the toadstools one by one, and making mysterious signs to them. "It is all very queer," whispered Judy to her grannie. "I wish I knew what he was saying."

"You will soon know, my dear," chuckled the tortoise who had overheard her. "I am almost ready."

For a few more minutes he continued to whisper and make his mysterious signs. Then he stopped, nodded to himself, and exclaimed: "Now I am ready."

He turned to Judy and her grannie, "Step out of the Ring, my dears, if you please, otherwise you may get an electric shock."

They stepped out and sat on the grass, watching him with wide-open eyes.

"I have to stay inside myself," he continued, "otherwise it would not work." He knitted his brows for a moment as though he were searching his memory. "I do hope there is nothing that I have forgotten." Then he made a gesture of impatience. "Of course — I knew there was something — the oak apple. Judy, my dear, run over to that big oak and fetch me one — a nice clean one with a long stalk."

Judy hastened to do his bidding and in a moment returned with the oak apple.

"Don't step inside the Ring," he cautioned her. "Stay where you are and throw it to me. There! That's splendid! Now I think we really can begin."

Judy and her grannie held their breaths.

The wood was very silent; the only sound came from far, far away . . . the melancholy "Too-wit-Too-woe!" of Mr. Justice Owl, meditating on the follies of the world. The moonlight shone down on the Fairy Ring, lighting up the faces of the toadstools till you would have said they were laughing, and casting a bright sheen on the back of the tortoise, so that his shell looked like a silver shield.

"Now!" whispered the tortoise.

He stepped forward to the first toadstool in the Ring, held the oak apple poised for a moment above it, and then touched it very gently on its head. As he touched it, a sweet chime rang out, like a silver bell, and at the same time the toadstool became luminous, and glowed like a tiny candle.

Judy clutched her grannie's hand in excitement.

Mr. Tortoise touched the next toadstool, and again there was the chime of a silver bell and the toadstool glowed and trembled. All round the Ring he went, touching them one by one, and soon there was a circle of soft, golden flame — like the rim that we sometimes see round the moon on summer nights, when rain is on the way. The tiny bells kept ringing, in the most delicate harmonies, up and down the scale, in tinkling sharps and trebles.

Very softly, through the chime of the bells, they heard the voice of the tortoise, chanting a secret spell. This is what he was saying:

> Ring silver chime
> In magic rhyme
> And tinkle, tinkle bell.

Glow golden star,
Shine near and far,
Your secret signal tell,
And send these hosts
Of ghouls and ghosts
Down the long steps to hell!

Little by little, the sound of the bells increased — growing sharper and more urgent; and the toadstools glowed more brightly, till they were so bright that all the undersides of the leaves in the trees high above were lit up as though by a bonfire.

And then — then came the most wonderful thing of all. Out of the pile of goods in the centre of the Ring there slowly rose a damp curling mist of poison . . . grey and cold like the breath of a snake. It coiled and twisted — it seemed to be trying to escape from the magic circle, and small pointed tongues of it darted this way and that; but each time they touched the ring of light, they fell back and were forced higher up . . . up, up, through the branches of the trees. The leaves withered and turned brown as the mist touched them, as though they were being blighted by a strange and evil frost.

And at the same time that the poison was being drawn up to the sky, high up towards the cleansing stars, so it was being sucked down, deep down into the earth. From all the little boxes and bottles and cases and tins there came trickles of poison, cold and grey; a grey that was the colour of all the world's dirt and despair; the grey of bat's wings, of filthy gutters . . . the grey of cowards' faces, the grey of dirty windows in forgotten slums. As it trickled, it turned and twisted, as though it too were trying to escape, and it writhed in black streaks towards the Magic Ring of the toadstools. But as soon as it came in the circle of the light, it plunged into the earth with an angry hiss.

The mist grew fainter and fainter, the streams of poison dried up one by one; at last the final wisp of grey floated through the branches, like a dirty rag, and the final trickle of poison vanished into the ground. Softer and softer sounded the chimes of the bells; the lights of the toadstools flickered away one by one.

And now there was only silence and the moon.

The voice of Mr. Tortoise recalled them to reality. It was hoarse and trembling, for he had used up all his strength in this great effort of magic. Yet he tried to sound light-hearted.

"Well, my dears," he said. "I don't think that was a bad job."

They were too overcome to speak.

Mr. Tortoise stepped slowly out of the Ring. "And now," he said, with a twinkle in his eye, "what about another glass of raspberry wine?"

VIII

It was nearly dawn before all the things were back in the shop again, and both Judy and her grannie were more tired than they had ever been before. But what did it matter? The poison had gone; the shop was clean and sweet; it seemed to feel utterly different — there was such a sense of kindness and goodness everywhere. The bottles sparkled so brightly in the moonlight that you would have said they were rejoicing, and the nests seemed to snuggle up together, warm and close, as though they knew that once again they would be a happy refuge for the birds. It was like the end of a bad dream.

"And to think that we owe it all to that funny little Mr. Tortoise!" whispered Judy to her grandmother.

"Ssh!" Mrs. Judy put her finger to her lips. "He may not look very much but he has obviously great gifts."

Judy nodded. "And the kindest of hearts," she agreed. "But with such talents why should he be so poor?"

Mrs. Judy shook her head. "Ah! my dear . . . that's his business. Maybe he prefers it that way. It isn't for us to ask. All we can do is to thank him."

And like a wise old woman she thanked him in the best possible way, with a final glass of the raspberry wine.

Mr. Tortoise, in spite of the large quantities which he had drunk, was in no way intoxicated. On the contrary he was grave and sober. He held up the glass to the light, and the first faint gleams of the sunrise caught it, and made it shine like a rose with the dew on it.

"I drink," he said, "to a memorable evening."

Mrs. Judy stifled a yawn, and puffed at a dandelion clock. Five puffs, and the stalk was bare. "Mercy!" she said. "It's almost a memorable *morning*. I must to bed." She turned to Mr. Tortoise. "Once again, my dear sir, our deepest thanks."

And with many a groan and a sigh she climbed up to her bed on the branches.

When Mr. Tortoise said good-bye to Judy he held her hand for a long time — much longer than was necessary.

"I think," he said, "that you need a protector."

She smiled. "I seem to have found one."

"Your grannie is old. And the Tree . . ." he looked up into its branches . . . "the Tree is old, too."

"You must not say a word against the Tree," protested Judy.

"I would not do so. The Tree is good and beautiful. But the Tree is old. And the Tree is tired."

Judy looked upwards. The sun was rising swiftly, and in the clean cold rays of morning the branches of the Tree

were wrinkled and haggard. The leaves — they were as
sprightly as ever, danced gaily in the breeze; but they hardly
seemed to belong to the Tree at all. They were like a crowd
of happy children frisking round an old man who sat
gnarled and still, dreaming his dreams, scarcely conscious
of the frolic all about him.

The quiet voice of the tortoise spoke again.

"I have not much power . . ." he began.

Judy bent down and touched him gently on his shell.

"It seems to me that you have *great* power," she said.

He shook his head. "Only . . . only now and then.
Only if . . ." he glanced at her with a strange expression
in his little eye . . . "only if . . . if I am working for somebody
I . . . I like very much." He blinked at her and shuffled
nervously on his tiny feet. In a gruff voice he continued:
"But I have a certain gift of foretelling the future. And I
see difficult times ahead."

"Difficult?" whispered Judy.

The tortoise nodded and pointed up to the Tree.

"It is very tired," he murmured, almost to himself.
"Have you ever thought that one day the Tree might be
so tired — so very tired — that . . ."

"That what?"

The tortoise hesitated. Then he said: "That it might
want to . . . sit down?"

Judy started. The idea seemed so strange that she could
not grasp it.

"What would you do then?" asked the tortoise. "Where
would you go?"

Judy shook her head. It was all so puzzling. And yet —
the Tree did look tired.

"Never mind," said the tortoise. "Do not let us meet
trouble before it comes. In the meantime, you still have
the bean I gave you?"

Judy had forgotten all about it. She felt in her pocket. Yes, it was still there.

"Do not lose it," he warned her. "There is more in it than you think. It is not just something to make you laugh. It will help you in many other ways."

"What ways?"

"If ever you are in trouble — very serious trouble — take it out and rub it three times."

"But what will happen then?"

"You will see."

Judy stared at him. But no, she did not stare at him — for he was no longer there! She rubbed her eyes. He had vanished.

For a moment she stood there, waiting, listening, wondering if he was playing some trick on her, if he had just darted away into the long grass. But no. He had gone.

From far away came the tinkle of bells. It grew fainter and fainter and finally vanished. And from high in the sky came the first call of the lark.

CHAPTER XIII

THE BOOK OF MAGIC

THE wonderful events in the Fairy Ring had given Mrs. Judy an idea. When she came down to breakfast on the following morning, she said:

"I shall be very busy for a few days, my dear."

"But, Grannie, what are you going to do?"

"Never mind." She winked mysteriously. "You will know in good time."

Judy did not like the thought of her grannie working so hard. "Don't you think you ought to have a rest?" she asked.

Mrs. Judy shook her head. "No. What I have to do must be done quickly. It must be finished before the cold weather comes, and that may be here at any moment now; the Chief of the Swallows told me."

"Are the swallows leaving so soon?"

"They are all packed, ready to go."

"Summer is so short," sighed Judy.

"Never mind, my dear, There are still a few days left, and as you know, the last days of Summer are more full of magic than any others. I must make the most of them."

"But are *you* going to work some magic, too?"

"Perhaps I am, perhaps I'm not."

With which Judy had to be content. Her grannie would say no more on the subject, but climbed slowly back into the branches of the Tree, saying that she probably would not come down again for several days. With her she took a quill pen, three bottles of ink (one gold, one silver, and one purple), and a big bundle of writing paper.

It was all very strange.

11

While Mrs. Judy is still up in the Tree, let us pay a visit to the swallows, who are so eagerly expecting the herald of Autumn, with his message summoning them to the warm lands of the South. Only when this message has been delivered can the swallows fly home; their flight is the signal for Summer to step from her throne of gold and for Autumn to mount her throne of bronze. It is a very beautiful sight, when the herald comes to the swallows, but unfortunately very few Humans can witness it nowadays, because it can only be seen through magic spectacles. Owing to wars, and a number of other human follies, it is almost impossible to find a pair of magic spectacles any more. Even if you do find any, they have probably been put out of focus because their owners have spoiled them by looking at ugly things and pretending that they are beautiful. That is one thing that you must not forget, if you are ever lucky enough to find a pair . . . *every time you look at an ugly thing, the glass is blurred.* And there is only one way to make it clear again, by wiping it with your own tears. It is because we have shed so few tears at the things which are ugly that so many of us are blind to the things which are beautiful.

For several weeks before Autumn finally decides to send her herald to the swallows, she has been busy dropping delicate hints that she is on her way. She begins by scattering silver visiting cards on the grass overnight, printed in frost that melts away soon after dawn. When she has scattered enough cards, she sends scores of tiny men with paint boxes, who swarm through the trees when the world is sleeping, dabbing the leaves with specks of crimson and yellow; when they have used up all the colour in their paint boxes, they take golden scissors from their pockets to snip off the ripe chestnuts, which go spinning and dancing down the forest paths in the greatest glee. Then Autumn sends for her jewellers, who fly far and wide, hanging the hedges with necklaces of crimson berries, and when the jewellers have finished, out come the drapers, with veils of mist which they spread over the lakes and the valleys in the most exquisite colours of violet and silver and grey.

At last the great day comes. On some dawn in mid-October, when the sky is flecked with red and the wind blows chill from the North, Autumn sends her herald to the swallows. Those who have caught a glimpse of him flying over the forest in the half-light, say that never have they seen a being so beautiful, for his face is painted gold with the last gleam of Summer's sunshine and his cloak is painted silver with the first sparkle of Winter's frost. It is a cloak that is woven from the petals of all the last flowers of Summer, which Summer has sent to Autumn as a parting gift — deep blue gentians, and autumn crocuses, pale asters and glowing dahlias, fringed with the dark red tassels of love-lies-bleeding. In his cap is set the last rose of Summer, which is the most fragrant of all the flowers of the year, and in his hand he carries a trumpet which is very slim and delicate, for it is moulded from the first thin layer of ice that has gathered by the edges of the lake. So fragile is this trumpet that it is shattered with a single note ... a note of strange sweetness, rich in echoes — echoes, not of the past but of the future, echoes of high winds through bare branches, of crackling logs on cottage fires, of the steady, peaceful fall of rain on moss. Most Humans would not hear the echoes in this note; indeed, only a few have ever heard the note at all. But here and there, now and then, a few Humans hear it, just as dawn is breaking on an October morning ... and they will tell you, these wise ones, that it is the loveliest music they have ever known.

While the herald is on his way, the swallows gather together, waiting for him in the light of the paling stars.

Says the Chief Swallow ... "I think the herald will come to-day."

"To-day! To-day!" There is a great twittering and fluttering under the eaves..

Says the Chief Swallow ... "Has everybody packed?" There is a stern note in his voice, as though he would stand no nonsense. And again, there is a great twittering and fluttering for, sometimes, everybody has not packed. There are often a number of giddy young swallows who have left things till the last moment.

"If not" ... and here the twittering and the fluttering ceases for a moment, and there is silence ... "if not", repeats the Chief Swallow ... "It will Be a Pity!"

And once more there is a great twittering and fluttering. For they all know what he means. He is referring to the sad case of a certain Miss Swallow who was so late in packing that she got left behind, and after fluttering aimlessly round Sussex for several weeks, was caught in an early snowstorm, and passed away with acute bronchitis, on the steps of the Hotel Metropole at Brighton.

This morning, however, everybody had packed. The last wing had been trimmed and polished, the last good-bye had been said to the nests. So the twittering and the fluttering subsided, and they sat there waiting, while the Chief Swallow stared fixedly to the North, for it was from the North that the herald would come

And then he came. He came from out of a stormy dawn, with a rustle of leaves and a sweep of clouds, and the colours of his cloak seemed to fly all over the red-rimmed sky, so that you would hardly know where he began and where he ended. He came to the swallows and hovered before them, between the earth and the heavens, a beautiful figure, like an angel, with the trumpet to his lips. They waited, their hearts beating high, their little bright eyes watching him. He lifted the trumpet and blew. "*To The South*" came the note, "*To The South*". The trumpet melted from his hands, falling to earth in scattered fragments of frost; the last rose of Summer shed its petals from his cap and drifted away on the wind; and with a wave of his hand, and a smile that was like a ray of October sunlight, the herald had gone.

"The Time has Come," said the Chief Swallow.

He turned and gazed over the hill, for the last time, the hills of England in which he had spent so many happy hours. It was sad to go ... could they not stay a little longer? But the wind blew cold, ruffling his feathers, and the clouds gathered thick and fast, so that the world was dark. Far, far away, at the end of their journey, there would be no clouds; a sky of blue would melt into a sea of deeper blue, and on the shores of that sea there would be roses. To this blue heaven they must go.

He stretched his wings. He took a last deep breath. "To the South!" he cried. A moment later the sky was alive with wings, skimming through the air like a flight of arrows.

Judy was wandering by the lake on the morning that the swallows flew, gathering driftwood for the fires that she would so soon be needing. She loved these early hours, when she could talk to herself without anybody overhearing her, when she was utterly alone, with the lake like a pale mirror sleeping, with the weary mists upon it.

And then, suddenly, she was no longer alone. Far off, she saw a gay black silhouette against the rising sun — a flock of wings dipping and darting and skimming and swooping in perfect harmony. "The swallows!" she cried, and waved to them. They swept down towards her, so

close that she could almost touch them, in one swift line of black, and the sound of their wings was like the rustle of a silken dress.

And then they were gone. But no — not quite gone. For she turned just in time to see the same lovely pattern repeating itself to the South, the same black, sweeping lines, rimmed with gold. Look! They are flying up, up . . . over the hills and far away . . . they are smaller and smaller . . . like leaves, like tiny specks . . . like . . . like nothing. The skies are empty.

The lake turned in its sleep. The steel-grey of its surface warmed to a delicate blue. The mists joined hands, floated away, disappeared.

"That was a beautiful dream," whispered the lake to itself.

"Autumn has come," sighed Judy.

She turned and made for home.

When she arrived, she found that Mrs. Judy had come down from the tree, and was sitting waiting for her, with a big parcel on her lap.

III

"Why, Grannie!" cried Judy, "whatever have you been doing in the last few days?"

Mrs. Judy pointed to the parcel. "This is what I have been doing," she said.

"But what is it?"

"It is my Book. And I have only just finished writing it."

Judy was quite astonished. "But I had no idea you could write a book."

"Neither, to be frank, had I," replied her grannie. "It was Mr. Tortoise who gave me the idea. When he was working those wonderful spells in the Fairy Ring I began to remember all sorts of little scraps of magic which I had been taught when I was a girl. It seemed a great pity that they should be forgotten, and so I decided to put them down. And here they are. . . ."

She undid the parcel, and handed the book to Judy, who exclaimed with delight when she saw its beautiful cover. It was made of delicately plaited grass, of many shades of green, and in and out of the grass Mrs. Judy had woven a design of buttercups; these had been pressed flat but they were still golden and glittering. Round the edges she had gummed all sorts of feathers . . . there were pale grey pigeon's feathers, and several red feathers from the robin-redbreast. There were copper-green drake's feathers and yellow canary feathers and some brilliant blue feathers that Judy recognized as coming from Mrs. Jay. And in the centre of the cover was a lovely glass marble, streaked with orange and scarlet and green.

"That is a magic marble, by the way," said Mrs. Judy casually. "It has a sea-serpent inside it."

"Oh dear!" Judy nearly dropped the book.

"You needn't worry," said Mrs. Judy. "It can't get out. It was put inside the marble and sent to sleep for a thousand years for trying to bite Christopher Columbus. That was in 1492, so it still has to go on sleeping for over four hundred and fifty years."

"But it's such a very small marble to have a sea-serpent inside it!" said Judy.

"It happened to be a very small sea-serpent," observed her grannie. "They are much the most dangerous."

"I never read about all this in my history book," said Judy.

"There are lots of things you don't read in ordinary history books. That's why I've written *my* book. Do open it."

Judy opened it very carefully, and turned to the title page. This is what she read:

MRS. JUDY'S LESSON BOOK

by

MRS. JUDY

author of

Witches I Have Known

Underneath was a little notice saying—

Mrs. Judy has also written the following books:

VOYAGES ON A SEA-SERPENT'S TAIL
MENUS FOR MIDDLE-AGED MAGICIANS
GNOMES — THE TRUTH
HOW TO TURN CROCODILES INTO STOCK-BROKERS
SIX SIMPLE WAYS OF CURING CLOVEN HOOVES
ELVES OF THE UNDERWORLD
ETIQUETTE FOR DRAGONS

"But, Grannie," cried Judy, "have you really written all these books?"

"Not exactly," replied Mrs. Judy. "But it looks well. All the best authors do it."

"But supposing somebody asked to see them?"

"I should say they were out of print. All the best books are."

"Wouldn't that be a little . . ." Judy hesitated for the right word. She had been going to say "untruthful", but it did not seem very polite to tell one's grandmother that she was untruthful.

"I know what you are thinking," said Mrs. Judy.

"You think it might not be quite honest to say I had written all those books when I hadn't. Well, there's a very simple way of getting out of that. I can just write on the title-page . . . 'This page is all fiction. All the rest of the book is true'."

"Well that *would* be a clever idea," said Judy.

"That's what I thought," Mrs. Judy smiled contentedly. "And perhaps if this book is a success I might write all those other books some day."

"I'm sure you *could*, if you really tried."

"So am I. I could certainly do the one about the witches. I've met dozens. And the menus for middle-aged magicians would be easy . . . so would the gnomes and the elves. I might have to take more trouble about the Etiquette for Dragons; it's so long since I met a dragon, and for all I know they may have changed. They may wear their scales shorter and they mayn't breathe fire any more. I heard all the latest dragons had had gas stoves fitted inside them, and when they wanted to breathe fire they just put in a penny, twisted their tails and lit a match. Of course it may be only a rumour; it would be interesting to find out."

"I hope you *won't* try to find out," said Judy. "It sounds very dangerous."

"Anyway," said Mrs. Judy, "that can wait for the future. The first thing we have to do is to publish this book and see if we can make it a success. Now I am going for a walk and I shall leave you to read it. When I come back I shall want to know exactly what you think of it."

Whereupon she put on her hat, gave Judy a kiss, and wandered slowly off into the wood.

Judy made herself comfortable against the tree trunk, opened the book, and began to read. And we are going to look over her shoulder and read the book too. For really it is a very important book and you will not be able to buy it anywhere else because it is full of magic, and you cannot buy magic any more in a modern book shop. There is a law against it.

So let us begin to read right away.

MRS. JUDY'S MAGIC BOOK

Chapter 1

Wizards and Spotted Dogs

NEXT time you see a spotted dog when you go for a walk, be sure to cross your fingers, because it will not be a spotted dog at all, it will be a wizard in disguise. If you do not cross your fingers you will have a pain.

The wizard's real name is Mr. Snooks and he changes himself into a spotted dog for two reasons — firstly because everybody likes spotted dogs, and wants to pat them, secondly because he can put a pain or a toothache into each spot, and when you pat his back, you get the pain, and the spot disappears. I once saw him run up to a group of boys and girls who all patted him with both hands. By the time they had finished they all had toothache and tummy ache, and all his spots had gone . . . when he ran away he was quite white.

If you cross your fingers you have nothing to fear.

This only applies to the *next* time you see a spotted dog. After that, all the spotted dogs you see really *will* be spotted dogs . . . unless, of course, they happen to be wearing peaked caps, in which case they would naturally be wizards.

CURE FOR BAD MEMORY

If you have a bad memory, and have to learn something by heart — say a poem or a piece of history — you can help yourself by a very simple piece of magic. Next time you eat a boiled egg, keep the shell, and put in it one lump of sugar, one tea-leaf dipped in vinegar, and a piece of paper on which you have written your own name. Then rub the shell gently backwards and forwards over your forehead. As you do so, you must repeat these lines:

Open, open magic door,
Teach me more and more and more.

As you say this, you can almost feel a little door opening in your head.

It had probably got stuck when you were asleep. I ought to explain that there are all sorts of doors in your head which normally open and shut of their own accord. There are the doors through which all the dreams dance at night. When you are well and good and happy, the right doors open and you have nice dreams. When you are not well, or when you have not been good, the wrong doors open, and you have bad dreams and wicked thoughts.

The memory door is one of the doors which you have to open yourself. As I said before, the magic egg-shell helps you to open it.

Now as soon as you feel the door open in your head, put the egg-shell in an egg-cup and cover it with a handkerchief. Then go into another room and learn whatever it is you have to learn. It will be much easier now. Go over it again and again till you know it. Then — and not till then — you can go into the next room. Go up to the egg-shell and repeat what you have learnt. If you have learnt it right, you will find that the sugar and the tea-leaf and the piece of paper have disappeared, and in their place there is a penny.

This means that you will never forget what you have learnt. But to make quite sure, take the egg-shell, and rub it over your forehead again, repeating these lines:

> Close the door of Memory,
> Shut it fast and turn the key,
> Then I never shall forget
> Any lesson I am set.

Rub the egg-shell once again. Then crumble it in your fingers. And you will always remember your lessons.

HAUNTED SHOES, THEIR CAUSE AND CURE

Lots of children are walking about in haunted shoes without knowing it. Shoes are very easy things to haunt; in fact the very first test given to any member of the Associated College of Witches,[1] before she can take a degree, is to haunt a pair of shoes. In America, the usual method is for the witch to disguise herself as a bootblack; she carries the spell under her tongue and spits it out into her hands and then rubs it into the shoe with the blacking ... which is not blacking at all but black earth, dug up from a cemetery at midnight, and baked in the skull of a goat. In England, where there are very few bootblacks, the witch usually flies in through the keyhole of the kitchen and smears the boot-brushes with a strange, invisible fluid made from the eggs of serpents and the stings of wasps.

As I said before, when you are wearing a pair of these shoes you may have no idea that they are haunted. But little by little you will find that your feet are carrying you into all sorts of places where they have no business to go; for instance, you may be on your way to school when you suddenly see a side-street which looks interesting, and before you know where you are, your haunted shoes are

---

[1] This College has since been amalgamated with the Wizards' Institute and the United School of Gnomes and Poltergeists.

running your feet down it, with the result that you are late for school. Or you may be standing at a street-crossing, waiting for the lights like a sensible person, when without warning your shoes begin to twitch and force you to run across too soon, and risk being run over. (Many children who have had accidents in the streets have been wearing haunted shoes.) Even when you are safely in the school-room your shoes may start to fidget and shuffle, however hard you try to keep them still.

All these are sure signs that they are haunted.

There is no easy cure for haunted shoes, because the witch has usually woven the spell right into the leather; you will need lots of patience and a good deal of time. However, they *can* be cured, if you persevere. The first thing to do is to clean them yourself, whenever this is possible. As you brush them, recite these lines:

> Blacker, blacker, ban and banish
> Wicked Witch's spell from leather;
> Brighter, brighter, witch will vanish,
> My two feet will stand together.

When you have finished, put on the shoes, and stand with your heels together, looking down at your shoes. If they are very bright, it is a sign that they are no longer haunted; if they are not very bright, it is a sign that you will have to go on polishing.

In order to keep the spell from coming back you must always see that they are clean. And when you come into the house on a muddy day you must wipe each foot *three* times on the mat before going inside, saying as you do so:

> As I wipe away the grime,
> So I wipe the witch's crime,
> As I clean away the mud,
> So I'm clean of witch's blood.

If you always keep your shoes bright and smart it is quite possible that one day a different sort of spirit may come along and haunt them, with very happy results; if you are a boy, for instance, a magician will put a spell into the sole which will make you able to run faster than you ever did before; or if you are a girl, a fairy may hammer in some invisible nails which will help you to be a beautiful dancer. (These dancing nails can only be seen under a very powerful microscope; they are made from the tiniest possible pieces of golden wire and at the end of each nail is the tooth of a goldfish.)

And so Judy read and read, with eyes that were wide with wonder; and the sun mounted higher and higher in the heavens, sparkling on the scarlet oaks and opening up the cups of the Autumn crocuses till they glowed like little magic lanterns.

What a wonderful book it was! If only she could remember everything she had read, she felt that all her troubles would be over — and she had hardly read half of it yet! However, it was growing late, so she closed the book, putting a golden maple leaf between the pages to remind her where she had left off.

As she rose to her feet she noticed with surprise that in spite of the brilliant sunshine she felt cold and stiff. And surely . . . surely, it was rather dark for the time of day? Puzzled, she stared about her. What could it be? Nothing had happened; everything was the same . . . and yet, *was* everything the same? Were not the shadows deeper? Did not the branches weigh more heavily to the ground? Quickly, moved by a sudden instinct, she looked up. And then she caught her breath. For the Tree was slowly drooping — drooping downwards to the earth.

Stifling a cry of alarm, Judy ran out into the sunlight.

Even as she did so, the drooping ceased; the Tree was still
again. It was as though a very old man, who had grown
weary of standing in one position, had leaned heavily
forward on his stick, sighing and muttering to himself, and
then had drifted back into his dreams. Judy stared at the
Tree; the fear faded from her eyes and gave place to pity —
pity for the Tree that was so tired and heavy with the years,
whose limbs were so gnarled and stiff and aching. The
words of Mr. Tortoise echoed through her head. "Have

you ever thought," he had said, "that one day the Tree may want to sit down?" She had paid small heed to him at the time, but now his words sounded like an urgent warning.

She went back into the shadows, and knelt down by the great trunk, patting it and fondling it, and murmuring gentle words. "Please Tree," she whispered, "please do not be so tired. Please Tree, try to rest, and do not struggle with the wind and the rain. Please Tree . . . if . . . if " — and here a lump came into her throat and she had to brush away her tears — "if you very much want to sit down, please . . . please do so; you have sheltered us so long, you have given us all your life, we shall manage somehow. But please . . . please if you *can* stand up a little longer, we should be so truly grateful!"

So she whispered, stroking the bark of the great trunk; and somehow she felt that the Tree had heard her, and had understood. For when she looked up again, all the leaves were dancing, and the branches were bathed in a golden light. A fresh breeze had risen, but the Tree no longer shrank before it, but greeted it as though it were a friend. And as the breeze blew, the voice of the Tree seemed to come down to her, firm and strong, saying, "Have no fear! As long as you need me, I shall stand!"

CHAPTER XIV

JUDY IN DANGER

SAM was growing angrier and angrier. In spite of Miss
Smith's efforts, Judy and her grannie were still carrying
on at The Shop Under the Willow Tree; and doing very
good business too. Mrs. Judy's Lesson Book had proved a
wonderful attraction; she had propped it up on a branch
near the Nest Department, charging a penny for reading it;
and there was always a long queue of animals waiting to
turn the pages. In fact, the queue became so long when Mr.
Snail was reading that she had to lift him off the book and
return his penny. It had taken him over an hour to read
half a sentence, and he had left a long, moist trail behind
him on the paper. "People like that," hissed Mrs. Hare
impatiently, "should not be allowed into libraries at all."

Sam wracked his brains, trying to think of something to
do. Should he write a book himself? But no — they would
think him a copy cat; besides, it would mean a lot of work,
and Sam didn't like work. He wanted quick results,
without too much trouble, which was why he had engaged
Miss Smith. But what had she done? A lot of promises, a
lot of talk, a lot of scurrying about with those darned toads
. . . but it all led to nowhere. Drat the woman! Unless she
could do something, and do it quickly, he'd give her the
sack.

He rose from the breakfast table, throwing an empty jam
jar at Bruno, who was patiently waiting on him, and went
in search of Miss Smith.

She was sitting at her dressing table in her cave, preparing herself for the day. She did not hear Sam approach,
and Sam watched her with a mixture of wonder and disgust,

for he had never yet seen her before she had made her toilet. The real Miss Smith, he now observed, was quite bald and toothless, with hardly any nose, no eyelashes,

and a skin the colour of old potatoes. But the way in which she transformed herself was extraordinary — at least, so it seemed to Sam, who had not had much to do with modern girls.

First she pulled a golden wig over her head; then she stuck an artificial nose on her face; then she opened her mouth and put in her false teeth. That was better, but she still looked a very ugly old woman. So she took two little clothes pegs, and pulled her cheeks tight on each side, to take away the wrinkles, sticking the clothes pegs under the wig so that nobody should see them. Then she took an eyebrow pencil and drew the most beautiful eyebrows on her forehead, and she cut two strips of false eyelashes — as long and as curly as a film star's — and gummed them on to her eyebrows. She was beginning to look almost pretty now, except for the colour of her cheeks, but that was an easy matter to arrange, for she smeared them all over with a rose coloured cream, and dusted them with a pale pink powder and when she had done that, she drew a perfect Cupid's bow where her lips would have been if she had had any. Now she was finished — but no, not quite, for she still had to dip her finger nails into a pool of scarlet lacquer, which was made from the blood of the descendants of a number of notorious pigs who had once rushed violently down a steep slope into the sea.

Suddenly, in the cracked mirror, she saw Sam's reflection. She was not too pleased; a girl does not like to have men prying into her secrets.

"Well," she sniffed, "I do think you might have knocked. What are you staring at? Have I got a spot on my nose, or something?"

"If you had a nose, you might have a spot on it," retorted Sam. "But as you ain't got a nose, you can't have."

"Really! That's a nice thing for a gentleman to say!"

"I didn't come here to pay compliments. I came to talk business."

"At this hour of the morning?"

"We've wasted too much time already," snarled Sam. "I'm sick of paying your wages for nothing. I want this job finished — see? Unless you get rid of those two witches under the Willow Tree . . ."

"Witches?" interrupted Miss Smith, in icy tones. "Did I hear the word witches?"

"You did. So what?"

Miss Smith tossed her head. "I was not aware," she said, "that Miss Judy and her grannie had any qualifications. A witch — " and here she began to tap her knee with her scarlet finger nails " — is a very definite title. It means somebody who has passed a great many exams. . . ."

"I shouldn't think you passed many of yours," sneered Sam.

Miss Smith ignored the interruption. "It means somebody with a very enviable position in the Underworld," she went on.

"Well, your position in the Underworld won't be much to write home about, not when they read the reference I shall give you!"

Miss Smith started; she had not thought of that.

"I shall tell 'em you're not worth your keep!" snapped

Sam. "I shall tell 'em you couldn't addle an egg, let alone haunt a house. I shall tell 'em you couldn't give anybody cross-eyes, let alone a hump. I shall tell 'em you couldn't even ride a bicycle, let alone a broomstick. . . ."

"Oh, this is too much!" cried Miss Smith, dabbing her eyes with a handkerchief which had been cut from the shroud of a duke who had suffocated both his nephews at Eton and Harrow respectively — "I will not endure such insults! Where are my darlings?" She looked around her wildly for the toads. "Where are my honey-pots?"

The honey-pots, who had been watching this scene from underneath their favourite cluster of toadstools, hopped forward to the rescue.

"Spit in his . . . " they began.

"Spit on my foot," retorted Sam rudely.

"Oh! What language!" cried Miss Smith.

"My foot I said and my foot I meant," shouted Sam, stepping towards the toads.

"Bite him, my angels! Spit all over him, my jewels!" screamed Miss Smith.

But the jewels were not so sure; Sam's boot looked heavy, and it had a sharp point on it. They shuffled backwards, glaring at him with their wicked eyes, longing to spit at him, but not certain whether they had enough poison to make it worth their while.

"Just you try!" yelled Sam, taking another step forward, and lifting his boot. "Just you try!"

The toads glared still more fiercely, but they took another step backwards — Sam's boot looked very sharp indeed. Besides, they were bored with the whole business; they hated the wood, they hated the cave, they hated the animals. They hadn't made a single friend since they came, except one old adder, and even he had hardly any sting left in him. They wanted to get back to the big, bad city, with its lovely gutters and its beautiful sewers, where their friends the Rats would be waiting to play all sorts of wicked games with them. They had no heart for a fight with Sam. They sat there, sulking.

"Want to go home," they croaked.

"So you shall, my poppets," cried Miss Smith. "This very instant!"

She snatched her bag, and opened it for the toads to jump in.

"Just a minute!" Sam put his hand on her arm. "If you go now, you get no wages."

"I don't care," sniffed Miss Smith.

But the toads cared. "No wages?" they croaked. "No rake-off?"

"You said it," snapped Sam.

"Then what about our pocket money?"

"You'll get it some other time, my sweets," exclaimed Miss Smith. "Come now! Hop into the bag!"

The toads drew back. "Nothing doing," they croaked, shaking their heads.

"But darlings, you said you wanted to go home." The toads were silent. "What *do* you want?"

"Dough," croaked the toads.

In spite of her irritation, Miss Smith could not help glowing with pride at the wickedness of her darlings. How terrible they were! How they scowled and frowned and sulked, the little angels! She could have hugged them. All the same, they were being very trying.

"I really don't know what I ought to do," she sighed.

"We know what you ought to do," croaked the toads. "Get our dough!"

With which they hopped angrily back to their toadstools, and prepared to go to sleep.

Miss Smith sat down on a log and fanned herself, for she

was feeling quite hot after this angry scene. "This is the most unpleasant job I've ever undertaken," she exclaimed.

"Then why don't you finish it?" retorted Sam. "All you've got to do is to get rid of those two and then you can go."

Miss Smith snorted. "That may seem very simple to you, but you don't understand. They're *good*, those two — and good people are very difficult to hurt, let alone destroy. Every time they say their prayers, they make it harder to get near them. I honestly think I shall have to give it up. Unless . . ." she paused, and an extra wicked glint came into her eye.

"Unless what?" demanded Sam.

Miss Smith looked over her shoulder to see that nobody could overhear her. Then she tiptoed across to the toads to see if they really were asleep. Yes — they were snoring, making the most beautiful noises, like muddy water being sucked into a drain.

She went back to Sam, and began to whisper in his ear. We dare not tell you what she said, for there are some things so wicked that if you try to write them down they scorch the paper; as soon as the ink touches the page there is a little puff of smoke, the paper bursts into flame, and instead of a page there is only a pinch of ashes. So we will not attempt to report what she said, because you would not like this book to look as though it had fallen in the fire.

But we can give you a rough idea of what she meant. You have heard of the old saying — "Set a thief to catch a thief"? It means that evil men understand one another; they have learned each other's tricks and weaknesses; they know the dark alleys down which they slink and the crooked doorways in which they hide. Just as this is true of Evil, so it is true of Good. "Set a saint to catch a saint" . . . that was the terrible lesson that Miss Smith was teaching Sam, and you will have to be much older and ... maybe ... much sadder before you can really understand it, for it is the sternest lesson in life, that only the good can hurt the good, that only the pure can pervert the pure.

However, we are not in the school room — we are reading a story book; so let us get on with the story.

"Do you really want to finish them off?" hissed Miss Smith.

Sam shuffled uneasily on his seat. "Well ..." he muttered, "it depends on what you mean by 'finish off'."

"*You* know what I mean."

And, indeed, he did. She meant — murder. It was an ugly word and Sam, who was a coward, did not like to face up to it.

"I want 'em . . . I want 'em . . . out of the wood," he growled.

Miss Smith chuckled and rubbed her hands together. "Then there's only one person who can do it."

"Who's that?"

Miss Smith clutched his hand and stared into his eyes. Her fingers were like icicles, but her eyes were like burning coals.

"Can't you guess?" she whispered. "We want somebody good, don't we? Well — who's good in this dump? Who's kind and truthful and honest — and all the rest of it?" She lifted her arm and pointed towards the furthest cave.

"Bruno!" gasped Sam.

"That's it!"

"Bruno's the one to do it!" he cried.

"Bruno's the one!" she echoed.

Sam leapt to his feet, put his fingers in his mouth and blew a shrill whistle. Out of his cave lumbered Bruno, and stood before them, waiting for his orders.

I I

A poisoned kettle, a bottle of poisoned acid drops, and a pair of magic gloves, embroidered on the back with grinning skulls — these were the terrible objects which were spread on the floor of Bruno's cave, and for three whole days and nights he had been staring at them.

When they had told him what he was to do, he had refused point blank.

At first they had tried to coax him.

"You don't have to *give* them to her," crooned Miss Smith, in the sweetest of tones. "You just have to leave them in the shop when she is out, so that she finds them when she comes back."

Bruno shook his head.

"Be a sport, Bruno!" chaffed Sam, trying to twist his scowling face into a smile. "It's only a joke."

Bruno shook his head again. He knew very well that it was no joke. Those hideous gloves, with their grinning skulls, were enough to tell him *that*.

"You're being very obstinate," said Miss Smith, trying to keep her temper.

"And you know what happens to obstinate bears?" growled Sam.

Yes — Bruno knew what happened. But he still refused to do their bidding.

So then they changed their tune; instead of trying to coax him, they used force, kicking him, beating him, scorching his fur with red hot tongs. It was no use; he would not do it. At last, they locked him up in the cave, with nothing to eat or drink. "And there you'll stay," screamed Miss Smith, "till you change your mind!"

But how *could* he change his mind? How could he go to the shop with those wicked things and leave them for Judy to find, knowing full well that if she used the kettle or ate the acid drops she would die of deadly poison? Why — they were so poisonous that he himself could only handle them if he were wearing the magic gloves, otherwise the poison would sink into his body.

"What can I do? . . . What can I do?" moaned Bruno. He had to make up his mind quickly for at any moment they would be coming for him. And if he said "No" again, Sam had sworn to take him back to the Circus. At the thought of the Circus, Bruno trembled all over and buried his face in his poor bruised paws. Surely anything was better than that? But was it? Was it better, for instance, to be a murderer? His head seemed to go round and round, trying to find a way out, but the more he thought the dizzier he became, for he was faint from lack of food and drink.

There was the sound of footsteps outside. Bruno stiffened. Here they were. Quick — quick — he must think! And suddenly Bruno's brain seemed to grow clearer — he seemed to see where his duty lay. He must go back to the Circus.

Yes, he must go back — back to the cage, back to the whips and the bright lights and the blaring music. He had borne it before, perhaps he would be able to bear it again. Perhaps even — once again — he might be able to escape, and find some other magic wood, and die in peace. But in his heart, Bruno knew that this was a very faint hope, for he was no longer young and strong, and his limbs were stiff and weary.

A key turned in the lock.

Quick — there was still something he must decide.

What was it? His brain was growing dizzy again. Ah, yes! He must warn Judy before it was too late. He must pretend to Sam that he was going to poison her; he must set off with the kettle and the acid drops, and go to the Willow Tree, and wait for her return, and then . . . .

"You there! Come out!"

There was no more time to think. The door swung open, and Sam stood there, with the witch by his side. He held a whip in his hand and she was brandishing a pair of red-hot tongs.

"Well," snarled Sam, "have you made up your mind?"

Bruno nodded.

"And which is it to be?" cried Miss Smith, waving the tongs so close to him that they almost singed his fur.

For answer Bruno drew on the magic gloves and picked up the kettle and the acid drops.

"He's going to do it!" yelled Sam, in delight.

"I'm not so sure," retorted Miss Smith. "He's got a

nasty deceitful look on his face." She threatened him again with the tongs. "Are you going to play straight?"

Bruno nodded again. And, indeed, he was going to play straight — with Judy.

"Well, don't you try any funny business, or it'll be the worse for you," she snapped. "Now let's see — have you

got everything? Acid drops? Kettle? Gloves? Then you can get going. Mind you fill up the kettle and put it on the fire so's it'll be boiling when she comes back."

"And be sure to leave a note, 'With love from Bruno' on it, so's she won't suspect," warned Sam, prodding him in the ribs.

Bruno turned to go.

"Wait!" screeched Miss Smith.

Bruno paused.

"Whatever you do, don't forget to bring back my magic gloves!"

For the last time Bruno nodded. And then, with bowed head and stumbling feet, he went his way.

III

If Judy had not found the mushrooms, on that fateful morning, our story would have taken a very different course. She would not have returned to the shop, she would not have surprised Bruno, and heaven knows what might or might not have happened.

As it was, hardly had she been walking for five minutes than she saw a gleam of white in a sheltered hollow, and there, on a patch of grass, with the sun glistening on them, was a wonderful clump of late mushrooms. Never had she seen such beauties — there were some the size of saucers, and some the size of buttons, and they were all as clean and sweet as if they had just had a bath. If there was one thing Judy liked for breakfast it was mushrooms, so she tied her handkerchief to the bough of a tree, to mark the place, scrambled up the bank, and hurried back to the shop to get a basket.

And there, to her astonishment, was Mr. Bruno.

He had his back turned to her, and he was taking little

shuffling steps, first to the left and then to the right, as though he could not make up his mind. For a moment Judy thought it must be a burglar; after all, it was Sunday, and all the animals knew that the shop was shut and that she and her grannie would be out. But then, as she tiptoed closer, she saw who it was.

"Why, Mr. Bruno," she exclaimed, "whatever are you doing?"

Bruno started back as though she had hit him, dropping the kettle and the acid drops. He stood there, panting, staring at her.

"I wasn't doing anything . . . I swear I wasn't . . . I only came to warn you!"

Judy could not think what he was talking about, but as he had dropped his things, she knelt down to pick them up.

"Don't touch them! Don't go near them!"

She looked up at him in astonishment. Then she noticed that the tears were streaming down his face.

"Why, Mr. Bruno, you're crying!" she whispered very gently, in a voice that was full of pity.

"It's nothing," he muttered, turning away his head. "Please don't touch those things — I'll do it. And then I'll go away, after . . . after you've heard what I came to tell you."

"But you mustn't go, Mr. Bruno. Not . . . not like that; not till you feel better. Besides, if I oughtn't to touch these things, though I can't think why, surely you oughtn't to touch them either."

"It's all right for me," he gulped. "You see, I'm wearing magic gloves."

Judy looked at the gloves and was more puzzled than ever. Such horrible gloves she had never seen, with their grinning death's heads. She shrank back in fear.

Mr. Bruno bent down and began to pick up the things.

But his eyes were so blinded with tears that he could not see properly, and he fumbled about hopelessly in the long grass.

Judy could not endure to see him like this; in spite of her disappointment when he had joined The Shop in the Ford she had never really had any hard feelings about him; she could not forget how kind he had always been in the past, with his gifts of honey and his little bunches of flowers; and though he was so strong she knew that he had never abused his strength — even if a bumble bee were to fall asleep on one of his bunches, he would lift it off, ever so gently, with his giant paw, and lay it to sleep on another flower, so softly that it did not know anybody had touched it.

And now — to see him like this, broken, terrified, in despair . . . and wearing those horrible gloves! No, no . . . there was some mystery here; and she was impatient to clear it up.

"Mr. Bruno," she said, trying to prevent her voice from shaking, for she, too, was feeling very near to tears. "What was it you wanted to warn me about?"

"If you only knew!" came the answer. He was still fumbling in the long grass.

"Then why don't you tell me?"

"I'm trying to tell you — honestly I am, Miss Judy. It's only that I . . . ."

"That you what?"

He shook his head; how could he explain? How could anybody else understand how terribly frightened he was? He was going to tell her — yes; but he was certain that the minute the words were out of his mouth, something dreadful would happen — Miss Smith would suddenly drop down from the sky, or Sam would appear with his whip, or a flash of lightning might strike him dead. Even if none of these things happened, it would make no difference in the long run, they would find out what he had done and punish him cruelly and send him back to the Circus. Oh yes, he was going to tell, but he wanted just one minute longer, just one minute.

Judy knelt down by his side. "Mr. Bruno," she whis-

pered, "don't be afraid. Aren't we . . . aren't we . . . friends?"

Friends! That magic word! He looked up and for the moment his great paws hung down by his sides, motionless. Friends! The air seemed to be full of a thousand echoes from a morning many years ago, when he had woken up from his long sleep of exhaustion, to find all the animals around him, staring at him with big wide eyes . . . and Mr. Justice Owl had said, "You are among friends."

Friends! How kind, how peaceful that word had sounded then — like a caress, like balm on a bleeding paw! He had not known what it meant in those days, all that he had known was that it was good; it was good in the same way that some other sounds were good — like the sound of wheat rippling in the sunlight, like the sound of sleepy kittens purring by a fire, like the sound of snow, spreading a shining mantle over a heap of withered branches, as though it were saying, "Even you . . . even you who are old and sapless and forgotten . . . even you are worthy of the finest cloak that can be woven from the silver looms of the sky."

Friends!

He moaned and threw himself on the grass, burying his face in his great arms. He could bear it no longer; he would tell her everything, this very minute.

Softly, as though he were a child, Judy began to stroke the back of his head. But after a few minutes, her hand was still, for she was rigid with horror and indignation at the story which Bruno had to tell her. Little by little it all came out — his escape from the Circus, his recapture by Sam, his imprisonment and the deadly plot which they had laid for her own destruction.

When he had finished she sprang to her feet. She was pale and trembling, but there was a fire in her eyes that boded ill for Sam and the Witch.

"Come, Bruno!" she cried, "get up! We have no time to lose!"

He blinked at her, wiping away his tears. "Must I, must I go back to them, now?" he stammered.

"Go back? You shall never go back!"

"But they may come for me!"

"Let them try!" She gave him her hand. "You have saved my life, Mr. Bruno." He shook his head. "Oh, yes, you have! And I shall never forget it. Go back, indeed! Even if we had no one to help us, even if we were all alone, you and I, we would fight them to the last. But we are not alone — we have friends, powerful friends, too! Watch!"

From her pocket she drew the magic bean. Before she rubbed it, she closed her eyes. "Please, Mr. Tortoise," she whispered, "Please do not fail us now."

She rubbed the bean, once, twice, three times. Slowly she opened her eyes.

There, on the grass before her, sat Mr. Tortoise.

"And about time, too!" he snapped. "I've been expecting this for days!"

"You knew?" cried Judy.

"I know everything, my dear. And one thing I know is that you have not sent for me a moment too soon!"

IV

"Magic is not enough," explained Mr. Tortoise, "not with desperate characters like these."

It was several hours later, and Judy and her grannie were sitting on the grass, with Mr. Bruno by their side, listening to the tortoise outlining a plan of campaign. They all felt very much better, for Bruno had drunk a whole bowl of milk and eaten two large honeycombs, and Mr. Tortoise had taken quite a number of sips of his favourite raspberry wine. Besides, to make sure that they were not disturbed he had shown Judy how to draw a magic ring all round the Tree, which would give Sam and the Witch a very sharp electric shock if they attempted to disturb them.

"Magic is not enough," he repeated, addressing his remarks principally to Mrs. Judy, for it was she who had expressed the opinion that since he had such wonderful powers, it would be simplest if he were to use them straight away. "Could you not turn them into toads, or something like that?" she had suggested — of course, with the greatest respect. "Or rocks? Or blasted oaks? Or might it not be possible to cover them up in a huge iceberg so that they would all freeze to death? Naturally — " she hastened to add, "you must be the judge — I was merely throwing out ideas at random."

Mr. Tortoise bowed. "Thank you, madam," he replied. "Toads, of course, could be managed — and blasted oaks would present no special problems, though the idea of the iceberg is perhaps somewhat ... somewhat academic. However, I think that we must use other methods — simpler methods, more human methods in fact. For in Sam, at least, we are dealing with a Human."

He lifted his glass and took a sip of wine, smacking his lips with relish as he did so. Then he went on:

"There are several reasons why I am against using pure magic, in this case. Firstly, because it would provoke counter-measures; every time I worked a piece of white magic they would work a piece of black magic; and though I have a very poor opinion of Miss Smith's abilities — in fact she strikes me as a very second-rate sort of witch ..." here he sniffed contemptuously, "the fact remains that even second-rate witches can cause a great deal of trouble, particularly when they are in a bad temper. And Miss Smith, I imagine, will soon be in a very bad temper indeed, if she is not in one already."

"Another glass, Mr. Tortoise?" inquired Mrs. Judy, who was enthralled by his words.

"If you insist, madam. Thank you." He took another sip, and continued: "The second reason why I am against using more magic than we can help is because, quite frankly, it will upset all the simple creatures in the wood, who only want to lead their lives in peace. They have already had quite enough to make them restless. The unfortunate episode of Miss Squirrel's tail, for example, and all the poison that has been spat out by the toads — to say nothing of the various tricks which have been played on them by Sam in his own shop. If this sort of thing goes on — and it well may — the animals will begin to lose all confidence; they will grow frightened; and before we know where we are they will retire into their shells, and stay in their nests, and hide in their burrows. Do you see what I mean?"

Mrs. Judy nodded. She could not help feeling a certain regret, because it would have given her great pleasure to see Sam and the Witch inside an iceberg . . . she would have gone and made faces at them through the glass, as it were. Yet she had to admit that there was a lot of common sense in what Mr. Tortoise was saying.

"And there is a third reason why I am against using magic as a weapon," said Mr. Tortoise.

"Yes?"

He hesitated and sighed. "I am afraid it is rather a personal one."

"Never mind, Mr. Tortoise," said Judy, "Please tell us."

"Well, my dear, to tell the truth, I am growing old. And . . . and to be frank, it takes it out of me. Oh yes, it does . . ." he went on, when she began to contradict him. "I have to make an effort, nowadays, to remember all the spells, and sometimes I have quite a sore throat after reciting them. That is why — in confidence, in strict confidence — I sometimes feel the need of a slight — a slight, how shall I say? — a slight tonic!" And once again his little beady eye fastened on the bottle of raspberry wine.

"Oh, Mr. Tortoise, why didn't you tell us before?" cried Judy, pouring him out another glass.

"He's been working himself to death for us, and here I am, trying to work him all the harder!" exclaimed her grannie.

"It's all my fault," muttered Bruno.

"Calm yourselves — calm yourselves, my dear people!" declared Mr. Tortoise, who, though he certainly was a little tired, was not quite as tired as all that. "I should not have mentioned it. However, since we are all friends together . . ."

He did not finish the sentence, but lifted his glass, and drained it at a single gulp.

And now, there was certainly nothing tired about Mr. Tortoise. In crisp short sentences he told them his plan. It was very simple. They were to appeal to the protection of the law.

"There is a Law of the Wood, is there not?" he demanded.

"Of course there is a Law of the Wood!" they agreed.

"There is a Court of the Wood, is there not?"

"But, yes!" they cried. "And it meets whenever there is any mystery or crime!"

"And there is a Chief Justice, is there not?"

"Mr. Justice Owl!" they exclaimed, in one breath.

Mr. Tortoise bowed. "Mr. Justice Owl!" he repeated. "A person for whom I have the highest respect. A person who is more than fitted to deal with this . . . with this outrage."

There was still a tiny drop left in his glass. He drained it down.

"Ladies and gentlemen," he cried, "we are going to Mr. Justice Owl — now — this very moment!"

CHAPTER XV

APPEAL TO THE LAW

MR. JUSTICE OWL lived in the ruins of an old barn that stood all by itself in a clearing on the highest part of the wood. In winter, when the trees were bare, you could see it for miles away; in summer it was completely hidden by the leaves, and you would not have guessed that there was a barn there at all unless you had actually stumbled on it. But though you could not see Mr. Justice Owl, nor his house, he could see *you* very clearly, and you might be sure that he would see you, if you were doing anything you shouldn't. At least, that was what Mr. Justice Owl said, though sometimes it may not have been quite true, because most of the day he was asleep. However, perhaps he slept with one eye open.

The barn was the only building in the wood that had been made by Humans, and as such it gave Mr. Justice Owl an extra feeling of authority. Who the Humans were and why they had ever come to the wood was a mystery; even old Mr. Parrot, who claimed to have lived in the wood for nearly four hundred years, had no recollection of them; they had been dead and buried long before he arrived. "And a good thing, too," said Mr. Justice Owl, who had little use for Humans. All the same, he was proud of his barn; it seemed to set him above his fellows, and over the crumbling doorway—from which the door had long since vanished—he had caused P.C. Monkey to paint, in large white letters:

MR. JUSTICE OWL

Underneath, in smaller letters, was painted:

THE TRUTH, THE HOLE TRUTH AND NOTHING BUT THE TRUTH
SWELPMEGOD

"Excuse me, sir, but what does Swelpmegod mean?"
inquired P.C. Monkey, when he was painting the sign.

Mr. Justice Owl blinked and regarded him with a cold,
legal eye. To be frank, he himself was not at all sure what
Swelpmegod meant; all he knew was that the Humans
were always saying it in Courts of Law; and since it sounded
very grand and professional he had decided to put it up.
However, he had no intention of betraying his ignorance
to P.C. Monkey.

"You spoke?" he demanded, sternly.

P.C. Monkey, who always felt nervous when Mr.
Justice Owl stared at him, began to scratch himself. "Yes,
Your Worship. Swelpmegod."

"What about Swelpmegod?"

"I was just wondering what might be the meaning?"

"It means," he proclaimed, "Thou Shalt Not Scratch
Thyself." Being a lawyer, he always had an answer ready.
However, he was not quite satisfied with this definition; it
sounded rather like what his colleagues would have called
a "quibble". And if there was one thing he hated, it was
a "quibble". So he closed his eyes again, and added:

"It is a Learned Expression."

Nobody could quarrel with that. It was an expression —
and since he had expressed it himself, it must be learned.
"Really," thought Mr. Justice Owl to himself, "I am a
remarkable person. Never at a loss — never! I am wasted
here, quite wasted — I should be in a far higher position,
where my talents would be properly appreciated." Of
course, he did not really mean a word of this; he loved the
wood so much that nothing would ever have persuaded him
to leave it, not even if he had been voted Lord Chancellor
of England.

It was nearly five o'clock in the afternoon before Judy, followed by Mr. Bruno and the tortoise, arrived at the foot of the slope leading up to the barn. In spite of the lateness of the hour, Mr. Justice Owl had only just breakfasted; it was only natural that he should spend most of the day in sleep, considering all the night work he had to do, patrolling the wood and making sure that nobody was getting up to mischief. However, he was secretly rather ashamed of these late habits, so when he saw our friends approaching he called out to P.C. Monkey to hurry up and clear away the breakfast things. "If it is an urgent matter," he said, brushing the last crumbs from his feathers, "you may say that I am in conference, and will be down in five minutes." With which, he fluttered off to his Study, which was really the remains of an old loft, comfortably furnished with soft wisps of hay which he refused to allow anybody to touch, although it was so old that it ought to have been sent to the cleaners long ago.

Mr. Tortoise made himself the spokesman of the party. "Will you please tell His Worship that it is a very urgent matter?" he said. P.C. Monkey remembered his instructions, and assured them that his Worship would be down in five minutes. So they sat down and waited.

After precisely five minutes he came, fluttering majestically down to them in a single swoop, and perched himself on the handle of an old plough that leant against the wall. He bowed first to Mrs. Judy, then to Judy, then to Mr. Tortoise, then to Bruno. After all this bowing, he closed his eyes, and in measured tones, he observed:

"This is most irregular."

"Indeed it is, Your Worship," agreed Mr. Tortoise, "but as the matter was so urgent. . ."

"It needs to be very urgent indeed. Otherwise . . ." He did not finish the sentence, but shook his head mournfully from side to side, as though dire penalties would be inflicted on them for disturbing him.

"It is a matter of attempted murder," said Mr. Tortoise quietly.

Mr. Justice Owl opened his eyes again with a start. "Attempted murder! Of whom?"

"Of Miss Judy, Your Worship."

"By whom?"

"By young Sam."

"Humans!" quavered Mr. Justice Owl. "Always Humans! Nothing but trouble, trouble, trouble!"

"Well, really!" snorted Mrs. Judy.

"Forgive me, madam," he protested. "I should have excepted the present company. None of us know anything but good about you and your charming grand-daughter. But as for the rest of your race . . ." He ruffled his feathers and blew through his beak, and shook his head once again.

"How is Mr. Bruno concerned in all this?" he demanded. "Was he an accomplice?"

"Oh, no, sir!" cried Judy, putting her arm round Bruno's shoulder, for at the mention of his name he had begun to tremble violently. "He was only an attempted accomplice. In fact, he saved my life."

"Attempted accomplice? Saved your life?" Mr. Justice Owl blinked several times in rapid succession. "I am bewildered." He turned to Mr. Tortoise. "Mr. Tortoise, kindly let us have the truth, the whole truth, and nothing but the truth. At once." And to make his command sound more effective he added as an afterthought . . . "Swelpmegod."

And Mr. Tortoise, who wanted nothing better, plunged straightway into his story.

When Mr. Tortoise had finished, there was silence. Mr. Justice Owl sat on his perch with his eyes closed, and Judy watched him breathlessly, waiting for him to speak. From outside she could hear the faint sounds of the wood she loved so much — the rustle of the leaves, singing their evensong to the winds of twilight, the murmur of the river, flowing down to the darkening valley, and the last greetings of the birds from the trees and the thickets where the mist was gathering. Night was drawing near; over the golden face of day there was drifting a veil of silver; and soon the silver veil would have turned to grey and it would be spangled with stars.

But still Mr. Justice Owl did not speak. Then, suddenly, he opened his eyes. And from his beak there came a long, low moan, "Too-wit, too-woe . . . too-wit, too-woe!" How often had he sent out that cry to the world, how often had the fateful slogan echoed through the sleeping glades! Too little wit, too much woe — that had been his constant call, and well we know that he had good reason for calling it. But never had he called it more fervently than to-night, never had the phrase a deeper meaning. For Mr. Justice Owl realized that he was face to face with Evil — real Evil . . . human Evil, which is so much more terrible than animal Evil. For human Evil is of the brain and the spirit, whereas animal Evil is of the flesh and of the blood. You will have to be grown up before you can understand what that means; and even then you may not understand it fully for grown ups are strange creatures, who are confused by words, and think that things are good or evil by reason of their names rather than by reason of their nature.

However, our story is too urgent for these reflections.

After Mr. Justice Owl had emitted his melancholy cry, he blew a shrill whistle, and P.C. Monkey appeared in the doorway.

"You called, Your Worship?"

Mr. Justice Owl fixed him with his sternest glare. "P.C. Monkey!" he proclaimed. "You have a grave duty before you!"

P.C. Monkey was very impressed by these words, and actually forgot to scratch himself.

"Have you your hand-cuffs on you?"

"Yes, Your Worship."

"And your truncheon, and your notebook?"

"Yes, Your Worship."

"In that case you will proceed at once to The Shop in the Ford. You will caution Young Sam. And you will arrest him for the attempted murder of Miss Judy."

"Murder?" gasped P.C. Monkey. "Miss Judy?"

"Attempted murder," corrected Mr. Justice Owl.

P.C. Monkey was so astonished that he automatically saluted and turned, as though he were about to rush off without further instructions.

"One moment," cried Mr. Justice Owl. "I have not finished yet. There is also the case of Miss Smith."

He turned to address his remarks to Mr. Tortoise. "In my opinion, it would be unwise to attempt to arrest this person. I gather that she might cause a great deal of trouble. She might, for instance, decide to become invisible, and the law about arresting invisible witches is, unfortunately, somewhat confused.

I think that Mr. Tortoise will agree with me?"

"Undoubtedly, Your Worship."

"In these circumstances," continued Mr. Justice Owl, "it seems wiser that we should caution her, and order her to attend as a witness, assuring her that if she does so, no futher proceedings will be taken against her, providing she leaves the wood the moment the trial is over. It is not an ideal solution — far from it. If I had my way I would put her in irons. However, as she could probably slip through any chains that we could put on her, we must use other methods. After all, the source of the whole trouble, the prime mover in this outrage, is Sam himself. Once we are rid of him, we shall have no more witches. It therefore seems wiser to me to attempt to enlist the co-operation of Miss Smith, however repulsive it may be to our real feelings. It should not be too difficult; I imagine that there is not much love lost between her and her employer. You agree, Mr. Tortoise?"

"A most wise and learned decision, Your Worship."

"There is one last thing." Mr. Justice Owl turned towards Bruno. "Mr. Bruno!" he said gravely, but not unkindly, "from what I can understand of your conduct in the past few months as outlined by Mr. Tortoise, you have been foolish and weak."

Poor Bruno hung his head and shuffled his feet.

"You were foolish, in the first place, to embark on a career of deception; you were weak to submit to the blackmail of a worthless Human."

"I was afraid . . ." muttered Bruno.

"Quite. You were afraid. And you had no reason to be afraid. You should have trusted the Law of the Wood to protect you."

Bruno hung his head even lower.

"However," — and here a warm note crept into Mr.

Justice Owl's voice, "whatever follies you have committed in the past have been amply paid for. And for your behaviour to-day I have nothing but the highest praise."

"Oh, Your Worship!" gasped Bruno, holding up his head for the first time, and gazing at Mr. Justice Owl with wide-open eyes.

"The highest praise!" he repeated. "At the risk of your own life, you refused to do the bidding of those who had ensnared you, and you stood alone against all their powers of black magic."

Mr. Bruno held his head still higher and his breast actually began to swell with pride.

"The wood shall hear of it, in due course. And the wood will be proud of you. In the meantime, I am going to give you a chance to prove your mettle, once again. Will you obey my instructions?"

"Indeed, Your Worship . . . anything, anything!"

"Good! Then you will go with P.C. Monkey this very moment and offer him every assistance in the dangerous task of arresting this criminal."

"Arrest Sam?" Bruno gave a whoop of delight.

"But Your Worship . . ." began P.C. Monkey, who did not like the idea of Bruno sharing his honours.

"There are no 'buts' about it," corrected Mr. Justice Owl. "You are agile, P. C. Monkey, and you are willing. But Sam is strong, and cunning, and desperate. I do not propose to take any risks. You should be thankful for Mr. Bruno's help." And since P.C. Monkey still looked doubtful, Mr. Justice Owl ordered, "I should be obliged if you would both shake hands and wish each other good luck."

Bruno grasped P.C. Monkey's hand in his big paw, and his grin was so infectious that P.C. Monkey grinned too.

"And now, the two of you, be off! You have just an hour left before the dark!"

III

Had you been strolling near The Shop in the Ford that evening, in the gathering dusk, you would have been excused for thinking that you had stumbled upon a lunatic asylum, in which all the lunatics were having a free fight. Cries of rage and fury rent the air; Sam was cursing and swearing, Old Sam was screaming murder, Miss Smith was having hysterics, and the toads were leaping here, there and everywhere, croaking as though they were demented, and calling on each other to spit in everybody's eye.

Why this uproar? The explanation was very simple. Sam had discovered that his plot had failed.

All day long they had been sitting around, waiting for the return of Bruno. As the hours passed, without any sign of him, Sam began to grow more and more restless; it was only the complete confidence of Miss Smith that prevented him from growing desperate.

"If anything goes wrong this time, we're sunk," he muttered.

"But, my dear sir, how could it go wrong?" demanded Miss Smith, with the brightest of smiles. "I gave you my *personal* guarantee."

Sam merely scowled at her. She smiled more brightly than ever. "That poison," she continued, "was deadly . . . but *deadly*. If you were to pour it on the ground it would sink right through the earth and come out on the other side and destroy large quantities of Australians."

"Judy ain't in Australia, worse luck," he snarled.

"I have no doubt she's in heaven by now," sniffed Miss Smith.

"Well, wherever she is, where's Bruno?"

"Oh, he'll come all right!" she tinkled. "You just wait and see."

So they waited.

And they waited.

And still they waited.

But they did not see.

It was shortly after five o'clock in the evening — at the very moment when Mr. Tortoise was unfolding the whole devilish plot to Mr. Justice Owl — that Miss Fox happened to trot by, on her way to Sunday supper. She could never resist a little piece of gossip, particularly when Humans were concerned (for after all, was she not the darling of the Humans, who were always chasing her in the most flattering manner?) and so when she saw Sam and Old Sam and Miss Smith and the toads all sitting on logs and looking miserable she frisked up to them to report the latest news.

"Peek-a-bo!" she simpered, peering out of the long grass.

"Shop's not open," growled Sam. "Sunday!"

Miss Fox did not think this was a very gracious greeting; however, her news was too good to waste, so she did not take offence.

"Guess who I saw to-night," she murmured, playing with her tail in the most affected manner.

"Don't care," snapped Sam.

"Spit in your eye!" croaked the toads.

"Really!" Miss Fox drew back and tossed her head. "I must say! Talk about manners! I come here to tell you the most interesting piece of news, about your Mr. Bruno and Mr. Justice Owl, and all you say is spit in my..."

She could not finish the sentence. A chorus of yells and curses greeted her; she was seized and shaken; question after question rained down upon her; and when she had at last managed to gasp out the news that she had happened to see Judy and her friends going in to call on Mr. Justice Owl, the scene of pandemonium which ensued was so

terrible that she took the first opportunity to dart away
into the long grass and escape, swearing never to have
anything to do with Humans again.

It was at the moment when the fight was at its fiercest
that two shadows fell across the grass. The shouting died
down, Sam took his hands from Miss Smith's wig, which
he had been trying to pull off, Old Sam stopped rubbing
his shins, which had been well kicked, and the toads
crouched panting, huddled together.

There, clear-cut against the setting sun, the two figures
of Bruno and P.C. Monkey confronted them. For a
moment, all was still — you would have said they were a
set of wax-works, waiting for somebody to come and
throw a dust-sheet over them.

And then P.C. Monkey stepped forward. He stood in
front of Sam.

"I have a warrant for your arrest."

Sam's voice was dry and harsh.

"What for?"

"For the attempted murder of Miss Judy."

IV

There was dead silence. P.C. Monkey, stood there
holding out the handcuffs, with Bruno behind him block-
ing the way.

It was at Bruno that Sam was glaring. "You — you
beastly hulk of a bear!" he spluttered. "You dirty, double-
crossing crook!" He took a quick step forward, and then
stopped abruptly; there was a look in Bruno's eyes that he
had never seen before; it was a look in which there was no
fear but only a fierce contempt. And instead of cringing
away from him, Bruno stood his ground, with his great
arms folded over his chest.

"I am waiting," said P.C. Monkey.

Sam ignored him and turned to Miss Smith. "Do something!" he cried. "Why don't you do something?"

She did not answer.

"What's up?" he screamed. "Are you deaf? Why don't you get busy — bewitch 'em, poison 'em, anything? Miss Smith . . . *do* something!"

His voice whimpered away into silence. He stood there breathing heavily, staring around him like a trapped animal.

And then the silence was broken by a ghastly sound— the sound of Miss Smith laughing. It was the real Miss Smith who was laughing now, laughing the Witch's Laugh, not the false Miss Smith, with her pretty tinkle, which she produced when she wanted to deceive her victims. No, this was the real Witch's Laugh, of all sounds the most sinister, for it is like the rush of the wind through lonely churchyards and the hiss of the sea round sinking ships; it has in it the echo of rattling bones and clanking chains; it is made up of the sighs of the dying and the damned.

Loud and long laughed Miss Smith, and her laughter seemed to echo far away over the topmost branches of the trees like a bitter wind, so that the birds who heard it paused in their singing, and were silent.

"Stop that darned noise!" yelled Sam.

"Ho-ho-ho! — He-he-he! — Ha-ha-ha!" she shrieked.

"Stop it I tell you. You're driving me crazy!"

She stopped as suddenly as she had begun.

"You little whippersnapper!" she hissed. "You little snivelling rat! You and your old man! Telling me to do something! Ho ho! He he! What've you ever done for me, I'd like to know?" She stepped towards him as though she were about to spring at his throat, and he shrank back in terror.

"I . . . I . . . paid you . . . ." he began.

"That's a lie! Not a cent have I had since I came. Nothing but kicks and curses! And now I'm told to do something. Ha ha! He he! That's rich. I'll tell you what I'll do for you! Give evidence against you! I'll see you hanged on the highest tree in the wood!"

Bruno and P.C. Monkey exchanged glances. That was exactly what Mr. Justice Owl wanted.

"You'll be hanged yourself," gasped Sam.

"Oh no, I won't! It'd take a good deal more than a rope to hang me! I know a trick or two, Master Sam. But you . . . you're as good as dead already!" And she put her fingers round her neck, and made a hideous face, as though she were being hanged, with the whites of her eyes staring up to the sky and her tongue hanging out of her mouth.

"So that's the way it is!" snarled Sam — and his face was so twisted that it was terrible to look upon. "All against me, eh? Just too bad!" He shook his head and a cunning look came into his eyes. "Seems as though there's nothing to do but to give myself up, eh?"

"You ain't got a chance, Sam," groaned his old grandfather, who had been skulking in the background.

Sam nodded. "So be it," he said, heaving a deep sigh.

He held out his arms for the handcuffs. P.C. Monkey stepped forward. As he did so, Sam brought down his hands on P.C. Monkey's shoulders, vaulted into the air, leapt clean over his head, dodging Bruno by the fraction of an inch, and shot into the forest shadows. It all happened like a flash of lightning, and for a second they both groped vaguely in the air, not knowing which way to turn.

Then, with a yell, P.C. Monkey darted after him. Bruno followed last — running as he had never run before. But his heart was filled with dismay. "Please — please," he breathed to the god of the Bears, "please, please help me this time ... please do not let me fail again!"

V

Faster! Faster! Would they never get him?
At one moment, it seemed as though he were their

captive, for he caught his ankle in a root, and P.C. Monkey, swarming over the branch of an elm, dropped straight on to his shoulders. But before Bruno could come up to them Sam had shaken himself free, and was off again.
Faster! Faster! Night was nearly on them, only a few faint gleams lit the tree trunks, and Bruno could hardly see where he was going. He was torn and bleeding, and his heart was thumping as though it would burst. If only he were a little younger, if only his legs were not so heavy, his coat not so thick! A ditch loomed before him — he tried to take it in a flying leap, but he stumbled and fell in head first. When he scrambled out he was half blinded with mud

and ran straight into the trunk of a tree. But still, swaying and tottering, he sped on.

The sounds of the chase were growing fainter — now and then he could hear the crack of a branch as P.C. Monkey swung overhead and a distant curse from Sam as he stumbled over a bramble — but he could no longer see them, he could only guess where they were. And suddenly, even the noises ceased.

Bruno stopped, panting desperately and stared wildly ahead. Where could they be? What had happened? Then he noticed that the ground on which he was standing sloped sharply upwards, and he remembered that ahead of him, behind a thick clump of pinewood, lay a little quarry, bounded by a sharp cliff. His heart sank. Had they fallen over it? Had Sam escaped? Was P.C. Monkey injured? Quick — quick — there was not a second to lose. He plunged ahead, scaling giant rocks as though they were the steps of a staircase, brushing aside thick branches as though they were matchwood.

At last! Here was the top of the hill, and the pinewood, and the wide open space of the quarry. He staggered to the edge of the cliff, and there, far below, was a sight that made his blood run cold.

Sam had got P.C. Monkey on the ground, and was kneeling on his chest with his hands round his throat, slowly throttling him to death! Bruno could just make out the whites of P.C. Monkey's eyes, rolling in agony. Sam's fingers were twisting tighter and tighter, and with each twist he was screaming out his rage and his hatred.

"This'll teach you!" he yelled. "This'll learn you!" Twist, twist! "Say your prayers, Mr. Monkey, say your prayers . . . say 'em for the last time . . . !" Twist twist! "One more twist, Mr. Monkey, and you'll be . . ."

He never finished the sentence. For at that instant,

Bruno made a supreme effort, summoned up his last remaining ounce of strength, and leapt like a gigantic rocket into the air.

There was a scream and then silence, broken only by the panting of Bruno and the low moans of P.C. Monkey. For a moment Bruno thought that Sam was dead, for he had landed straight on his back, and might well have broken his spine. But no — the wicked heart was still beating. And by and by he came to, and glared around him with murder in his eyes.

But now it was too late. For Bruno had taken the handcuffs from P.C. Monkey's pocket and locked them firmly round Sam's wrists.

An hour later, bruised and battered but triumphant, they delivered their prisoner to Mr. Justice Owl.

CHAPTER XVI

THE NIGHT BEFORE THE TRIAL

TO say that Sam's arrest caused a sensation would be to put it very mildly indeed. From the moment that it was known, the whole wood resounded to such a twittering and grunting and squeaking as had never been heard before.

The first official announcement was made on the Notice Board which P.C. Monkey nailed up every Monday morning outside Mr. Justice Owl's barn. As a rule there was nothing on this Notice Board at all, so that it read something like this:

COURT OF THE WOOD

PERSONS FOR TRIAL TO-MORROW MORNING   Nil.
    Offences   Nil.

By Order
Mr. Justice Owl
Swelpmegod.

Usually Mr. Justice Owl added a few words of praise for the animals' good behaviour, chalking them in under his signature, such as "Very Good" or "Quite Satisfactory — Keep it Up," as though he were writing a school report. When he was not in a good temper he wrote words of warning, such as "The Eyes of The Law are Watching You," or "Crime Never Pays," which was felt by the animals to be somewhat harsh, for as they had committed no crime why should they be reminded that it did not pay?

From time to time, of course, there was an offence, and then Miss Fox was always the first to spread the news, for she was the greatest gossip in the wood, and made a point of frisking up to the Notice Board every Monday to see who had been getting into trouble. It was not often that she found anything very serious; most of the cases were very old offenders, such as Mrs. Cuckoo, who had been had up no less than twenty-seven times for laying eggs in other people's nests. Sometimes, however, there was a mild excitement, such as the celebrated Beaver Case, where two rival families of beavers had both built dams across the same stream. The masterly manner in which Mr. Justice Owl had settled this problem had aroused the admiration of all the animals, but it is too complicated to describe in these pages.

Never in the whole history of the wood, however, had there been anything like a murder case, and when Miss Fox first saw the announcement she was so flabbergasted that for several moments she sat staring at the Notice Board with her eyes as round as saucers. This is what she read:

COURT OF THE WOOD

PERSONS FOR TRIAL TO-MORROW MORNING.

Miss Glow-worm. Offence: Ignoring lighting Regulations.

Master Sam. Offence: ATTEMPTED MURDER OF MISS JUDY.

Witnesses for the latter trial, including Miss Judy, Mr. Bruno, and Miss Smith (W.I.T.C.H.) must be in their seats by 9 a.m. The prosecution will be conducted by

Mr. Tortoise. The jury will consist of the following persons:

> Mr. Peacock (Foreman)
> Mrs. Hare
> Mrs. Fox
> Mr. Manx
> Mr. Pouter Pigeon
> Mrs. Dove
> Mr. Squirrel
> Mr. Chameleon
> Mrs. Zebra
> Miss Crow
> Mr. Beaver
> Mrs. Rabbit.

By Order
Mr. Justice Owl
Swelpmegod.

As the dreadful news slowly sank into Miss Fox's little brain, the fur on her back began to rise, and her brush swelled and swelled, till it stuck out behind her like a huge brown feather. Then, with a long-drawn howl, she flew homewards screaming "Murder! Sam! Murder! Miss Judy! Help! Murder!" She ran so fast that when she reached home she was quite exhausted and could only sink on the floor, stammering, "Murder . . . murder!"

"You wicked girl!" cried her mother, "You've been playing with those Humans again!"

"Murder!" gasped Miss Fox, once more.

"Just as I always told you!" snorted her mother. "Well, perhaps this will teach you a lesson!"

Miss Fox could only shake her head, and it was a long time before she convinced her mother of the truth. When Mrs. Fox finally understood, she was suitably shocked.

But her horror of the crime was somewhat blunted by her indignation at the fact that her name was third on the Jury List, below that of Mrs. Hare. "Really," she muttered "the way that creature pushes herself forward! Anybody would think she was royalty!"

Which shows that animals are really very like ourselves; even in times of danger and disaster, it is the little things that worry them most.

II

In view of the extraordinary succession of events which took place during the following twenty-four hours — a period which left its mark for ever on the history of the wood — it is a pity that we could not have had the services of a little army of reporters, scurrying here, there and everywhere, noting the manifold details of the drama as it was unfolding itself.

242

What a story they would have had to tell! They would have shown us Bruno, hurrying home to his distracted family, hugging Mrs. Bruno and all the little Brunos as they had never been hugged before, and lying back, like a conquering hero, to receive the homage of all the animals who had heard about his great adventures. They would have shown us Mr. Peacock, all of a flutter, opening and shutting out of sheer nerves, at one moment peevishly asking Mrs. Peacock what the Foreman of the Jury was supposed to do, and as soon as she attempted to tell him, ordering her to hold her tongue and not to meddle in affairs which did not concern her. They would have shown us P.C. Monkey strutting up and down in front of the Notice Board, before an enraptured crowd, spinning his truncheon in the air as though it were a bandmaster's staff and occasionally allowing Miss Squirrel to adjust the bandage over his eye. Miss Squirrel adored fixing the bandage, partly because, by doing so, she felt that she was scoring off Sam, who had played so wicked a trick on her tail, but principally because it gave her an opportunity of displaying the tail itself, which had grown again, far softer and shinier and more feathery than it had ever been before.

And they would have shown us the enemy! Stiff and sullen, with his pale cheeks fixed in a mask of hatred, Sam crouched in the darkest corner of the barn, chained to an old post. It was his own fault that he was in this uncomfortable position; no less than three times Mr. Justice Owl had sent down to inquire if he would take any refreshment. A glass of milk? A slice of bread and honey? Sam had sent back a snarling refusal.

As for Miss Smith — whole pages could have been written about *her*! For instead of being depressed or anxious or in any way afraid, she was filled with glee at the thought that at last she would be able to get even with

Sam, the nastiest employer she had ever had. Oh — th
things she would say about him! She would say that peopl
like him did not deserve to have a witch at all — that if sh
had known, she would never have come — that she ha
been insulted — and that the toads had not only bee
insulted, but positively *attacked*. . . .

"Darlings!" she cried to the toads . . . "didn't he kic
you?"

"He sure did!" croaked the toads.

"And aren't you bruised all over?" she demanded.

"Black and blue," they echoed. "Can't sit down."

"Show me!"

The toads staggered round in a circle, making mournfu
noises.

Miss Smith clasped her hands, and shook her head
"It would melt the heart of a stone to see you like this!"

"So what?" croaked the toads, who were getting bore
with staggering round.

"Only this, my dream birds." And here Miss Smith'
voice took a sharper note. "Mind you do all that befor
the Judge to-morrow."

The toads winked. "Sob-stuff, eh?"

Miss Smith nodded. The toads winked again, an
hopped off to their favourite toadstool, in the highest c
spirits.

Miss Smith heaved a long sigh of contentment. What
heavenly trio they were! In Hollywood, they would b
a sensation. In fact, they were *made* for Hollywood. On
day, perhaps, she would be able to take them there. An
after that, they could all retire and live in a lovely dam
cave full of bones and delicious skulls, within easy reach c
a commodious cemetery.

The only persons who were fairly calm and collected o
the eve of the great trial were Judy and her grannie. The

spent most of the day resting under the Willow Tree, listening to Mr. Tortoise as he outlined the probable course of the trial.

"It should not take long," he said. "The evidence is overwhelming, particularly as Miss Smith has decided to come in on our side."

"Shall I have to be a witness?" asked Judy.

"Of course, my dear. But you need not be afraid. All you have to do is to tell the truth."

"I don't like it," she sighed. "I wish — at least I *almost* wish that we could let Sam go."

Mrs. Judy snorted. "What? And all be murdered in our beds the day after? No thank you!"

"Justice must be done," Mr. Tortoise reminded her. "And it will be soon over."

"Sam will be a slippery customer," was Mrs. Judy's comment.

"I flatter myself that he won't be too slippery for *me*," retorted Mr. Tortoise. "In fact, there's only one thing I'm worried about."

"What is it?" they both demanded.

Mr. Tortoise did not answer for a moment. He was looking up through the branches of the Tree, as though he were searching for something, staring with narrowed eyes at the sky, as though it held some secret that he could not unravel.

Judy followed his gaze. "What are you looking for, Mr. Tortoise?"

He still did not answer her.

"You'll give me the creeps if you go on like that," sniffed Mrs. Judy. "To say nothing of a crick in the neck."

Slowly Mr. Tortoise looked down again.

"I don't understand it," he said, shaking his head.

"Understand *what*?" cried Mrs. Judy.

"The weather," he murmured absently.

"Is *that* all?" Mrs. Judy gave a croaking laugh. "Who ever *did* understand the weather, I'd like to know? Good heavens, I thought it was something serious!"

"For all we know, madam, it may be very serious indeed."

His tone was so grave, and he looked at her with so strange an expression, that she stopped laughing.

"What *is* it, Mr. Tortoise?" asked Judy, in a gentle voice. "Even if it is something dreadful, I think we ought to know.   e shan't . . . we shan't be afraid."

Mr. Tortoise sighed. "It may be only my fancy," he said, "but no less than three times to-day I could have sworn I saw his face in the clouds."

"Whose face?" they demanded in astonishment.

Once again Mr. Tortoise stared up to the sky.

"The face of the Clerk of the Weather!"

There was a breathless hush; they seemed to be waiting for something.

And then it came. From its deepest roots to its highest branches, the Tree trembled. There could be no mistake about it. There was not a breath of wind; the air was so still that the lightest feather would have sunk straight to earth. Yet the Tree shook and trembled — its thousands of leaves, some still green, some already golden with the coming of Autumn, shivered and skimmered in the sunlight, and many of them fell at that moment, spinning and drifting down towards them.

"You see?" whispered Mr. Tortoise. "The Tree feels it too!"

"But what does it mean?" asked Mrs. Judy in a scared voice.

"It means that the Clerk of the Weather is up to something."

"I didn't even know there was such a person," confessed Judy.

"Then the sooner you learn, the better." He took one more look up to the sky. There was a single dark cloud, floating rapidly towards the sun, but he could not see any face in it. "Yes, he's certainly up to *something*."

"Do you think the Witch has been putting ideas into his head?"

Mr. Tortoise laughed scornfully. "The Clerk of the Weather has no need of witches. He's more powerful than all the world's witches put together."

"Please tell us about him!" cried Judy, who was eager to learn more of this remarkable person.

"Yes, *please* do!" urged Mrs. Judy. "It'll take our minds off this dreadful business to-morrow." Since he still hesitated, she added . . . "And, perhaps, before you begin, a little sip of raspberry wine?"

Mr. Tortoise bowed. "Well madam, if you absolutely insist. . . ."

She filled his glass.

III

The Clerk of the Weather — so Mr. Tortoise told them — is of all persons in the world the most moody, the most fickle, and the most difficult to please. Many, many hundreds of years ago, he was an angel; but he was turned out of heaven for the most extraordinary reason. "In fact," said God at the time, "nothing like this has ever occurred in heaven before, and I sincerely trust that it will not occur again." For whereas most people are dismissed from heaven because they are not good enough for it, the Clerk of the Weather was dismissed because heaven was not good enough for *him*.

It happened like this. One afternoon, the Clerk of the Weather — whose name at that time was Claud — was strolling about the courtyards of heaven, listening to the Harp Orchestra, which played regularly from four till six. For various reasons he was feeling restless; the harp had never been an instrument of which he had been particularly fond, and after listening to it for several thousand years he was beginning to hanker after something a little more robust, such as a saxophone, or a big drum. To add to his irritation, he had been fitted with a new pair of wings that morning and they were much too tight round the neck.

But the principal cause of his discontent was the weather. It was, of course, very wicked of him to complain of it, for it was in every sense of the word *heavenly* weather — which means that the sky was as blue as a china plate and the sun as bright as a golden coin and the breeze was as gentle as the breath of a kitten. If Claud had been really the right sort of angel he would have gone on adoring this sort of weather to all eternity. But he was not the right sort of angel; he wanted a change; and in a mad, rash moment he said so.

"Oh God!" he suddenly shouted. "I wish it would rain!"

There was dead silence in the courts of heaven . . . even the harps were still.

"Or snow or hail or blow or come out in a good old peasouper!" he yelled. And the echoes of his voice rang far and wide . . . "pea-souper . . . souper . . . souper . . ." down long corridors lit with diamonds, through ante-rooms hung with pearls and emeralds, till finally it echoed faint but clear, like the last ripple of a spent wave, to the steps of a Golden Throne.

God heard the echo — as He hears all echoes, great and small.

"He shall have his wish," said God. "He shall have all

the weather he wants. In fact—he shall be the Clerk of the Weather."

Three hours later the angel Claud sped like an arrow through the gates of Heaven, hovered for a moment in the stainless blue, and then dived sharply to earth. Only a very few angels saw him go. They were puzzled to note that in spite of his disgrace he looked strangely happy.

IV

"All these things" — said Mr. Tortoise — "happened a very long time ago."

"But where is he now?" demanded Judy, who had followed his story with the utmost interest. "How does he work? What does he *do*?"

This is what Mr. Tortoise told her.

The Clerk of the Weather has three houses. One at the North Pole, one at the South Pole and one on the Equator. The houses at the North and South Poles are both made out of blocks of ice; but the house on the Equator is more like a huge tent. The principal piece of furniture in all the three houses is an immense desk. It is so large that if you were to clear it of all its books and papers you could play tennis on it.

Each of the three desks is divided into five sections, representing the Continents of America, Europe, Asia, Africa and Australia. And each of these five sections has five inkpots and five pens.

There is an inkpot full of chilled water, with a pen of ice — — which never melts — so that when the Clerk of the Weather wants some part of the world to be very cold, he writes the word "Freezing" in the ledger, against the country in question.

There is an inkpot that is full of bubbles, with a goose's

quill which never stops whirling round and round; and the Clerk of the Weather snatches it when he feels he wants the wind to blow, and writes — "Wind" over some page of the book (He has to hold tight to the pen while he is writing, or it might fly out of his hand).

There is an inkpot full of ordinary rain-water, which of course is for "Rain", and another full of very hot red ink, which is for "Heat".

But perhaps the most remarkable of all the inkpots is the one for "Earthquakes", because there is no ink in it at all. It is merely a pen standing in a jar, and it looks quite harmless; but if you were to touch it you would find that it gave you a sharp electric shock. Even when the Clerk of the Weather uses it his fingers tingle so fiercely that he can only hold it for a very few moments, which is the reason why earthquakes are usually so short. This pen writes with jagged, sweeping strokes that jump all over the page, and the nib is so sharp that often it digs right into the page.

There are all sorts of other exciting things to be found at the headquarters of the Clerk of the Weather. For instance, there is a whole aviary full of Fog Birds, who are the most remarkable creatures, with bodies made out of grey mist and long draggled wings that are really wisps of clouds. Nobody has ever caught a Fog Bird, because as soon as you try to catch it, it melts away. When the Clerk of the Weather wants to start a fog he opens the door of a cage and sends the Fog Bird on its journey. It drifts off into the sky and when it has found the right place it hovers around looking for a small cloud. Then it makes a nest in the cloud, lays an egg, and flies home again. As soon as the egg is laid, it grows and grows, and swells and swells, till finally it bursts and out of it pours a dense fog which spreads far and wide. The Fog Birds are moody, restless creatures, and the Clerk of the Weather has never been able to train them as strictly as he would have liked. For some reason or other, which he has never been able to understand, they have always been very attracted to the City of London, and when he has sent them to France or Russia or Norway they have disobeyed him and flown straight off to London instead. Sometimes, on a raw November morning, when a yellow tinge creeps over the sky, and the streets grow so dark that the lamps must be lit at noon, you can look up and see — very faintly — the draggled wings of the Fog Birds, fluttering among the clouds, preparing to lay their eggs.

All these things, and many more, the Tortoise told to Judy and her grannie; by the time he had finished it was quite dark. So he bade them an affectionate good-night and left them, like sensible people, to get a good night's rest before their great ordeal on the morrow.

CHAPTER XVII

JUSTICE IS DONE

THE great day dawned at last, and it was a day of rising wind and angry broken clouds.

"I should say it was going to rain," said Mrs. Peacock as she called her husband in the early light of morning.

"You always say it is going to rain," he snapped, blinking his sleepy eyes. Which was quite true; Mrs. Peacock was so afraid of his Opening in bad weather, and spoiling his tail, that she always feared the worst.

"When were you thinking of Opening?" she inquired, timidly.

Mr. Peacock snorted. "Really! What a question to ask before breakfast!"

"I only wondered if it would be before or after the verdict?"

To tell the truth, Mr. Peacock had been wondering the same thing himself. Ought he, as Foreman of the Jury, to Open as soon as the judge appeared? If so, it would be difficult to close again, without looking disrespectful. And it would be very fatiguing to keep Open throughout the entire trial. On the whole, he thought it would be better to Open at the precise moment that he delivered the verdict. He had acted the part many times in his own head. Mr. Justice Owl would say:

"Have you reached a verdict, Mr. Foreman?"

"Yes, Your Worship," he would reply.

"And what is it, Mr. Foreman?"

And here, Mr. Peacock thought, he would pause, with the eyes of the whole Court upon him. And very slowly, very deliberately, he would Open, so that his tail would be like the glittering shield of Justice itself. And out of that blaze of colour, that bonfire of blues and reds and greens, would come his voice:

"Guilty!"

For he had no doubt whatever that Sam was guilty. If anybody was so silly as to suggest that he wasn't, he would just sit down and sulk and refuse ever to Open again.

He did not say all those things to Mrs. Peacock; she would not have understood. He merely said:

"Kindly leave matters of law to those who understand it."

Mrs. Peacock sighed; he was very trying before breakfast. However, she did not really care, for this was the proudest morning of her life. Of all the honours that had been heaped upon Mr. Peacock, none had been so high as this. "Mr. Foreman Peacock" — how grand it sounded! Perhaps they would be able to keep the name for good? "Mr. and Mrs. Foreman-Peacock." She would suggest it to him when he was in a better temper. In the meantime, she would have to leave the question of Opening to settle itself.

Similar little squabbles and arguments were in progress all over the wood, as the animals swallowed their breakfasts and hurried to the Court. Long before nine o'clock it was full to overflowing; there was not an inch of grass nor even a tiny log to spare, and the branches of the trees were so heavily loaded with birds that they seemed to be laden with strange exotic blossoms. Even Mr. and Mrs. Seagull had flown inland for the occasion, and were perched on the end of an apple-bough, where they looked very white and elegant against the red fruit.

II

Meanwhile, Mr. Justice Owl, who had been sitting up all night poring over the facts of the case, was watching the sand trickling through the hour glass and feeling — though nobody would have guessed it to look at him — exceedingly nervous. There were a number of features about this trial

which he did not like at all, features which disturbed and bewildered him. Miss Smith, for example. He had good reason to suppose that Miss Smith was on the right side, and would do all in her power to bring Sam to justice; none the less, she was a Human — at least she was *shaped* like a Human — and since she was also a witch, there was no knowing what tricks she might not play.

"Humans!" moaned Mr. Justice Owl, moving restlessly up and down on his perch. "Heaven deliver me from Humans!"

"You called, Your Worship?"

It was P.C. Monkey who spoke. He had just been out to take a final look at Sam, who was still as sullen and silent as ever.

Mr. Justice Owl blinked at him. "How much longer is there to go?" he demanded.

P.C. Monkey glanced at the hour glass. "About seven minutes, Your Worship." Then, in a timid voice, and with a nervous grin, he murmured ... "This is a great day, Your Worship."

"Indeed?" Mr. Justice Owl raised his huge black eyebrows. "In what respect is it a great day?"

P.C. Monkey started to scratch himself, and then stopped abruptly, under the warning glare of those piercing eyes. "Well, Your Worship ... the trial, and the murder. . . ."

"*Attempted* murder," corrected Mr. Justice Owl.

"Just as you say, Your Worship," he stammered. "And Sam, and all these Humans."

"Humans!" Mr. Justice Owl closed his eyes, and assumed the most pained expression. "Humans!" he repeated. "Do not speak to me of such creatures!"

All the same, P.C. Monkey was very glad that he *had* spoken of such creatures, for he knew his master well enough to realize that it was just the sort of subject that was needed to take his mind off things.

"They certainly are a queer lot," he ventured.

"Queer?" snorted Mr. Justice Owl. "Did you say queer?"

"I *think* I said queer, Your Worship."

"A most inadequate word," retorted Mr. Justice Owl. "The word you need is '*mad*'."

"Mad." P.C. Monkey nodded respectfully. "Yes, Your Worship. Mad."

Mr. Justice Owl glanced once more at the hour glass; there was still five minutes to go ... just time enough for him to deliver a last, devastating attack on the Humans who had caused all the world's trouble, the Humans who had broken into the magic circle of the Wood, and shattered the peace and the quietness.

"Humans!" he cried. "How wonderful the world would be without them! The other day I read a report in the paper . . . needless to say it was a *Human* paper . . . in which a number of Humans were blamed for 'behaving like sheep — going about in herds and not thinking for themselves.' Did you ever hear of such impertinence? It is an insult to the noble and peaceful family of Sheep. It is the *Humans* who go about in herds and don't think for themselves! Look at the way they make war! Sheep would never be so foolish, nor would any other animal. Did you ever hear of a lot of sheep suddenly leaving their homes and their pastures and going off to fight, let us say, a herd of zebras whom they'd never even met, just because some silly sheep had told them that the zebras wore striped coats, and that anybody who wore a striped coat must be their enemy? That is exactly what Humans are doing all the time. Look at their dreadful way of waging war in the air. If I have a fight in the air, it is because I am attacked. I fight for my life. But what would you think of me if I were to take a rock and fly off with it to a farmyard and just drop it in the middle of a basket of eggs? That is what the Humans call 'bombing'. They all do it, and they think it is wonderful, and they give medals to the Humans who break the most eggs. To me, it is all sheer folly and wickedness. I have very little hope for the Human race . . . very little. It will take them at least a million years to reach the level of animals . . . and long before then, I am afraid that they will all have killed each other off."

He closed his eyes once more, and shook his head.

There was silence, except for the moan of the rising wind.

P.C. Monkey looked at the hour-glass.

"Your Worship," he said, "it is time."

Mr. Justice Owl blinked, ruffled his feathers, and cleared his throat. When he spoke again, his voice was clear and cold, the perfect voice for a judge.

"We will proceed."

He fluttered down from his perch.

"You have my papers?"

"Yes, Your Worship."

"And my glasses?"

P.C. Monkey produced them.

Mr. Justice Owl put them on, and glanced at the first paper on the list. By now, he was completely master of himself, and was no longer feeling nervous; in fact, he was beginning to enjoy himself immensely.

"Where are we?" he asked, with studied carelessness. "Ah yes! I observe that there are two cases before the Court to-day. The first . . . let me see . . . the first is Miss Glow-worm."

P.C. Monkey nodded.

"Quite. Miss Glow-worm. An habitual offender." He sighed heavily. Then he waved his claw. "You may lead the way."

III

Poor Miss Glow-worm.

Of all the days in the year . . . to choose *this* day to be arrested!

On all the previous occasions when she had appeared before Mr. Justice Owl, the Court had been empty; there had been no spectators except Miss Fox, who could hardly be said to count. And so her ordeal had been quite easy to endure — just a few words from the judge, a warning to try to be a better girl, and then, she had gone away again, with nobody the wiser.

But to-day it was very different. Just because that wicked Sam had been arrested, the Court was packed to suffocation, and her weakness would be exposed before the prying eyes of everybody in the wood. It was too cruel, and she wished the earth would open and swallow her up.

The Court rose at the entrance of Mr. Justice Owl, who fluttered up to his judicial perch in the shelter of an overhanging rock. Judy, her grannie, and Mr. Tortoise walked over to a bench reserved for them by the side of the Jury Box. (Sam was still chained up in the barn.)

For a moment there was silence. Then, in ringing tones, Mr. Justice Owl cried: "Swelpmegod!"

And everybody sat down.

P.C. Monkey stepped forward. "The first case on the list is that of Miss Glow-worm, Your Worship."

Hundreds of eyes turned to stare at Miss Glow-worm, who was sitting all alone on a big cabbage-leaf in the middle of the Court. They could not see very much of her, she just looked like a bright spark, and so they could not guess how nervous and unhappy she was feeling. In fact, Mrs. Hare, who did not approve of glowing, on principle, hissed to her neighbour: "Really, you'd think she would have the decency to tone herself down a *little* . . . on a day like this!" Which was not quite fair, for poor Miss Glow-worm could not tone herself down, however hard she tried.

P.C. Monkey read out the charge, as follows:

"At midnight on the night of Thursday last, Your Worship, I was going my rounds when I saw a bright light at the foot of the old Pear Tree. I hurried across, and saw that the light came from the defendant, Miss Glow-worm."

Mr. Justice Owl: "What was she doing?"

P.C. Monkey: "She was glowing, Your Worship."

Mr. Justice Owl: "Nothing else?"

P.C. Monkey: "No, Your Worship. Just glowing, very bright."

Mr. Justice Owl: "Proceed!"

P.C. Monkey: "I cautioned defendant, and told her to

put her lights out, because otherwise she'd be waking everybody up. She said, 'I can't'. I replied, 'It is the law'. She said 'I don't care what the law is, I can't'. I tried to reason with her. I said, 'Look at me . . . *I* don't go walking about as if I'd swallowed an electric light bulb. *I* don't glow'. To which she replied, haughty like, 'You couldn't if you tried'. So as it wasn't any use arguing with her, I issued a summons and told her to come here to-day. And here she is."

P.C. Monkey was so pleased with his long speech that he began to scratch himself violently, until he caught Mr. Justice Owl's eye, which made him stop, and stand to attention.

Mr. Justice Owl (turning to Miss Glow-worm). "Have you anything to say in your defence?"

Miss Glow-worm (in a nervous little squeak): "Yes, Your Worship. I *can't* stop glowing."

Mr. Justice Owl: "Speak up! And do not shine so brightly or I shall be forced to charge you with contempt of court."

The effect of these words upon Miss Glow-worm was to make her still more nervous, so that she kept on glowing by fits and starts, as though somebody were switching a light on and off. Mr. Justice Owl, seeing her plight, leant forward, and in gentler tones said:

Mr. Justice Owl: "Dim yourself, madam. That is all I ask . . . *dim* yourself."

Miss Glow-worm (squeaking a little louder, but still flashing on and off): "I *can't* dim myself any more. I have dimmed myself till I am almost ill."

Mr. Justice Owl: "But my dear Miss Glow-worm, all the other animals obey the regulations."

Miss Glow-worm: "What about the Firefly Family?"

Mr. Justice Owl: "Never mind the Firefly Family."

Miss Glow-worm: "And Mr. Tiger? His eyes were shining so brightly the other night that you could have seen them a mile off."

Mr. Justice Owl (sternly): "The conduct of other animals is no concern of yours. It is your own conduct that we are discussing. And your conduct is far too bright. You will be the cause of an epidemic of insomnia if you go on like this."

Miss Glow-worm: "But it is my *nature* to be bright. It is a matter of temperament. There is something inside me which I cannot repress."

Mr. Justice Owl: "We must all make sacrifices in the general interest."

Miss Glow-worm: "I am perfectly prepared to make sacrifices. But I simply *cannot* dim myself any more. If I do, I shall die."

And here, Miss Glow-worm's voice trembled so pathetically, and she sniffed so loudly, that the Court was visibly affected, and even Mr. Justice Owl had to dab his eyes with a mouse's tail which he always kept handy for such occasions.

Mr. Justice Owl: "I have no wish to be harsh. But I cannot allow you to walk about at night in your present condition. You are a nuisance to the whole community. Have you tried wrapping yourself up?"

Miss Glow-worm: "I should suffocate."

Mr. Justice Owl: "Or sitting underneath a cabbage leaf?"

Miss Glow-worm: "If I sat under a cabbage leaf all night I should starve. Besides, I should shine *through* the cabbage leaf. My temperament is so bright that you cannot conceal it."

As she said these last words, she glowed even more

brightly, as though to prove the truth of her claim. She looked like a brilliant jewel, or a dewdrop with the sun shining on it.

Mr. Justice Owl blinked at her, and then closed his eyes. The whole Court waited tensely, to hear his verdict. There was silence, except for the sound of Mr. Beaver's heavy breathing, and an occasional buzz from Mr. Bee.

Then Mr. Justice Owl opened his eyes again.

Mr. Justice Owl: "I see only one course open to me. You must submit to a medical examination."

"But Your Worship . . ." gasped Miss Glow-worm.

"There is nothing to be afraid of," observed the judge. "A brief visit to Dr. Leech, that is all."

"Oh, not Dr. Leech, Your Worship, *please.*"

"Then you may visit Mrs. Leech."

Miss Glow-worm shook her head, and dropped several tears. Even her tears were bright and sparkled down on to the grass where they twinkled shamelessly.

"That is all, Miss Glow-worm."

She looked as though she were about to speak again, but P.C. Monkey gently tipped up the cabbage leaf so that she was obliged to slide off it. She made her way through the long grass to the back of the Court, and disappeared into the shadows of the wood. But "disappeared" is not quite the right word; long after she had gone Judy could see her out of the corner of her eye — a spark that grew tinier and tinier, glowing like a distant star.

IV

"It is our turn now," whispered Mr. Tortoise.

Judy started; she had been so absorbed in the case of Miss Glow-worm that she had almost forgotten her own affairs.

"I feel afraid," she murmured.

"You need not. When it comes to your turn, all you have to do is to tell the truth."

There was no time to say any more, for already P.C. Monkey was calling for silence. The next few minutes seemed to pass in a dream. She saw Mr. Tortoise walk slowly to the centre, and bow to Mr. Justice Owl, who returned the bow and proceeded to address a few carefully chosen sentences to the Jury, explaining the nature of the case and telling them to keep their minds open and to return a fair verdict.

"That is all I shall say for the moment," he said. "I leave the case, for the time being, in the able hands of my learned friend, Mr. Tortoise."

Even then, everything seemed misty and unreal; Judy had a curious sense that these things were not actually happening, that she was only listening to somebody telling her a story. She saw Bruno lumber up, and take his place in the box as the first witness, and she heard him stammering out the story of all the uncanny events of the past few weeks . . . but though she knew that he was speaking nothing but the truth, the voice seemed to come from a great distance, and it was as though he were speaking of somebody in a fairy tale rather than her own self.

It was only when Bruno had finished his evidence and stumbled down from the witness box that Judy really woke up. It would indeed have been difficult for anybody to remain aloof at that moment, for the whole Court burst into applause — never did you hear such a clapping of paws and tapping of beaks and thumping of tails. Bruno stared around him, bewildered, the tears starting to his eyes, and then hurried over to sit with Mrs. Bruno, who clasped his paw in silent sympathy.

"Order! Order!" cried Mr. Justice Owl. "If there are any more demonstrations, I shall clear the Court." He glared at them all very fiercely from under his glasses. "Next witness, please!"

"Miss Smith!" cried P.C. Monkey. "Forward, Miss Smith."

As his voice rang up to the trees, it seemed to echo and echo through the branches, and every echo was a hiss, like the hiss of a snake — Miss s s s Ssssssmith — Miss s s s Ssssssmith! Far and wide spread the echoes, rising and falling, and they were caught up by the wind which had grown fiercer and colder as soon as her name was called.

Suddenly Judy felt a trembling hand on her shoulder. It was her grannie.

"What is the matter, Grannie?"

"I don't like the look of things," she whispered. "I have just seen his face!"

"Whose face?"

"The Clerk of the Weather!"

Judy stared quickly up to the sky. "I can see nothing."

"No — he's gone again. But he was there a moment ago — when they called her name."

"What was he like?"

"I only saw the face. But it was like a great mountain through the clouds — and it was grey and sharp and angry."

"Why should he be angry?"

"I don't know. But he obviously *is*. Listen to this wind!" She shook her head and muttered, "I don't know how the Tree will stand it!"

But even as she spoke, the wind died down again, and in the sudden hush the voice of P.C. Monkey was heard once more crying, "Miss Smith!"

This time there were no echoes, and at last Miss Smith appeared.

She stepped out from behind the big pear tree where she

had been hiding, putting the finishing touches to her appearance. As she walked forward, the animals gasped with astonishment; never had they seen so beautiful a young lady. For Miss Smith had dressed herself to kill; she had on a brand new nose; she had sprinkled gold-dust on her wig, and had put magic drops in her eyes to make them very large and sparkling. Her dress was made of a shimmering silver brocade, and in her hair — or rather her wig — she wore a diamond tiara. It was not really made of diamonds of course, but of glass; however, the animals could not be expected to know that.

"Quite an aristocrat," whispered Mrs. Peacock, who had noticed that Mr. Peacock was preening himself and turning his tail so that Miss Smith should see it to its fullest advantage.

Mr. Peacock was inclined to agree, but he did not like to have his opinions given to him by his wife. So he snapped, "Quite . . . they are always the worst," thereby causing poor Mrs. Peacock to feel that once again she had said the wrong thing.

Miss Smith mounted the box, murmuring "Swelpme-god" as though it were the most natural thing in the world, and Mr. Tortoise proceeded to examine her. The following dialogue ensued.

Mr. Tortoise: "Your name?"

Miss Smith: "Miss Smith."

Mr. Tortoise: "Age?"

Miss Smith (simpering): "Three hundred and eighty-three." (Sensation in Court, interrupted by P.C. Monkey brandishing his truncheon and calling "Order! Order!")

Mr. Tortoise: "You will agree, then, that you are old enough to know better?"

Miss Smith: "Oh no! I am old enough to know *worse*. Bad, worse, worst. That's my motto."

Mr. Tortoise: "In that case, you have no desire to deny your profession?"

Miss Smith: "Deny it? Certainly not!"

Mr. Tortoise: "Will you tell the Court what you are?"

Miss Smith: "With pleasure. I'm a witch." (Renewed sensation in Court.)

Mr. Tortoise: "Fully qualified?"

Miss Smith: "Of course! In fact, I got honours in Aches and Pains."

Mr. Justice Owl: "Aches and Pains? What is that?"

Miss Smith: "It is like First Aid, Your Worship, only the other way round. Instead of knowing the best way to cure a sprained ankle, I know the best way to make it worse."

Mr. Justice Owl (in disgusted tones): "Proceed!"

Mr. Tortoise: "How did you first come in contact with Young Sam?"

Miss Smith: "Through the *Witch's Evening Wail*."

Mr. Justice Owl: "The *Witch's Evening* what?"

Miss Smith: "*Wail*, Your Worship. My favourite newspaper. I read Sam's advertisement in it. Here it is."

She took out a cutting from her bag and handed it to P.C. Monkey who passed it up to Mr. Justice Owl. In a sombre voice he read it out: "Witch wanted for Country Shop. Must hate animals, old women and children. Extra wages if prepared to be thoroughly disagreeable."

Regarding Miss Smith coldly through his glasses, he said: "This, I take it, was inserted by Young Sam?"

Miss Smith: "Yes, Your Worship."

Mr. Justice Owl: "And you felt that it was a position you would be able to occupy without . . . without distaste?"

Miss Smith: "Distaste? Why — it was *made* for me!"

Mr. Justice Owl made no comment. He merely passed the cutting to Mr. Tortoise.

"Kindly file this among the evidence," he observed.

"And remind me, before I sum up, that I wish to make a few observations on the pernicious influence of the modern Human press."

Mr. Tortoise bowed, and continued with his cross-examination.

It did not take very long. Miss Smith was an admirable witness — if the word "admirable" can be applied to anybody so wicked. She made not the least effort to conceal her dreadful gifts, in fact she was indignant at the idea that anybody should doubt them. For instance, when Mr. Tortoise questioned her about the quality of the poison which the toads were in the habit of spitting, and suggested that they might have to spit quite a great deal before the results were fatal, she grew pink in the face, and retorted:

Miss Smith: "Really! I didn't come here to be insulted!"

Mr. Tortoise: "I am merely trying to get at the facts."

Miss Smith (with heat): "Well, then, here are the facts. One drop of poison in your eye will make you blind. One drop on your foot will make you go dancing mad, so that you spend the rest of your life hopping up and down, like a jitterbug. One drop in your soup and you will have the most horrible pains, from your top to your toe. And one drop . . . on your heart . . ."

Mr. Tortoise: "Thank you, madam . . . I think that is sufficient."

Mr. Justice Owl: "More than enough!"

Mr. Tortoise: "As a matter of form, Your Worship, I think that the toads should be called."

Miss Smith: "But they *must* be called! I *promised* them they'd be called! It's their *treat*!" (She kissed her hands to the toads, who were sitting together close to the Jury box.)

Mr. Justice Owl: "Let the toads be called!"

V

It was from this moment that the drama mounted more and more swiftly to its extraordinary climax. Sitting there, watching and listening, Judy felt, once again, that she was a figure in a dream, over which she had no control. And she was conscious of all sorts of things and people, far away, who were being inevitably drawn into the circle of events; although she could not see him, she was conscious of Sam, straining and snarling in his chains, and of Old Sam too, who — though he was miles away, and far out of sight — was packing his bags, muttering and nattering in his beard, preparing to escape for ever from the wood. But most of all she was conscious of the Tree. Through the wide clearing she could see it in the distance, and she knew that it was in great distress. It had a tragic droop; its great branches were sunk towards the earth; its arms seemed to move blindly, groping for support, as though it were crying to her, "I can bear no more! If the wind rises again, I am finished!"

Judy clasped her hands and breathed a silent prayer. As she looked up to the skies, there was a parting in the clouds. What . . . what was that? That thin grey shape, looming out of the mist? She peered forward, narrowing her eyes. Could it be . . . ? But the clouds had closed again. Judy still stared. "A face," she whispered to herself. "I *did* see a face. Like grannie said. Grey and sharp and angry." She closed her eyes. "Oh, please, Clerk of the Weather," she breathed, "be kind to the Tree. Blow where you will, do what you must, but please be kind to the Tree!"

There was no answer, save the slow wail of the wind.

And then, for the last time, everything seemed to grow

clear and matter of fact. There was a gleam of sunshine. P.C. Monkey advanced towards the centre.

"Your Worship," he cried. "The toads!"

VI

The appearance of the toads created one of the greatest sensations of the day. To celebrate the occasion Miss Smith had tied pink ribbons round their necks and dabbed powder on the end of their noses; this only made them more hideous than ever, and when they hopped out into the centre and glared around them with their cross eyes, they looked like three wicked circus clowns who were about to play some very unpleasant trick on their audience. Many of the animals shrank back in disgust and even Mrs. Hare, who never lost her dignity, edged nearer to the shelter of Mr. Peacock.

"I trust," she murmured, "that there will be no . . . ahem . . . no . . ." she wanted to say "spitting" but it did not sound a very lady-like word.

"No what, madam?"

"No — ahem — demonstrations."

"Have no fear, madam," proclaimed Mr. Peacock, gallantly. "I will protect you."

All the same, he was just as anxious as Mrs. Hare that there should be no "demonstrations". If one of the toads were to spit on his tail he was quite sure that it would burn a hole in it, and then, he felt life would hardly be worth living. He decided that on no account would he Open until the toads were safely out of the way; in fact, with all these queer things happening, it might be safer not to Open at all.

When the toads had been sworn in, Mr. Justice Owl spoke in a loud stern voice:

"Say swelpmegod," he demanded.

The toads shook their heads.

Mr. Justice Owl could hardly believe his eyes. "Did you hear me?"

"We heard you, boss," croaked the toads.

"Then say swelpmegod at once," he cried sternly.

"Nope," croaked the toads.

"Of all the monstrous impertinence . . ." began Mr. Justice Owl.

The toads interrupted him. "Not swelpmegod, boss. Swelpmesatan."

"Swelpmewhat?"

"Swelpmesatan," they repeated. "More in our line."

Mr. Justice Owl looked as if he were about to explode. Not only was he furious at the toads' disobedience, but he was all of a fluster because he had no idea what swelpmesatan meant. For all he knew it *might* be a Learned Expression, and it *might* be something that Humans were in the habit of saying, and if it were, he would look a pretty fool if he refused to allow it. The situation was awkward in the extreme, and it is difficult to imagine how he would have got out of it had not Mr. Tortoise once again come to the rescue.

"If you will forgive me, Your Honour," he murmured, popping his head over the edge of the box.

Mr. Justice Owl bowed, and attempted to smooth his ruffled feathers. To tell the truth, he was glad of the interruption. "Proceed!" he grunted.

"We all know the meaning of swelpmegod, I take it," observed Mr. Tortoise, looking round the Court.

There was a good deal of shuffling and fluttering at this statement, for none of the animals had any idea what swelpmegod meant, though of course they would not have dreamed of admitting their ignorance. Mrs. Hare put on a haughty expression, and stared fixedly at Mrs. Rabbit, who lowered her eyes and went pink in the face. Mr. Peacock assumed a fierce glare, and held his head high as though to say, "Fancy anybody doubting whether I knew it — why I invented it!" As for Mr. Justice Owl, he closed his eyes, and prayed fervently that Mr. Tortoise would not ask *him* to define it.

"It means, of course," continued Mr. Tortoise, "So help me God."

There was an audible sigh of relief. Mrs. Hare nodded, very publicly, so that everybody should understand that she had known all the time. Mrs. Rabbit, poor thing, tried to nod too, but she was so embarrassed that she only managed to let out a loud sneeze. Mr. Peacock gave a faint flutter to his tail, indicating approval.

"I trust Your Worship will agree with my definition?" inquired Mr. Tortoise.

Mr. Justice Owl opened his eyes again, thankful that at last the mystery was solved.

"Quite correct!" he boomed. "So help me God. Proceed!"

"The other phrase — swelpmesatan — means — as Mr. Justice Owl would be the first to tell you — So help me Satan!"

Mr. Justice Owl opened his eyes very wide. "So *that's* what . . ." he began, and then checked himself. He had nearly given himself away, and he was all in a muddle again. "So help me Satan," he spluttered. "Correct." And then, since all the animals were waiting for him . . . "Most irregular!"

"Indeed, Your Worship, it is most irregular, but I would submit. . . ."

"Most irregular!" repeated Mr. Justice Owl, who felt that he was on safer ground.

"Your Worship is right to insist on the point. At the same time, I would humbly submit that these three witnesses . . ." here he pointed to the toads . . . "are *themselves* most irregular. . . ."

"You've said it!" croaked the toads.

"Silence!" boomed Mr. Justice Owl.

"And that therefore," continued Mr. Tortoise, "it would be better to allow them to use their own oath. Sad as it may seem to decent, law-abiding folk like ourselves, these three witnesses take their orders from . . . from . . ." his voice sank almost to a whisper, "from Satan."

"Good old Satan," croaked the toads.

"For the last time, silence!" thundered Mr. Justice Owl.

"Satan is their master," proclaimed Mr. Tortoise. "And, therefore, if they say swelpmesatan, they are more likely to tell the truth. That, Your Worship, is my humble submission."

Mr. Justice Owl said nothing for a few moments. He was too bewildered. It was lucky for him that thanks to his huge eyebrows, his massive beak, and his remarkable gift for staying completely still, he always managed to *look* very wise. Even when his mind was a complete blank he *looked* as though he were pondering all the riddles of the Universe and had gone a long way towards their solution. When at length he said "Proceed" — (it was the only word he could think of) — he said it with such dignity and such weight that it sounded like the last word in wisdom. "A remarkable brain", murmured Mrs. Hare to Mrs. Fox, who nodded gravely.

We will not linger long over the evidence of the toads; it is enough to say that it completely confirmed all that Bruno had said. Only one thing worried Mr. Tortoise — how was he to *prove* that they were as wicked as they claimed? They chattered so much and boasted so loudly that the

Jury might think it was all a lot of childish talk, like silly boys pretending to be gangsters. If he could only get them to spit, all doubts would be removed. But he was sure that if he were to ask them outright, they would only sulk and shut their mouths, just to annoy him.

So he thought of a very clever idea. He said:

Mr. Tortoise: "I understand that there are only certain times of the day when you are able to produce this poison?"

Toads: "Times of the day, my fanny! Any time's spitting time!"

Mr. Tortoise: "Any time . . . let us say . . . after midday."

Toads (indignantly): "No, you old dope — *any* time!"

Mr. Tortoise (smiling and shaking his head): "I'm afraid you cannot expect the Court to believe that."

Toads: "D'you want us to prove it?"

Mr. Tortoise (shrinking back in mock alarm): "Certainly not!"

Toads (fiercely): "You asked for it!"

Before anybody could prevent them, they had burst into song.

> With a splash and a spatter and a ho ho ho
> What does it matter if the world's our foe?
> With a stab and a sting and a ha ha ha
> We spit as we sing to the evening star!
> With a lick and a spittle and a he he he
> Quick fire at his little an-at-o-my!

And without pausing for an instant they threw back their heads, took a deep gulp, and spurted a stream of bright green poison straight at Mr. Tortoise. Happily for him he had known that it was coming, and by some miracle he managed to turn a clumsy somersault which landed him just outside their range.

Even so, some of the poison would certainly have splashed on him, had it not been for a sudden gust of wind that blew it to one side. During the whole time that the toads had been giving evidence the wind had almost died away, but at the very moment that the toads spat, it whirled down through the trees as though it had been a wild beast crouching to spring. So strong was it that even Mr. Justice Owl in the shelter of his cave found himself gasping for breath. When he recovered his self-possession he blinked down at a most extraordinary sight.

There on the grass where the toads had spat was an ugly bare patch which rapidly grew larger and larger and deeper and deeper; and from the centre of it rose thin streaks of grey vapour that twisted and twirled like the heads of snakes, flicking tiny tongues of fire.

"Order! Order!" cried Mr. Justice Owl, as though this might have some effect on the ghostly snakes. Since it had none at all he called loudly for P.C. Monkey. He made a grand gesture towards the disturbance. "Arrest those . . . those . . . ahem!" he demanded. He had no idea what it was that he wanted P.C. Monkey to arrest, and he was very doubtful whether P.C. Monkey would be able to arrest them, but since he was the judge he had to say something.

Once again the situation was saved by Mr. Tortoise. Advancing rapidly to the very edge of the ring he muttered a few words — what they were, we shall never know — and the coils of vapour began to quiver and flicker and drift back into the pit. Then he walked all round the edge, still muttering to himself, and the grass ceased to smoulder and the earth stayed still.

He turned to Mr. Justice Owl.

"The situation is in hand, Your Worship."

Mr. Justice Owl was profoundly relieved. Never in all his experience had he known so many awkward situations.

"If this sort of thing continues," he thought, "the trial will develop into a circus." It was high time that he asserted his authority.

He addressed the Court at large.

"We have just observed," he proclaimed, "an example of Witchcraft."

"You've said it," croaked the toads.

"Silence! Another word from you and . . ." He did not finish the sentence, but stretched out his wings to their full extent, and ground the upper and lower parts of his beak so fiercely together that even the toads were alarmed and took a step backwards.

"I permitted this demonstration," he continued, "in order that the Jury might have ample opportunity to judge for themselves the type of person whom they are engaged in trying. I imagine that they have now seen enough to enable them to make up their minds." He turned to Mr. Peacock. "Is that correct, Mr. Foreman?"

"Most certainly, Your Worship."

"Good! In that case, there is only one more witness to be examined before the prisoner is brought to trial."

P.C. Monkey stepped forward.

"Miss Judy!" he cried.

Slowly she rose to her feet.

CHAPTER XVIII

THE STORM—AND AFTER

BY the time that Judy rose to give her evidence the wind had grown so fierce that the uproar in the branches overhead threatened to drown the evidence; it was as though a great chorus was thundering through the trees crying "Justice! Justice!"

"We shall be blown from our seats!" muttered Mrs. Hare, trying not to lose her dignity while snuggling more safely behind the shelter of a log. Mrs. Rabbit had long ago forsaken all thoughts of dignity, and was clutching the drooping branch of an old ash, while many of the smaller animals were clinging to twigs and tufts of grass, with their tails streaming out behind them, like flags straining at the mast. Even Mr. Peacock had long ago folded up his tail, for fear of being blown up to the clouds like an inverted umbrella.

The only two who seemed unaffected by the tempest were Mr. Tortoise and Mr. Justice Owl. Mr. Tortoise's shell was so thick, and his body so streamlined, that it would have taken an earthquake to disturb *him*. As for Mr. Justice Owl, he was protected from the elements by the warm dry niche of his judicial seat, and he sat there looking quite unmoved, with not a feather ruffled, gazing around him with majestic superiority. All the same, in spite of his apparent calm, he was anxious; he did not like the look of the sky at all; he had never seen it such a strange colour— a sort of indigo, streaked with an angry red. As for the wind, it was really beyond a joke; if it grew any worse he would have to shout to make himself heard. And since it showed no signs of abating, but seemed to be fiercer every second, he sent a hasty summons to P.C. Monkey.

"Go to Mr. Tortoise at once," commanded Mr. Justice Owl, "and tell him to make his cross-examination as short as he can, so that we can bring Sam before the Jury at the earliest possible moment. Otherwise the case will have to be adjourned."

P.C. Monkey scrambled down and delivered the message, holding on to his helmet with both hands. Mr. Tortoise nodded.

"Tell His Worship that I am only going to ask Miss Judy a very few questions," he said. Then he nodded to Judy, who stepped into the box without any further delay.

Now it is a curious thing, on which many of the animals afterwards commented, that as soon as Judy began to speak, a lull seemed to come into the storm, and the howling of the wind died down to a low moan, as though Someone — Someone very important — was anxious to hear every word that she was saying. You and I may perhaps guess who that Someone was, for now and then we have caught a glimpse of his face, high up in the clouds.

Mr. Tortoise gathered his papers together and turned to Judy.

Mr. Tortoise: "We are all familiar with your story Miss Judy, and I take it that the accounts given by Mr. Bruno and the other witnesses are substantially correct?"

Judy: "Yes."

Mr. Tortoise: "In that case I do not think that we need go over them again. In fact, there is only one question I want to ask you. What was your *motive* in bringing this action against Sam?"

Judy: "I do not quite understand."

Mr. Tortoise: "Perhaps I can help you. Am I right in suggesting that whatever your motive may have been, it was *not* one of revenge?"

Judy: "Oh no — not revenge!"

Mr. Tortoise: "Nor of hatred?"

Judy: "I don't think it is hatred — though I hate the things he stands for."

Mr. Tortoise: "Then would you tell the Court your motive? Is it to bring justice?"

Judy (a little puzzled): "I do not know if I would call it Justice. I am not sure if I know what Justice is. I am not sure if *anybody* knows what Justice is . . . (here she turned to Mr. Justice Owl) . . . if His Worship will not think that disrespectful?"

Mr. Justice Owl (kindly): "Proceed."

Judy : "I think — though I do not wish to take up the time of the Court — I think that my motive is really . . . love."

Mr. Tortoise: "That was what I suspected. But would you please explain a little more fully?"

Judy felt herself blushing; she had never made a speech before, and she did not like to push herself forward. But the things she had to say were very dear to her heart, and perhaps it would not matter if she said them — just once — and then held her peace, for the rest of her life. So she conquered her shyness and spoke as follows:

"You see," — and here she turned so that she faced the main body of the crowd — "I *do* love you all, very much. I know I try to sell you things . . ." she smiled for a moment, and brushed back her hair, which was tumbling into her eyes . . . "but I've tried to sell you nice things, that were good for you, and to make them as cheap as I could. And always, I've tried to remember that though . . . though I'm Human and you are not, we are really all just the same. It's just . . . just . . ." — she paused, for she did not want to offend them, "just a matter of *education.* I've been very lucky in mine . . ." and here she smiled at her grannie . . .

"luckier than some of you, and I've tried not to take advantage of it.

"That was what I meant when I said I hated the things Sam stood for. I'm afraid a lot of Humans stand for those things; they have learned things that you have not learned, they have discovered ways in which they can hurt you and fight you and . . . kill you, without using their own bodies . . . mean ways, cunning ways, in which you have no chance at all . . . and . . . ."

She faltered, for she wondered if she was talking nonsense. But Mr. Tortoise gave her a smile of encouragement, so she went on:

"I don't want you to think that all Humans are like that; there are lots like Grannie and me; and . . . and I don't think I could help loving you even if I tried." She looked up to the trees, with their burden of wings — white wings, and red and grey — black wings, green wings, smooth and ragged, sleek and sombre. "I love you *all*. For instance . . . I love the birds — I want their wings to be swift and strong — I want them to be free. If they fly to the old Willow Tree, I want them to fly there because they feel that it is a place of rest for them, a place of peace, where the storms will not reach them. I love the birds — the little birds . . ." she paused, and smiled shyly at a row of sparrows, who were huddled together on a bramble bush, listening with tense excitement . . . "and the great birds too . . ." and her eyes flickered for a moment to the majestic figure of Mr. Justice Owl . . . and then past him, to the Seagulls, gleaming white against the red fruit of the apple tree, till they rested on the proud figure of Mr. Peacock.

"I am detaining the Court, Your Worship," she murmured, nervously clasping and unclasping her hands.

Mr. Justice Owl shook his head; he was too affected to speak.

"You are very kind," she whispered.

She took a deep breath. But the words she was going to say were never uttered. For at that moment the strange lull in the storm was broken, and the wind hissed over them like a mighty wave, as though the Someone who had been waiting to hear what she had to say, had heard and understood, and was impatient to act, to bring the drama to its final conclusion.

Judy gasped, and tried to speak — there were so many things she wanted to say, but they were little things, tiny things, that could not be shouted — things that could only be whispered and hinted. She wanted to tell them of all the things about them that she loved — the gold-dust on the wing of a moth, that was more precious to her than gold in the bank — the sheen on the breast of a dove — all silver and blue and grey in the early morning — the curves the swallows made against the blue, like the sweeping lines of an enchanted pen.

But she could not speak.

And suddenly she felt frightened of the wind; she felt that it was blowing blindly and cruelly; it was a wind of revenge . . . and in her heart there had not been any thought of revenge. There was not even a trace of bitterness against Sam; it had all melted away while she had been speaking. She knew nothing but a great pity that any boy should have taken to such evil ways.

Panic seized her. What would the animals do to him? They might hang him! And even if they did not hang him, they would shut him up for many years in a dark, cold cave. She could not bear it. She would never feel the same again if she knew that somebody had been hanged, for her sake, or was spending the long years of his youth chained in the dark when he should have been playing in the sunlight.

She beat her hands on the witness-box.

"No-no!" she cried. "Please leave him alone!"

Her voice was lost in the howl of the gale.

"Your Worship!" she shouted. "Listen to me . . . oh please listen!"

But Mr. Justice Owl could not even see her, let alone hear her. As for all the animals — if they had noticed her at all they would only have thought that she was calling for help.

Her voice rose to a scream. "Your Worship—anybody — Mr. Tortoise — please do not hurt him!"

It was hopeless; the words were blown back through her own lips; she could only gulp, and make frantic little signs which nobody understood.

Desperately she looked around her. Was there nobody who could help? In a few moments, P.C. Monkey would be leading in his captive, and once he was in the dock, once the animals had seen him, she was sure that they would never let him go. Judy knew something of the cruelty of crowds — whether they be of animals or of men; a herd of animals will trample down the weakest of their number, just as a mob of men will attack the humble and the sick. We are all much nicer by ourselves than we are in a crowd, for it is only in silence that we can hear the voice of God.

Judy knew all these things by instinct (though she could not have put them into words) and it was for this reason that she was frightened of the mob.

Why, oh why, had she not thought of this before? Why had she let things go so far?

Was there nobody — *nobody* — who could stop it?

She clasped her hands and looked up at the sky. And as she did so, her heart leapt with excitement. For there was his face again — the face of the Clerk of the Weather — and she knew that he had heard her, and that at last he had understood her true meaning, and that he was going to help.

How long she stood there, gazing up at the sky, no one will ever know; it may have been only a few seconds; but for Judy it seemed that time stood still. None of the others saw him; he was showing his face for Judy alone . . . and how grand, how awe-inspiring it was! Like a great mountain, with the white clouds streaming over it — a mountain made of mist and rain, that suddenly seemed to smile, with all its crags and valleys twisting and turning in the heavens. Now from out of this gigantic image there came a Voice, borne on the wind. . . .

"It shall be as you wish, my child."

One last smile. And then, a change swept over the Face. Dark clouds blew over the giant brow, lightning flashed from the misty eyes, the cheeks swelled and swelled and swelled. . . .

High above the tumult there came a sound of splitting wood and rending timber, and with it the sharp jangle of snapping chains.

A second later a shower of planks and beams hurtled over their heads twisting and tossing as though they had been withered leaves. Then, through the storm, there came one shrill cry — the strangest cry Judy had ever heard, for it was the cry of an animal set free from a trap, and yet, it was a Human cry . . . the cry of Sam. And even as the cry rang in their ears they saw him lifted high above them, clinging to a plank, tossing and turning like a man in a whirlpool. For a brief second there was a lull and the plank dropped sharply down; then the wind grew madder and madder, rolling him round and round. He was very close to Judy now. He seemed to be trying to say something. She could see his lips moving in a desperate effort to make her hear. And at last she heard. Just the words "Thank You!"

It was enough.

She knew she had won. She knew that Sam was saved.

A last gigantic gust that seemed as though it would blow the very earth into space, like a glittering ball of glass, to join the distant stars. The plank swept away, tearing Sam with it . . . high over the trees, farther, farther . . . till it was only a black dot in the clouds. At last it was gone.

"He has escaped from us . . . he has escaped from us!"

The cry of the angry crowd mingled with the wind.

"I, too, am glad."

Judy started. It was the voice of Mr. Tortoise, who had come to her side.

"He has escaped from us, yes. But perhaps he has also escaped from himself. And out there, in the great world, he may be able to begin again."

But before she could reply there was another cry behind her. She turned and saw her grannie, who was pointing with a trembling finger into the distance.

"The Tree!" she wailed. "The Tree!"

Judy stared down the glade . . . and then her heart sank. Far away she could just see the outline of the Tree, and it was drooping slowly to the ground. Branch by branch, limb by limb, like an old, old man who has no longer the strength to meet the storms of the world.

For a moment Judy was stunned by the shock; she could neither move not speak. Her grannie was sobbing by her side, and saying something, but she could not listen to her. All she heard were the words of Mr. Tortoise, and though they were only whispered, they echoed clearly through the storm:

"It has happened at last," he was saying. "The Tree is sitting down."

Had Judy been less dismayed, less bewildered, she might have heard something strange about this voice — for it had in it not the faintest echo of grief; instead it sounded happy. And in his eyes there was a sparkle that was more of laughter than of tears.

But she noticed none of these things. All she knew was that the Tree was in mortal danger, if indeed it was not already dead.

Without another word she ran swiftly from them, into the teeth of the storm.

II

Judy stood by the Tree, panting and staring wildly about her. Far and wide its great limbs were strewn, like a giant taken in battle. The two main branches were stretched at full length, as though they had been flung out in a last passionate entreaty to the gods. The massive trunk was torn and twisted, like the body of a wounded soldier. And all around were scattered the goods and chattels of the shop, blown helter skelter in hopeless confusion.

Judy stared and stared. And gradually she realized that

a very strange thing was happening — or rather, that three very strange things were happening.

Firstly, the storm had completely died away. A moment ago, the whole world had been in uproar, and the skies had scowled with angry clouds. Now there was no breath of wind; the leaves hung still as on a midsummer's eve. Looking up to the sky she saw a patch of blue, that was growing larger and larger and would soon spread all over the heavens. "There is magic at work, somewhere," thought Judy.

Yet she was not afraid.

Secondly — and even more strangely — she realized that she was quite alone. Nobody had followed her; there was no sign of Mr. Tortoise nor of her grannie, nor of P.C. Monkey. Indeed, there was no sign of any of the animals — no bird stirred in the branches, no insect hopped in the grass, not a bee buzzed among the flowers. For the first time in her life she was in utter solitude.

Yet she was not lonely.

Thirdly, came the strangest thing of all. Here before her lay the wreckage of all her hopes. Her home had gone; all the precious little things which she had gathered with such loving care were scattered beyond recall. She had lost her oldest friend — for the Tree, surely, must be called a friend; and this friend lay torn and dead at her feet, never again to shelter her with his strong arms, nor to whisper to her with his gentle wisdom.

Yet she was not unhappy.

No tears came to her eyes — not a sigh drifted from her lips. Instead, she found that she was smiling quietly to herself. For here there was no sense of destruction nor of death; instead, she felt that something had been created, that it was at this very moment springing to life.

But what?

She took a step forward — and then stopped. Was not that the sound of music, far away? She listened intently, holding her breath. But yes — there it was again, faint but clear, now very sweet. It was coming closer. She could hear the sound of flutes and violins and the tinkle of cymbals. They seemed to be playing a sort of serenade, for there was the sound of voices, too, drifting up from the valley, rising and falling, but growing clearer all the while. Who could they be? And what was it they were singing? She strained her ears to catch the words. At first she could not understand them, but after a few moments they came to her distinctly.

> "Time is a flower that will never fade
> If you pluck that flower with love,
> A bird that will always sing, sweet maid,
> If you hark to him with love . . .
> Time is a friend, be not afraid,
> For Time was made to love."

What a sweet song it was! But what did it mean? And why could she not see the singers, though their voices were so close? Were they hiding somewhere behind the trees? That must be it. She would go to greet them.

She took another step forward — and then she stopped again, very sharply indeed.

For she had trodden — not on the grass, but on a carpet!

She stood there motionless, with one foot poised in the air, hardly daring to look down. Then, very gently, inch by inch, she lowered her foot. At last it grazed the ground. Summoning up all her courage, she pressed it firmly down. As she did so she gave a little scream. For it sank deep into the softest carpet she had ever known.

Wide-eyed with astonishment, she looked down. Yes — it was a carpet, rich and bright, glowing in the sunlight, a

deep wine-coloured red. Only a little strip of it had been
unfolded — a great bundle lay before her. But even as she
watched it was slowly unwound by invisible hands, and it
rolled and rolled away as though it were inviting her to
follow it.

"This must be a dream," thought Judy, "but it is such a
beautiful dream that I do not mind. I wonder if I dare
tread on the carpet, or if it will sink under me, and throw
me into some dreadful pit?" But there was such a feeling of
happiness everywhere, and the music rang so sweetly, that
she forgot her fears and walked along the carpet, which was
so warm and silky that it seemed to caress her feet.

And then, once again, she stopped dead, and stared in
front of her.

For the carpet had stopped unrolling, and had come to
rest at the foot of the shattered trunk of the Tree. That
would have been strange enough, in any case, but what
was far far stranger was the fact that the trunk slowly
seemed to straighten itself, to widen, and to form itself into
an arch. The arch grew taller and taller and wider and
wider, and as it changed its shape so it changed its colour.
Little by little it shed its dull greeny-grey and was tinged
with yellow; the yellow spread and deepened, glowed and
sparkled . . . till it was the colour of buttercups, of daffodils,
of sheer gold. In fact — it *was* gold.

And through the arch, waddling awkwardly towards her,
came Mr. Tortoise.

III

"Oh, Mr. Tortoise!" cried Judy. "I am so glad you have
come!"

He did not answer her, but only stared at her, with the
strangest look in his little beady eyes.

"This is such a lovely dream," she went on. "And it only needed you to make it perfect!"

He still stared at her. Then he said: "Are you *sure* it is a dream?"

She laughed softly. "Of course it is a dream," she said. "What else could it be . . . with the music and the arch and the lovely carpet?"

"Supposing you were to wake up?"

Her face fell. "Oh, please, don't say horrid things like that. I don't want to wake up."

"Never?"

She thought for a moment. "Well — that depends. If Grannie could come into the dream, and all my friends, and . . ."

"And what?"

"And *you*, Mr. Tortoise . . ."

He was looking at her very eagerly.

"Yes?"

"Then I don't think I should ever want to wake up at all."

"You think we could be happy together?"

"I *know* we could."

"That was all I wanted to know."

"But why are we talking like this?" she asked him. "Why can't we just go on dreaming? We might fly like the birds and swim like the fishes and go on listening to the music. . ."

Mr. Tortoise cut her short. "I am afraid," he said, "that we must wake up."

"So soon? Oh, please, Mr. Tortoise . . ." She held out her arms to him, pleading.

"No, my dear, it has to be."

She sighed and said nothing.

"But perhaps you will find . . ." He stopped, as though he were searching for words.

"Yes?"

"Perhaps you will find, when we do wake up, that the reality is better than the dream. People often do — brave people. And I think you are brave."

"I wonder."

"You will need all your bravery now."

"Why — is something going to happen?"

"It is happening," he said. And as he spoke his words seemed to echo and echo, so that the trees caught them up and whispered, "it is happening . . . happening," in time to the music. "Happening . . . happening . . . happening!"

And indeed it was happening. For the most extraordinary change was coming over Mr. Tortoise. A moment ago he had been just a little brown blob of a tortoise, framed in a golden arch. But now his shell seemed to be blurred and trembling, like a reflection on the surface of a lake, and it was spreading upwards and outwards, taking to itself a silver sheen. It grew and grew, glistening in the sunlight; the tiny arms unfolded from their casing, the crumpled legs quivered and stood erect; from the withered pointed face the wrinkles fell away; the bald skull shivered and swelled; and with a sudden rush a thick mop of fair hair swept over the little eyes, which opened wider and wider, and gazed at her with adoration.

Before her stood a Prince.

CHAPTER XIX

HAPPY ENDING

"M R. TORTOISE!" gasped Judy. And then . . . as "Mr. Tortoise" was obviously an unsuitable name for the wonderful young man who stood before her . . . "I mean . . . I mean 'Sir'!"

"Call me John," he said gently.

"Oh, I couldn't!" She looked at him with dazzled eyes, marvelling at the golden plumes on his hat and the sparkling rubies on his sword.

"You're too . . . too grand."

He smiled. "You're not exactly shabby yourself."

"Please don't make fun of me."

"I'm not. Look at yourself."

Judy glanced down and her eyes opened wide with astonishment. Her feet — which a moment ago had been bare — were shod in silver embroidered with emeralds, and she had stockings of cobwebby silk, faintly shot with the palest green. Her dress was of rich velvet, and as she stepped this way and that, marvelling at it, she saw that a hundred shades of green had been woven into its glowing fabric — the green of the sea, the green of shadows under an apple tree, even the green of dark cedars in the moonlight. As a contrast to all this green, the blouse was thickly embroidered with tiny precious stones, in a design of brightly coloured leaves — there must have been thousands of little sapphires and diamonds and aquamarines and fire opals.

"Do you like it?"

"Oh, Sir!" breathed Judy.

"The name is John," he reminded her.

"John," she whispered shyly. "It's too wonderful."

"I'm glad you approve. As a matter of fact I designed it myself. I always think of you in that colour, somehow, with a background of leaves and trees, and green shadows."

"But how can I ever thank you?"

"You don't have to. After all, it's only payment for an old debt. Don't you remember?"

She shook her head.

"Don't you remember mending my shell?"

She laughed. "Oh, *that!*"

"Well," he said, "that was the beginning of it all. I swore that when I came into my Kingdom . . . ."

"Kingdom?" she interrupted. "Are you really a Prince?"

"I'm afraid so. Does it matter?"

"I don't know. It seems so strange."

"It seemed much stranger to be a tortoise," he chuckled.

"Why were you . . ." she began, and then stopped. It seemed rude to ask him why he was a tortoise. However, he saw the question in her eyes.

"I'll tell you why I was changed into a tortoise in a minute," he said. "But first, what do you think of the Palace?"

"Palace?"

"If you turn round, you'll see it. It's been gradually becoming visible all the time we were talking."

Slowly Judy turned. And then all words failed her. For through the golden arch a palace of white glittered in the sunlight, with marble columns as slim as the stems of white narcissi, and staircases that were as graceful as a flight of sea-gulls. In the courtyard played a fountain whose many jets and sprays danced in the wind like silver feathers.

But there was something even more wonderful. There, in the centre of a smooth-shaven lawn, stood the Tree —

her Tree — the Tree that had sat down — the Tree that by some miracle had stood up again, green and strong, and rejoicing in its eternal youth.

With a cry of happiness Judy ran through the golden arch, and a burst of music echoed as she passed.

II

An hour later, the Prince and Judy were sitting under the Tree, drinking sherbet out of cups of solid gold. Mrs. Judy, who had suddenly appeared in the most wonderful costume, with a train three yards long, thickly embroidered with garnets, had retired to rest in one of the towers, which she had chosen as her apartment because she said it reminded her of her old bedroom in the Tree. So for the moment they had it all to themselves.

"Do you really want to know why I was turned into a tortoise?" asked the Prince.

"Not if you don't want to tell me," replied Judy. "Though I do think it would be interesting."

He smiled. "It's quite simple. When I was very young . . ."

"But you're very young now."

"Well, when I was just a kid, I used to be pretty wild."

"I'm sure you were always very nice, whatever else you may have been."

"No, Judy my dear, I wasn't. I . . . I . . . hurt people." He saw the look of reproach in her eyes, and he seized her hand. "Mind you, I didn't really mean it. But I was just out for a good time. I thought I was being smart. I got hold of a pistol and pretended to hold people up. I laid traps for people, and laughed when they fell into them. I even . . . ."

"You even what, my dear?"

He blushed. "I even drank a little too much."

"Oh, John!" Judy suddenly remembered. "The raspber . . ."

"Quite, the raspberry wine. Well, I'm through with raspberry wine." He held up his goblet. "Hence the sherbet."

"It's much nicer," she said. "Don't you think?"

"I do indeed. Particularly with you by my side."

He held her hand a little closer.

"Anyway," he continued, "what with one thing and another, my guardians decided that I had to be taught a lesson."

"But couldn't your father have spoken to you, John?"

"My father died when I was a baby, Judy. And my mother too. Perhaps that's why I was so lonely."

He sighed — and held her hand still more closely. "So you see, I just had to put up with a lot of old guardians. And by the way — that reminds me. Do you remember the Clerk of the Weather?"

"As if I could ever forget him!"

"Well, he's a sort of uncle of mine."

"So that explains it!" Judy clapped her hands together . . . she had remembered the face in the clouds.

"Explains what?"

"Never mind for the moment," she said. "Go on about being a tortoise."

"Well, the guardians got together and they made a bargain with me. Either I had to give up being a Prince for ever or else I had to prove that I was worthy of my trust. And I could only do that by being turned into a tortoise."

"But why a *tortoise*?"

"Because I had to learn three lessons. And two of those lessons were the sort only a tortoise can learn. First, I had to learn to go slow. Well . . . a tortoise isn't exactly a speed-bug. Second, to rely on my real self and not on my . . ." He paused, and a blush mounted his cheeks.

Judy smiled and put her hand over his. "Go on, my dear. You mean you were very nice to look at, and you had to forget about it."

He grinned and scratched his head, with a very unprincely gesture.

"If you put it like that. Anyway, a tortoise isn't exactly handsome."

"And third?" asked Judy.

"Third," he said, "was you."

"How?"

"I had to meet a girl with a golden heart."

Judy blushed. "And do you think you've met her?"

"I don't think. I *know*."

He bent down and kissed her hand.

Many other things he told her, in that enchanted interlude, when the last glow of Autumn seemed to brighten again into the first flush of Spring; but the most important thing he told her was that he had loved her all the time, and didn't she think that the sooner they were married the better?

To which Judy could think of only one reply. Which, of course, was "Yes".

III

Now in a few minutes we shall be able to write the words with which all true fairy stories must end — the words . . . "And they lived happily ever after." For very soon they were married, and the wedding was quite wonderful, with Mr. Bruno as best man, and Mr. Peacock as chief page, and a whole bevy of bridesmaids led by Miss Squirrel and Miss Fox — and of course, Mr. Justice Owl to give the bride away.

However, it would take a whole book to tell you about these things, and time is growing short. So we must content ourselves with a little tidying-up. There were quite a number of people whom we deserted in the middle of the storm, and it would be rude to leave them without saying good-bye.

For instance, what happened to Sam, and Old Sam, and Miss Smith and the toads, and all the rest of them?

Well, Sam was blown out to sea. For a whole day and night he tossed and twirled in the clouds; and it was not till dawn on the second day that the Clerk of the Weather decided that he had learned his lesson, and allowed the wind to drop. Then he fell swiftly through the air, and dropped with a bump straight on to the deck of an oil tanker bound for Venezuela.

"Where the deuce did you come from?" demanded the Captain, startled by this strange apparition.

Sam explained as best he could.

The Captain snorted. He was a huge man with red whiskers and red eyes and a red nose; in fact, everything was red about him, even his language.

"Well," he growled, "if you want to come along with us, you'll have to earn your keep — see?"

Sam saw.

"Get along to the kitchen, then, and start peeling potaters."

So Sam got along, and did the first honest day's work of his whole life. And strangely enough he felt much happier for it.

Old Sam? Well, to be frank, we don't know what happened to him, nor do we very much mind. He was always a bit of a bore. He probably got blown over the Atlantic and landed on some island. For all we know he may be a respected citizen by now, giving lectures on fairies. Who cares?

A word, however, must be said about Miss Smith. She got into dreadful hot water when she reported back to the Witch's Employment Bureau. "A complete failure, Miss Smith, that's what you are," hissed the Chief Witch, in the crossest of tones. "I shall have to put you in the Warts Department." Now this was a terrible come-down for Miss Smith; it meant that all she would be allowed to do was to fly through the windows of poor old women at night, and put warts on their noses when they were asleep. Very monotonous work, and very badly paid. So Miss Smith tossed her head, remarked that she hadn't come to *that*, thank you very much, and stalked out. For some time she was out of work and then, one evening she was strolling down the Street of the Wicked Newspapers when she heard the sound of music coming from a public house. She walked in, followed by the toads, and — to cut a long story short — they offered her a job in the cabaret. She was quite good at it, for her voice was exactly like the voice of a popular crooner — which, as we all know, is one of the favourite noises in hell (in fact, there is a special corner of hell reserved for very bad cases, where ten thousand crooners moan all day and all night without stopping). So if you should ever take the wrong turning in one of your dreams and find yourself drifting down the Street of the Wicked Newspapers, you will be sure to hear Miss Smith crooning, with the toads croaking in chorus by her side.

So much for the bad characters in our story; now for the good. The only real trouble was caused by Mrs. Judy, who found it very difficult to get used to living in a palace, doing nothing. It was very nice to begin with, when she was trying on her new dresses, and wandering through all the wonderful rooms, and exploring the kitchens which were full of exciting things which she had never seen before, such as Frigidaires and electric irons and washing-up machines. But after a little while, time hung heavy on her hands and she decided that she would start another shop.

She was out walking in the grounds when she came to this decision and she happened to meet Mrs. Hare, who — needless to say — had been one of the first people to call.

"I think I shall be opening The Shop again, Mrs. Hare," she said, "as soon as the young couple are nicely settled."

Mrs. Hare looked extremely shocked. "Oh, *madam!*" she cried.

Mrs. Judy blinked. "Why d'you call me madam, all of a sudden?"

"Well, madam, your new position. . . ."

"Haven't got a new position," snapped Mrs. Judy. "Same old position. Stand-ing up in the daytime and lying down at night."

"But, madam," insisted Mrs. Hare, "surely trade... when you might have to be a lady-in-waiting?" She did not finish the sentence, but stood sniff- as though she were a duchess looking for a drain.

Mrs. Judy left her in a huff. When she returned home Judy could not think what was the matter with her. At last it came out.

"I ought to be back in The Shop," she muttered suddenly. Judy had no idea that she really wanted to go back; she thought she was just suggesting that she was not needed in the palace; so she said:

"But Grannie darling, that's absurd . . . we want you here."

"I've kept a shop all my life," insisted Mrs. Judy. "And I shall go on keeping it, princesses or no princesses."

And she mumbled and muttered to herself, and her old eyes were very near to tears.

"But Grannie, if you really want to, nobody suggested that you should stop. . . ."

"Oh yes, they did," she interrupted. "Everybody suggested. You suggested . . . Mr. Tortoise . . . I beg his pardon . . . His Royal Highness suggested . . . Mrs. Hare suggested. . . ."

"So Mrs. Hare has been talking to you, has she?"

"Well, she said that of course I couldn't go on with The Shop, not now. She said I'd have to be a lady-in-waiting, or something awful. I won't be a lady-in-waiting. I'm not sure if I'm a lady, and I hate waiting, so why should I?"

"Grannie, you shan't. All we thought. . . ."

"I don't care what you thought . . . I won't give it up!"

It took Judy quite a long time to calm down her old grannie, but at last she succeeded, and in the end Mrs. Judy was as happy as she had been miserable. For now she saw all the wonderful possibilities of The Shop as it might be in the future, with the Prince helping her.

"Just *think* of the things we shall be able to do," she said. "I've always hated having to ask for money, when I know how hard it is for the animals to pay . . . and now I shall just say . . . 'Oh, that's quite all right, we'll put it down to your account.' And then, of course, I shall lose all the accounts, and nobody will have to pay anything at all."

"It will be a lovely shop, Grannie."

"It will indeed."

And it was. The Prince had it specially built under the shadow of the Tree, and though it was much more comfortable than the old one had been, and had a great many more things in it, it was still a shop, and Mrs. Judy felt quite at home in it. She even deserted her bedroom in the Tower, and went back to her hammock in the Tree, where she might be seen swinging happily every night, watching the lights of the palace go out one by one — the lights in the dining room, the lights in the ballroom, the lights in the guard room where the sentries slept, and at last, the little light in the furthest tower, where Judy and her prince lay dreaming.

And now, we must put the lights out, too. For darkness is drawing over our magic wood, and it is time to say good-bye.

Let us take a last look at it. There it lies sleeping over the hills and far away, with the shadows creeping down its glades, and the night wind sighing down its valleys. Mr. Bruno slumbers in his cave, Mrs. Hare is yawning at the Burrows, Mrs. Rabbit is counting her little ones to see that they are all safely home. There is a twinkle under a fern . . . it is Miss Glow-worm going for her evening walk . . . a frisk through the undergrowth . . . it is Miss Fox, giddy as ever . . . a flash of jewels in the moonlight . . . it is the last flutter of Mr. Peacock's tail, folding up for the night. Through the silence echoes the melancholy cry of Mr. Justice Owl — too-wit, too-woe — proclaiming the follies of the world, and slowly, in the heavens, rises the evening star. A very golden star, a very special star, that shines for the wood alone.

One day, maybe, if you search the skies, you may find that star. And if you follow it, it may lead you to the wood. Maybe yes, maybe no. For it is not easy to follow a star. But it is always worth trying.